Home Field Advantage

ALSO BY
DAHLIA ADLER

Novels

Cool for the Summer

Behind the Scenes

Under the Lights

Just Visiting

Last Will and Testament

Right of First Refusal

Out on Good Behavior

Anthologies (as Editor):

His Hideous Heart:
13 of Edgar Allan Poe's Most Unsettling Tales Reimagined

That Way Madness Lies:
15 of Shakespeare's Most Notable Works Reimagined

Home Field Advantage

DAHLIA ADLER

WEDNESDAY BOOKS
NEW YORK

First published in the United States by Wednesday Books, an imprint of St. Martin's Publishing Group

HOME FIELD ADVANTAGE. Copyright © 2022 by Dahlia Adler. All rights reserved. Printed in the United States of America. For information, address St. Martin's Publishing Group, 120 Broadway, New York, NY 10271.

www.wednesdaybooks.com

Designed by Devan Norman:
Case stamp illustration © Shutterstock.com

The Library of Congress Cataloging-in-Publication Data is available upon request.

ISBN 978-1-250-76584-0 (hardcover)
ISBN 978-1-250-76585-7 (ebook)

Our books may be purchased in bulk for promotional, educational, or business use. Please contact your local bookseller or the Macmillan Corporate and Premium Sales Department at 1-800-221-7945, extension 5442, or by email at MacmillanSpecialMarkets@macmillan.com.

First Edition: 2022

10 9 8 7 6 5 4 3 2 1

*To everyone who needs a cheerleader, a strong arm,
or an open heart every now and again.*

And to Yoni, for always being all three.

Home
Field
Advantage

Chapter One

-AMBER-

Ready, steady, go!

I've heard those words so many times they've practically lost all meaning. But then again, I'm always ready and always steady. They're requirements for an Atherton cheerleader, and that goes quintuple for an Atherton cheerleader with aspirations of getting a captain's C on her sweater.

This year, those words will be coming out of Crystal Miller's lips every practice. Last year, they came out of Jamie Rhodes's. The year before that? Tia Ferrera's. And next year, unless I do something utterly egregious, like light a match within fifty feet of Sara Copeley's hair spray nest, they'll be coming out of mine.

I crushed it at cheer camp this summer. The new tennis shoes I used all my birthday money on are so clean, you could lick the morning dew off 'em. (And I can name at least three football players who'd do it on a dare, too.) I'm one of the only two cheerleaders (the other being my best friend, Cara) who's been on varsity since freshman year, and *still* I've watched videos of the routines at least once a day on my (refurbished, shhh) iPhone.

It's my first day as an official junior, the year everyone will be scrutinizing me to see if I have what it takes to be captain next year, and this feels like a test I've been studying for my entire life. (Honestly, the only one, some weeks.) Especially because, according to Crystal, she's got big news.

I instinctively double-check every inch of my body to make sure I'm in compliance with the squad's No Jewelry rules, even though I know I have practice prep down to a science, and yank my long chestnut ponytail extra tight.

A quick glance in the mirror reveals that I look like a flatter version of brunette Cheerleader Barbie, and that's exactly how it should be.

"Ammo!" A screech way too loud to come from such a tiny body breaks into my self-reflection. "Amber, come on. We're gonna be late."

"I *know* Cara Whelan, Our Lady of Perpetual Tardiness, is *not* calling me out on matters of punctuality," I shoot back, but

I jog after her, because she's right and because being my best friend means she's genuinely watching out for me.

Probably.

Anyway, Cara is the squad's smallest and highest-flying member, which means she can get away with pretty much anything. If she were remotely capable of organizing a damn thing, I'd be worried about her as competition for captain, but Cara readily admits she'd be a disaster at the job, if her parents would even let her do it. (Spoiler: Pastor and Mrs. Whelan absolutely would not let her do it.)

We pile into the gym, and though most of us have been seeing one another all summer between cheer camp, shrimp boils, and road trips to the beach and Wakulla Springs, we fall on top of one another like it's been centuries. "Your hair looks amazing!" I tell Ella Chow, who apparently chopped off about six inches since having us over for a barbecue last week. "I can't believe you didn't post a pic *immediately*."

"The surprise is so much better," she says with a grin, twirling around while her cousin Virany whistles. "Of course, I just did it yesterday, since there was no way I was keeping it from y'all for more than twenty-four hours."

"Speaking of keeping things quiet," Claire Marlow says with a pointed look at Taylor Broussard, who immediately blushes while everyone else laughs. Taylor and her boyfriend, Matt Devlin, captain of the Alligators, weren't exactly private about hooking up at Diana Rivera's pool party a few days ago.

"Ahem." It isn't even that loud, but at the sound of Coach

Armstrong clearing her throat, we snap to attention. "Welcome back, girls. Sounds like y'all had a fun summer. But I hope everyone watched the videos I emailed and y'all kept up your conditioning around all that partying. You made me proud at camp, and now it's time to outperform yourselves. As y'all may have heard, there's some big news today. Miller asked to be the one to tell y'all, and I think she's earned it." She gestures at Crystal, who flashes a bright white smile as she faces us.

"Just please tell me we're gonna get outside today," Diana begs. "It's actually halfway nice out."

I'd been hoping for the same thing, so I'm glad one of the seniors speaks up. While the Panhandle isn't nearly as gross as South Florida during the rest of the year, August is like living in a sweaty gym sock. If we *have* to come in before school to practice today, the least we can do is take advantage of the fact that we're only at about 80 percent humidity.

"We'll go out soon," Crystal promises, smoothing down her already perfectly pressed black ponytail, "but first, we need to have a private team meeting." The way she says it sends a little shiver down to my toes, and I throw up a prayer that she isn't announcing she's transferring. She'll recommend me for captain for next year, I'm sure, but if she left early and someone else (her BFF, Nia Johnson, almost definitely) took her spot, who knows what would happen?

Okay, I'm getting paranoid. I need to stop getting paranoid.

"Well?" Zoe Remini asks when Crystal has drawn out more than enough suspense.

Crystal huffs at her, as if her entire dramatic delivery has been ruined. "*Well*, as we all know, it's been two months since Robbie's, um, since Robbie." A somber mood settles over the squad at the reminder of Robbie Oakes's fatal car crash at the beginning of the summer, and even tough-as-nails Crystal can't hide how Atherton's still feeling the loss in more ways than one. But she presses on, captainly to the core. "And the Alligators' attempts at a replacement haven't exactly been cutting it."

That's an understatement. We've all been watching the football team's unofficial summer practices and pickup games at the park, especially since the backup quarterback, Drew Henley, up and moved without a word to anyone the week after Robbie died. Now everything rests on Tim Duggan, and everyone knows his throwing arm works for about three passes before it descends into limp noodle state.

Robbie wasn't exactly a superstar—the Alligators haven't had a winning season since . . . ever—but at least he had endurance. And though the Spring Showcase game—Robbie's last before hitting a tree with a blood alcohol level of twice the legal limit—proved that this coming fall wasn't gonna be the season they finally made the playoffs either, news (and blooper videos) of Tim's particularly atrocious performance at their week of two-a-days has been making the rounds.

"So, what's happening?" Sara Copeley asks, because the girl has the patience of a mosquito.

"Sundstrom found a new quarterback at football camp."

Crystal smiles, her pride at having the scoop before anyone else glaringly obvious. "From Butler. He starts today."

The entire room erupts.

"Is he hot?"

"Is he single?"

"What's his name?"

I let the voices wash over me as I pick at my laces. New guys don't exactly get me excited any more than old ones, if you know what I mean. Even if I was interested, the quarterback is automatically the captain's domain; the other girls only have a chance if Crystal decides she doesn't want him. And Crystal's been single and horny (she's a good church girl, but we all know) ever since her boyfriend moved up to Virginia for college, so if the new guy is even a little hot, it's hands-off for the rest of us.

Besides, this is about more than just a guy—this is a whole shifting dynamic. How's it gonna work, having someone new? How's someone gonna join without having sweated it out with Matt Devlin, Dan Sanchez, and the rest of them all summer? And how the hell is this the first I'm hearing about it? What's the point of having a boyfriend on the football team if he's not gonna pass along insider info?

Okay, so Miguel Santiago isn't exactly my real boyfriend, but he's still in big trouble.

"His name is Jack Walsh. Isn't that cute?" says Crystal, and the other girls agree that it is. "Anyway, that's all the info

I have for now; the team's been really tight-lipped about it. But this is where y'all come in. We've gotta do up Jack's locker just like we did the rest of them. Official Atherton welcome. Even if we don't have time to make cookies at home. Let's just split up and do what we can to make sure Jack Walsh is *very* happy here."

So, this is how I get to prove myself today—not with my splits or lifts or even my lungs, but with my impeccable puffy paint skills. No problem. My puffy paint skills are second to none. Whatever my squad needs.

Gooooo Alligators!

- - - - -

We end up staying in the gym for the entire practice, and by the time I drag my butt to first period, I'm cranky from lack of my usual Monday morning endorphins. Apparently, it shows on my face, because Austin Barrett promptly looks over at me and says, "Hey, Ammo. I'd ask how your summer was, but, uh, looks like your morning's been a little rough. You okay?"

"You look like crap too, Barrett."

He laughs. I'd be more pissed, but Austin hasn't exactly made it a secret he thinks I'm hot, and an extra bit of sleepiness in my eyes or whatever isn't going to make that go away. Not that I'd mind if it did.

"Ever the sweetheart. You okay?"

"Yeah, thanks." I like Austin—something I feel lucky to say about a guy I've turned down at least twice—but rare is the non-athlete who understands the necessity of my active morning routine. "Just tired."

"You don't look it," he says seriously.

"Too late, bro."

"Damn it." He grins. "I tried."

I return the smile, then go back to pulling my books out of my bag. I like Austin, but he *likes* me, which is reason number one jillion for Miguel's and my little fauxmance. Austin is such a sweetheart that sometimes I get tempted to slip in the truthier truth behind it all, but that would be a really, really bad idea. For so many reasons.

"Who's that?"

I look up at the sound of Austin's hushed voice and see a girl I don't recognize stop in the doorway and glance around the room. "No clue," I whisper, scanning the solidly built newcomer from head to toe. Her dirty-blond hair, still wet from a shower, is pulled back into a tight knot on top of her head, and she's wearing a sleeveless hooded shirt layered over a tank top that shows off ridiculous arms—the girl's got guns. There's no other word for 'em. I'm a base, and I've got pretty strong arms myself, but she looks like she could throw me in the air with one hand and send me flying higher than Cara.

I'm pretty used to the heat after living here for sixteen years, but I suddenly feel the need to fan myself.

With the addition of her and the new QB, that makes two

new kids joining our small class in one year, which is definitely not typical. But if the Walshes moved here for Jack to play ball, I guess he could have a hot sister who moved with him.

She walks right past me and Austin and takes an empty seat in the back, paying no mind to how everyone's watching her go. She pulls out a notebook and immediately starts scribbling while we wait for class to start, her biceps flexing lightly enough that I probably wouldn't notice if I weren't staring like a creeper. But I'm just curious what she's drawing, obviously, because—

"Good morning, class." I whip around as Mr. Thompson drops his bag on his desk, the bell ringing. "Welcome back to Atherton. I trust y'all had wonderful summers during which you read and loved *The Good Earth*. Now, let's see who I'm dealing with here. Aronson, Peter?"

"Yo," Pete calls from behind me.

"Barrett, Austin?"

"Heyo."

"Bates, Aisha?"

It continues on down through "McCloud, Amber"—aka me—without the new girl speaking up, so my "new QB's sister" guess is holding up pretty well. It's confirmed when Mr. Thompson says, "And finally, Walsh, Jaclyn?"

"Jack, please."

Mr. Thompson says something in response, but I can't hear it over the sound of gears turning in my head, loud static in my ears.

Jack Walsh. The new quarterback. Is a girl.

9

A hot girl.

Well then.

-JACK-

I've survived another night of sleeping in my new "bed." I've survived my first practice with my new team. I've survived my first class at my new school. At this point, I should feel like I can survive anything.

Instead, every minute of this day is just one wave of nausea crashing while another begins. If there's one message everyone seems to be sending my way, it's that I don't belong here.

Tell me something I don't know, Atherton.

Starting at a new school sucks enough. Starting at a new school where you're walking onto their football team and replacing their beloved dead quarterback? That's a whole other level.

Not a single guy on the team made eye contact with me on Saturday. I'd think they didn't even know I was there, except that ignoring me didn't stop them from whispering, each one a bigger condescending shit than the last, betting on what would make me crack. Big money was on running lines, like I don't wake up early to run around the nature preserve every single morning. The dicks who thought their little mat drills—burpees and high-knees and push-ups—were gonna do it clearly have no idea who they're dealing with. And while it was fun to watch *them* gas out and get reamed for not keeping up with conditioning, it's clearer than ever why they pulled in someone from outside Atherton to play QB.

Class was the opposite—every single person in the room was trying to get an eyeful, judgy eyes burning through my shirt like laser beams, no one uttering a word. I woke up this morning determined to channel the nerves of steel my best friend Morgan used to march into their first day of junior high in Northern Florida and promptly declare their pronouns were they/them and they wouldn't respond to anything else, but I can't not give a fuck what people think about me when my being here depends on their ability to see me as a leader.

At least I didn't let Mr. Thompson call me Jaclyn.

I'm out of my seat the second the bell rings, hoping I can grab a few minutes of texting Morgan and our other best friend, Sage, by my locker, but . . . huh. I thought my locker was third from the left of that bank, but that one's covered in green paper and stripes of yellow ribbon. I definitely did not pretty up my new locker today.

I step closer and see there's a green number 6 right in the middle of the locker, my new number. (It should've been 1, which is Atherton tradition for QB1, but since that was Robbie's, it's been retired.) I approach slowly, like an actual alligator might leap out and bite my ass, and sure enough, the numbers on the lockers on either side of the decorated one confirm that this is locker 204.

Which is exactly the number on the sheet of paper folded up and tucked into the back pocket of my cutoffs.

Weird.

I'd seen stuff like this at Butler—cheerleaders doing all sorts of nice shit for football players—but it didn't occur to me that might happen for me, too, especially after the cold shoulder from the guys this morning. It still doesn't feel like this is my school, though I know I should be ridiculously grateful to them for taking me onto the team when Butler would never, ever entertain the idea of a girl on the field. I've wanted to play football—*really* play—since my dad taught me how to throw a spiral when I was four, and now, finally, I'm going to.

I should be kissing the damn linoleum.

I would be if "Are you fucking kidding me?" weren't still ringing in my ears from practice.

You knew it might be like this, I remind myself as I walk up to my glittery locker and spin the dial with my new combination. I'm about to yank it open when I see a flash of green out of the corner of my eye and hear, "Excuse me, that's Jack Walsh's locker."

"Yep, it is," I say, pulling it open before turning toward what I now see is a group of three girls, all in cheerleader uniforms, led by a Black girl about my height with a *C* on her sweater and legs for days.

The one next to her, considerably shorter and sporting the highest and longest ponytail I've ever seen, crosses her arms. "What are you doing at his locker?"

"Who are you?" asks the third girl, who looks like she's sending a spray tanner's kids to college. "Don't tell me he brought a girlfriend to Atherton."

"Don't—What? Who's *he*?" What the hell is going on here?

"Okay, all y'all need to pause," says another voice, and I turn to see yet a fourth cheerleader, and why are these girls all so pretty? This one's white with sun-streaked brown waves and eyes the color of the ocean, and I swear they make cheerleaders look like this just to fuck with me. I'm about to pull my eyes away when I realize she looks . . . familiar. "This *is* Jack—Jaclyn—Walsh." She offers me a small smile. "You're in my English class. I'm Amber, and this is Crystal"—the captain—"Diana"—dead ringer for Ariana Grande—"and Zoe"—extra from *Floribama Shore*. "We're all cheerleaders, obviously"—she gestures down at her uniform—"so you'll be seeing lots of us. Welcome to Atherton!"

Human beings can't seriously be this peppy, can they? But at least Amber is trying to be nice, which is more than I can say for the three looking at me like they have no idea what to do with a new human in their midst. "I'd introduce myself, but it seems like y'all have already gotten that memo."

"You're the new quarterback?" Diana asks, arching a razor-sharp eyebrow.

Despite the derision in her voice, it still gives me a thrill to hear those words. "I'm the new quarterback," I confirm. "I don't suck. Promise."

Amber laughs. No one else does.

"Of the boys' team?" Zoe's eyes widen.

"Of the only team, as far as I know."

The girls all exchange glances I don't know how to read. "Okay," Crystal says slowly, and the others look deferentially to her as if it'll tell them how to feel about this. "That should be interesting. We have to get to class, but enjoy the cookies, I guess."

The other girls mumble something along those lines and retreat, except for Amber, who lingers as I turn back to my locker and see the cookies in question. I'd expected a box full of homemade or something, since that's what the guys at my old school always got, but instead, it's a bag of Famous Amos straight out of the vending machine. Oh well—beggars can't be choosers, and these happen to be my favorite.

"They're nice girls and great cheerleaders," Amber says as I tear open the bag. Chocolate chip. Yum. I hold it out to her, but she shakes her head. I stick one between my teeth and stuff the rest of the bag into my backpack. "They—we—just expected someone a little different."

"A guy."

"Well, yeah."

At least she's honest. "Sorry to disappoint."

She blushes a little and, damn, she really is cute. But the whole "nice" thing . . . I'm not falling for it, and I don't have time for bullshit. It feels like a game of good cop/bad cop and that's not the sport I signed on to play. "I didn't mean—"

"Look, Cheer Girl—"

"It's Amber," she snaps, aqua eyes flashing as the nice girl mask finally drops. Well, that didn't take much.

"What the fuck is the difference?" I'm being an asshole, but in my defense, everyone else was being an asshole first. "Listen, I get that I'm not what y'all had in mind, but I can play ball just fine without a dick to swing in the locker room. And I don't need any cheery shit to do it either, okay? So you can go follow your friends. I'll find my own way around."

I turn back to my locker, expecting to hear her stomping away, but no such luck.

"Not having a dick doesn't mean you need to *be* one, FYI." She waves imaginary pom-poms. "Rah-rah and a sunny fucking day to you, too." *Now* she storms off, her little skirt swishing behind her, and for a quick stupid moment, I consider calling her back and apologizing. But I'm not ceding any ground here, certainly not to a cheerleader, even if she has more of an edge than I first thought.

I may not love Atherton, but I do love football, and if all I get is two years to play it, I'm gonna do it while keeping my mouth shut.

- - - - -

By lunchtime, it's clear that word of my identity has spread, and I can't go anywhere without seeing gawkers and hearing whispers. Hiding in a bathroom stall to eat isn't my style, and Lord knows I need to carbo-load before practice, but I don't know where the hell to sit in this place. Certainly not at one of the two tables of football players and cheerleaders holding court in the middle.

I'm not the sentimental type, but the whoosh of missing my friends from Butler comes fast and fierce. Sage and Morgan, the best of the best, have been texting me all morning, wishing me a great day and sending pictures of everything from their morning Starbucks orders to classmates' new haircuts. I hate that I had to leave them behind, hate that I did it for a team and school that doesn't even want me.

I know they're hurt that I left, even though they get it. They both have passions of their own—Sage *will* be on one of those absolutely ridiculous baking shows one day, and Morgan's love for LARPing and cosplay is outshone only by how fucking talented they are at crafting and design. They both plan to pursue those passions after high school.

I just happen to have jumped ship a little earlier to pursue mine, leaving them behind in the wasteland that is Butler High. Which means I can't let them know that, so far, things here are Quite Shitty, Actually.

And that's just my friends. I broke my family in half for this, my mom moving with me to Atherton since she can work remotely as a customer service rep, and my dad staying behind with my brothers, who refused to move. That means as far as everyone's concerned, this must be the most worthwhile thing I have ever done, and I'm proving it with a uniform selfie, a locker photo, and anything else that screams "I am Atherton's new Golden God."

I have to make this work, for all of them.

And yeah, for myself, too. This is my shot. My *only* shot, since while select high schools might be making exceptions for female players, the chance at playing in college is even closer to one in a billion. There may come a day I can't name every single girl who's done it, but for now, I chant some of their names in my head like a mantra of possibility, even though I know being a placekicker or safety isn't like being a QB. *Katie Hnida. Sarah Fuller. Morgan Smith. Toni Harris.*

Each name is a deep breath, getting me back to where I need to be, which is being able to face a lunch crowd. I'm never gonna be a team leader if I can't even do that, so into the masses I go.

Any minute now.

Okay, really, I should spend lunch reviewing the plays in those videos Coach Sundstrom sent me.

Yeah, that's what I'm gonna do.

I'll make friends tomorrow.

Probably.

Chapter Two

-AMBER-

Cara's seven minutes late meeting me at my car after practice, but that's no surprise. She's late for everything, always; it's a wonder she even still has a job. Now I'm gonna have to drive like a maniac to get her there on time, praying I don't get yet another ticket. My car isn't anything fancy—an old Nissan Altima handed down by my dad when he and his then-new wife, Angela, upgraded (always upgrading, that father o' mine!)—but if I lose the ability to drive it, I can kiss every single thing in my life outside of school goodbye.

I scroll through my phone while I wait, flipping through

pictures from cheer camp this summer, feeling the corners of my lips lift up at the memories. I may be a dork, but I love everything about it—jump contests on the beach, impromptu dance parties, Spirit Night—and yeah, managing to sneak in some time with a certain cheerleader was definitely a seasonal highlight. . . .

"Hey! Sorry!" Cara runs up to me, breathless, and I nearly drop my phone, as if she can hear my thoughts. The picture I was looking at wasn't even *of* Veronica, but it still feels like too close a call. Not that Cara doesn't know I made out with a cheer captain from Tally—unfortunately, too much adrenaline and a poor location choice means *everyone* knows—but it's been written off as cheer camp shenanigans, fully endorsed by my Extremely Heterosexual Horndog Boyfriend, Miguel Santiago, star Wide Receiver of the Atherton Alligators.

And yeah, okay, maybe I encouraged that thinking.

After all, Miguel and I both benefit from this arrangement as we figure our shit out and just try to survive this place. The cheerleaders are like my family, but it'd definitely be testing the limits of that bond if they knew I was queer, and the football team would be much worse. Plus, if there's one person I can safely assume would *not* be cool with it, it's Cara Whelan.

Daughter of Pastor Whelan.

That Pastor Whelan, of the fire and brimstone and all the other shit that keeps his church running.

Cara's been one of my best friends ever since we were

little kids, back before I realized her parents constantly trying to get me to join her at church against my atheist single mom's wishes wasn't cool. Despite their house already being packed with kids, they took me in when my mom was working nights or just needed a little space to get through nursing school. I learned to pump on their swing set, bake cookies in their kitchen, and plant flowers in their garden. I still miss their Friday movie nights, even though it's all rated G, all the time. But "it's complicated" is an understatement, and if I ever want to watch *The Prince of Egypt* with them again, I'll keep both of these tennis shoes firmly in the closet, thank you very much.

There's no question Cara's been there for me through a lot, including picking up cheerleading with me when I didn't want to try out alone as an incoming freshman, even though we both thought it would be a way bigger fight with her parents. She held my hand through every step of my father getting remarried, letting me sleep over when I was feeling the loneliness extra hard and making sure we always had fun distractions like letting her little sister Mary give us makeovers. (Of course, since all the makeup in their house had to be approved, it was mostly just drugstore blush and Chap-Stick, but we still made it fun.) And she always sneaks me free drinks at work when they get returned by picky customers. But she's been raised with some shitty ideas and values that don't go with having a queer best friend, and I don't know what she'd say if I told her Veronica wasn't the first girl I've kissed and hopefully won't be my last.

I hate, hate, hate that.

"Can we hurry?" she asks, throwing open the car door, as if I don't know she's running ridiculously behind schedule, as always. "Geoff will kill me if I'm late again."

I don't bother answering, just jump in right alongside her. "What was it this time?" I ask once we're on the road. "Mrs. Kweller pulling you aside again to fangirl over your dad?"

"Just got caught up in a conversation with a couple of other girls about Jack," she replies, her fingers making a rapid-fire braid out of her fine reddish-brown hair. "What to do about it and everything."

Oh, I do not like where this is going. "What does that mean? What is there *to* do? She's the quarterback."

Cara snorts. "Come on. That's a joke. A really, really cruel joke, if you ask me. I can't believe we all spent so much time decorating that locker and then found out it was for *her*."

My jaw clenches. This is what I mean. She doesn't even realize how messed up this sounds. But apparently, she's not alone, and that's even *more* messed up.

Some girls just really love to hate themselves. Which only makes it harder for them to understand liking other girls "in that way."

Also, come the fuck on. We spent half an hour, tops, on that locker. It's not like we baked snickerdoodles.

"Why would it have been less of a waste of time if it were a guy?"

"Because—Shoot, you're gonna hit the red if you don't speed up."

"I'm not getting another ticket this year because you're late, C." I try to say it gently, but between this conversation and the fact that she didn't even offer to chip in for the ticket I got the last time I rushed her to work, I'm getting pissed. "And I really hope y'all decided Jack should be treated like any other quarterback."

She huffs out a breath as we pull up to the red light, but thankfully passes up whining about my driving for returning to our earlier conversation. "You know that's not gonna happen, Ammo. She's *not* like any other quarterback. Especially because no one wants to get into her pants."

God, it's like Cara is pushing every rainbow button of mine today. I can't even respond to that comment, which, by the way, feels like pretty big talk from someone saving herself for marriage. My tongue suddenly feels too big for my mouth.

"People are really pissed about Robbie being replaced by a girl," she says, tugging on the cross that hangs around her neck. "Which is obviously understandable."

Is it? Because unless Jack sucks—and there's no chance in hell she'd be here if she did—it sounds like this is just full-on misogyny. The words are clear in my head, but I can't get them out of my mouth. I've already had more than one tense confrontation with Cara about Robbie since his accident, and I'm not eager to get into another one. It's obviously sad anytime a seventeen-year-old kid dies, but I can't join Cara and the rest of Atherton in the "Robbie was an angel" mindset—not knowing what an asshole he could be.

But then, unveiling Robbie's sins means unveiling a whole lot more than that, so, into the vault it goes.

"I bet she thinks she's gonna hook up with one of the guys on the team," Cara continues, pulling down the sun visor to apply lip gloss in the little mirror. "At *least* one. Who do you think will go for her?" She doesn't wait for me to answer. "The sad thing is, I bet someone will. I mean, they all hate her because of the Robbie thing, but, like, you know how those guys are."

I keep my mouth shut and let Cara babble on, because if Jack's butch vibes aren't setting off anyone else's gaydar, I'm damn sure not gonna be the one to mention it. Besides, right now I'm more worried about how neither the team nor the squad seems willing to give her a shot than Cara's insecurities about a new girl showing up.

A quarterback can't function without a team that trusts them, and Robbie may have had an only passable throwing arm, but he had the team's support 110 percent. This rejection isn't just gonna suck for Jack; it's gonna be misery for the Alligators, their fans, and the twelve people responsible for psyching them up at every game—twelve people I hope to be captaining next year. Whoever manages to keep the squad in one cohesive piece is gonna be the most likely to get the top spot.

I need that to be me.

Cheer captain is the only thing even close to impressive I could hope to have on my college applications, and I *need* something impressive if I'm going to get out of here and actually be able to live out and proud at someplace like FSU rather than whatever life I'd have at Atherton Community College. And while I absolutely do not care what my dad thinks about anything, cheerleading *is* the only thing he ever wants to talk about during our once-a-month (if that) phone calls. It reminds him of being a stud in high school, or something. The glory days before he knocked my mom up at prom and then abandoned her to join the Air Force before either of them could finish college.

It's never been a question that I need this title to be mine. But if the squad is united under the banner of ousting Jack, does that mean whoever captains them has to fall in line?

"You're awfully quiet," says Cara as I turn onto the street where she pushes lattes at the Bean Counter three afternoons a week. "What do you know? Has Miguel told you something?"

"I don't know anything," I say honestly. "I'm just thinking about how much this whole situation sucks."

She seems to accept that, and then there's no more conversation because I switch on the radio and let Drake take over.

As soon as the light turns green, I shoot through it, and in another couple of minutes, we're safely at the Bean Counter. "You coming in?" she asks, a foot already out the door.

It's a reasonable question—I join her often, for the free cast-off drinks and to gossip or get help with my homework (you wouldn't guess it, but Cara's an evil math genius) when there's a lull. But right now, there's someone else I need to talk to, so I just say, "Can't, promised Mom I'd give her a full rundown on the first day," and let her blow me a kiss and dash inside without further questioning.

It's only a partial lie; I *did* promise that to my mom. Her nursing shift at the hospital just happens to end at eight o'clock, which means I've got a solid three hours to kill before I see her.

I open my texts and tap out a chicken emoji—shorthand for Miguel's favorite code phrase, "The hen is in the rooster house"—followed by a coffee cup and a water droplet. He'll be at practice for another half an hour, so I slip my phone into my bag and pull out of the lot, singing at the top of my lungs until the rest of the day disappears.

- - - - -

The Bean Counter is the only coffee shop in Atherton, but just over the city line in Barkley there's a much less trendy one called Drip that's not nearly as popular. Which is exactly why it's Miguel's and my favorite hangout.

The worn velvet armchairs at the back are both empty,

and Rick's behind the counter, which means no one will be bugging me for sitting here without a new drink in my hands. He knows exactly who I'm waiting for, and he's probably just as eager to talk to Miguel as I am, though for much flirtier reasons.

There's blessedly little homework the first day of school, so I finish quickly and switch over to the videos of the routines our assistant coach, Josie, sent out that we're supposed to know backward and forward. I'm so engrossed in mouthing along with the chants that I don't notice Miguel has arrived until a sweating cup of iced caramel mocha blocks out the view of my phone screen.

"Thank you, my love," I say, clutching it in grateful hands. "I owe you one."

"You actually owe—"

"I was talking to the coffee." It's sweet and cold and delicious and exactly what I've been craving. "God, I needed that."

"Guessing your day went about as well as mine did," he mutters as he settles his long limbs into the chair opposite me with his own iced mocha I know is full of extra sugar.

"The cheerleaders are going bananas over the whole Jack thing. I'm guessing the football players are too, huh? I can't *believe* you didn't tell me they replaced Robbie with a girl."

He snorts. "You think they told *us* a second before they had to? They knew how that was gonna go over. She didn't practice with the team until Saturday, and we all thought it

26

was a joke when she showed up, some sort of grand statement by Sundstrom telling us to shape up because we were playing like girls."

"Lovely."

"Yeah, well, Sundstrom isn't exactly known for his human decency." He swipes his fingers against his palm, spreading around the condensation from his cup. "When he said he found a dual-threat at football camp who conveniently happened to be moving to Atherton—and we all know that second part is a bullshit cover for recruitment—he made it sound like he'd found the next Tebow. She was . . . not what any of us were picturing, though it makes sense that the only way he'd be able to get someone that good to move is if it were someone who'd never be able to play at their own school. Anyway, no one thought she'd last the day, let alone come back."

Well, that all tracks. So much for my righteous anger at being left in the dark. "But she did. *And* y'all think she moved here specifically to play. And even with all that . . ."

"Yep, team's still acting like she's stomping on the flowers of Saint Robbie's grave," he says as he finally unwraps his straw and jams it into his cup. I don't think he realizes he's stabbing it in repeatedly as if it were human flesh until I put a Gator-green-nailed hand over his and hold it in place.

"He's gone, Mig." I keep my voice as soft as possible in the crowded space.

Miguel takes a sharp breath, and then his shoulders slump and his hand relaxes. "Sorry."

"You don't need to apologize to me. I know who Robbie was. You're not talking to a member of his fan club."

"I know." He turns his hand upside down and clasps mine, just for a second. "Thank you."

We sit quietly, thinking, remembering, neither of us daring to say another word out loud. Finally, my curiosity gets the better of me and I break the silence.

"So, is she better than he was?"

"Oh, hell yeah. It's a pretty low bar, but she's got him beat in every way. Honestly, the Tebow comparison isn't that far off, and Robbie was *not* a scrambling QB. She outran everyone but me and Devlin, and her arm is incredible. She also knows all our plays stone-cold, which Duggan sure as fuck didn't. If she were a guy, they'd all get the fuck over it. Instead, the prick who went through my shit looking for deodorant and used my personal property to threaten me for months gets to remain the team hero."

It truly is extremely fucking unfair, and nobody at school knows about it—how Robbie blackmailed Miguel right up until the crash by demanding everything from homework assignments to voting his way on team matters to cash Miguel didn't have in order to keep him in the closet. I certainly can't blame Miguel for being royally pissed that even having a great new quarterback won't make the Sainthood of Robbie Oakes disappear, because the only thing more useless to the team than a dead quarterback is a female one. But still, my heart sinks.

Without Miguel's support, there's no one on my side, which means this *can't* be my side. And yeah, Jack hasn't exactly given the sweetest first impression, but she still deserves a chance, and the *team* deserves the chance she'd be giving them.

That she's hot is definitely not a factor here.

Especially with that attitude.

Even with those arms.

"What's that face?" Miguel asks suspiciously.

"What face? There is no face." I take a long, noisy sip of my drink and arrange my features into the picture of innocence.

"There is absolutely a face. It was a little bit of a dreamy face, if I'm being honest. The kind of face that makes me wonder if someone was maybe thinking about the new QB for a second there."

"You're the one who just told me she's a good quarterback," I remind him, but I can tell that I'm blushing and he obviously can too.

"Oh my God. Loud McCloud has a crush on the new girl."

"Loud McCloud does not crush on Atherton girls, thank you very much."

Miguel waggles his thick eyebrows. "Hey, you didn't think you'd hook up at cheer camp, either, and look what happened."

If I could literally rip a smile off someone else's face, I would. Instead, I go back to slurping at my coffee extra-hard and let my death glare do the talking.

"So that's . . . three girls in a row now?" he continues as

if I'm not trying to destroy his insides with the power of my retinas. "Interesting. Verrrry interesting."

"I haven't had enough of this coffee to deal with your biphobia, Santiago."

He holds up his hands. "Hey, you're the one who said you weren't sure how you identify."

"Yeah, and I'm still not. It's not my fault Elliot Page won't return my calls. Not that my sexuality matters in this case because—say it with me—I do not crush on Atherton girls."

"'I do not crush on Atherton girls,'" Miguel echoes like the smart-ass he is. "Normally I would point out that you're totally self . . . what's 'cock-blocking' when you don't have a cock?"

I hate that I actually have an answer to this, thanks to Veronica. "Clam-jamming."

Unfortunately for Miguel, he'd taken a sip of his drink, and he coughs it up so hard, he almost chokes. "That's horrible."

"I know, but anyway, you know you're my one and only, boo. Even if you're going behind my back with that skank."

Miguel rolls his dark eyes. "I'm going to tell Malcolm you called him that."

"Don't you dare." I love Miguel's new boyfriend, but more than that, I love that Miguel has actually dipped back into dating again, even if he's gotta keep it on the DL. Robbie's blackmail bullshit destroyed his last relationship, and it took him being dead for a month for Miguel to work up the courage to use the phone number left for him by the cute boy who'd been hanging out around Miguel's lifeguard stand all summer. Mal knows everything, from Robbie's blackmail to our fauxmance, and he's still sticking around, so as far as I'm concerned, he's the perfect guy.

Honestly, bonus points if he truly is a little skanky. Miguel deserves it.

"Maybe someday we'll go on a double date," Miguel teases, and it's my turn to roll my eyes.

"Yeah, right." But now that he's in a good mood, I can't help shifting the conversation back to the question that's been on my mind even more than the new QB's arms. "You know I'm dying to be captain, right?"

"Literally everyone in a fifty-mile radius knows you're dying to be captain, sweetheart."

"Okay, well, I'm thinking that if I can be the one to bring the squad around to welcoming Jack into the fold, be the great harbinger of unity or whatever, that's gotta make them see me as a leader, right? Especially if it means Atherton's first winning season in forever?"

He sighs heavily, a sign that my last stab at this isn't gonna go anywhere. "I guess, but the squad isn't gonna get on board with her unless the team does, and I do *not* see that happening anytime soon. Doesn't help that she wasn't around for two-a-days or clinic or anything. People keep talking like Tim put in the work and then got shafted. Never mind that he's been *getting* a shot to prove himself all summer, and he sucks."

"They're not seriously pretending they wish he was still QB, are they? I thought they were bordering on mutiny."

"They were, *and* he basically begged to be put out of his misery, but they'll pretend it's about anything other than that she's a girl who's better than Robbie ever was," he says sourly, his fingers doing that nervous flicking thing they do when Robbie comes up.

"So, what do I do?" I ask. "How do I make them see that they're being beyond stupid and blowing the first shot they've had in years of actually going somewhere?"

"Trust me," says Miguel, "if I knew, I would've done it a hundred times already. I am not looking forward to a year of nauseating hero worship of the devil *and* another losing streak." He takes a long, noisy sip. "Please can we talk about something else? *Anything* else."

Deeply unsatisfying as his responses have been, I get why he is capital-*D* Done talking about Robbie Oakes. Fortunately, our little Rainbow Alliance always has plenty else to discuss. "So, like, does this mean you're finally ready to tell me about the magical one-month anniversary date? Because details on that were miiiighty stingy, my friend."

Miguel looks around like he wishes he had something on hand to throw at me. "*If* you're ready to finally spill some salacious details about cheer camp."

"Jesus, Santiago. You're a jock. Don't you know you're not supposed to know words like 'salacious'?"

"I guess that answers whether you're still jealous of my SAT verbal score," he says casually.

"I hate you."

"You love me."

"I do." I lace my fingers through his, and we fall quiet, and I know we're both thinking how much easier life would be if we were The Thing everyone thinks we are. But Miguel is gayer than spring break in South Beach and I may be into multiple genders, but that does not include my taken best friend, or any other cis boys, as far as I can tell. So. Here we are.

Maybe someday I'll have my own Malcolm. A Veronica outside of cheer camp. A pair of incredible arms to hold me that aren't attached to the most controversial student at Atherton High. A *real* relationship I can be out and proud with.

But then, I'm already going for cheer captain, and how many dreams does one girl get in this life, anyway?

-JACK-

Another day, another infuriating practice of no one giving a shit what I have to say and no one praising a damn thing I'm doing except for Coach Sundstrom's muttered "Good job today, Walsh" out of earshot of anyone else on the team—a far cry from the praise he heaped on at camp. I know he does that on purpose, so he won't piss off the rest of the guys, and I really fucking hate that I end up preening at those scraps like a stray cat because it's all I'm gonna get.

I let myself into my new "home" quietly and wave at my mom, who's sitting at our small dining table and wearing a headset to take customer service calls. She gives a wave back without breaking her rhythm and I disappear into the bathroom and strip off my sweaty clothes.

A good, long shower helps scrub off a little of the maddening memory of the afternoon. It's also a welcome break from the nonstop texts from Sage and Morgan that I know are meant to keep me in the loop but are starting to depress me. Ordinarily I'd appreciate Morgan's LARPing drama and I'd be there for Sage's venting about her parents fighting, but all it does is make me miss everything, and I can't afford to miss anything.

I can't afford to miss the inside jokes and knowing exactly where my place was in the cafeteria and who I'd be hanging out with on Friday nights. I can't afford to miss the old movie theater with reclining seats and the most horribly watered-down sodas and playing *Dragon Age* in Morgan's basement and swimming in the lake in our sports bras and throwing the ball around with my brothers in the cul-de-sac, nothing but wide-open space except for the Hecker kids driving their bikes around the flat circle. I can't afford to miss having my own room instead of sleeping on a pull-out couch in the living room with flimsy blinds that wake me up with too much sun.

I can't afford to miss any of that because I made my choice and it broke my family in two and took away Morgan and Sage's best friend and changed everything for everyone I love and I am grateful I am grateful I am grateful.

I *am* grateful, is the thing. I've poured my heart into football for so many years, even though there was never a space for me on the team at Butler. As soon as it became clear I was better at throwing, catching, and running than your average kindergartener—hell, than your average elementary school kid—my dad doubled down on the drills, bringing in my brothers as soon as they got old enough to join. Whatever self-consciousness I had that I wasn't "growing into" liking dolls and princesses and playing dress-up melted away with the knowledge that there was somewhere I belonged, even if it wasn't where the other girls were.

Then it became a Sunday morning tradition, our version of church. A gathering of us, neighbors, and cousins playing every week, no one saying shit about a second-grade girl playing QB for one side. Summers were filled with football camp, open to everyone because it meant more funding that way. I kept on failing at liking what I was supposed to—the right clothes and hairstyles and music and gender—but it was okay, because I liked something I was really fucking good at.

And then high school hit, and with it the reminder that this wasn't a sport for me, even if it felt like the most Me thing in the universe. Maybe the *only* Me thing in the universe.

Our Sunday morning games slowed to once a month, so I got a job at the Hat Hut and sold Jaguars caps until I could pay my own way to a much fancier football camp in Panama City. Technically it was only supposed to be for kids on actual school teams, but Morgan insisted we send in a few videos of me playing to get them to make an exception, and it worked. Then boom—the last day of camp, one of the coaches lets me know he's in desperate need of a QB who can run and throw like I can, and if my family happened to be picking up and moving to Atherton (because of course he wasn't *recruiting*; that would be verboten), he was sure they could find a spot for me.

And now we're here. The number six. And an upcoming Sunday where the only football that'll be thrown around in my presence is the one on my TV.

But Friday nights I'll be under the lights, and that makes everything worth it.

I think.

I am grateful I am grateful I am grateful.

I keep repeating this to myself as I examine my skin to see if any new bruises have shown themselves yet, then pull on a tank top and pajama pants. I am grateful for this opportunity, and I am grateful that my parents are behind me, and I am grateful that they were able to afford a one-bedroom rental on top of their mortgage, and I am grateful I am grateful I am grateful.

I'm grateful enough that I force myself to text my brothers, even though neither one has spoken a word to me since my mom and I pulled away from the house a week ago. They won't wanna chat—and I don't either, really—but with the twins, it's all about meeting them where they live. *LOTE?*

Busy, Jason responds. It's more than I get from Jeremy, who doesn't even bother responding to my offer to play their favorite video game. Under normal circumstances, I'd leave them alone, but I can't have them icing me out on top of everything else.

This time, I don't bother texting; I go straight to video chat.

"What?" Jason throws out sullenly. "I told you, we're busy."

"You know it's a video chat, Jase. I can see you're not busy. You're sitting at your computer, and don't pretend you're doing homework."

"You're not here. You don't know."

I sigh deeply. He's not even trying. This is so ridiculous. On a normal evening at six, my brothers definitely aren't having heart-to-heart chats with Mom, but they're acting like I stole away the only person either of them has ever loved. In fact, there's a decent chance that at this hour at home, Jason would be playing *Legends of the Empire,* like I just offered to.

In fact, it probably *is* what he's doing.

"I've been gone for a week, Jase; I'm not off to sea. Come on. Just half an hour. I could really use it," I try.

Definitely the wrong way to go. "Oh, well, if *you* need

something, then I guess everyone has to drop everything," he snaps.

Some variation on that remark has been his response to pretty much everything I've said since my parents told the twins we were moving, so it barely even stings at this point. Barely.

Fine. I'll just take a deep breath and sidestep that. "Where's Jer?"

"'Studying' at some girl's house." At least he engages long enough to make those obnoxious finger quotes.

Some girl's *house??* Jesus, even my little brother has more game with girls than I do. God, this is sad. But okay, not the point.

"You've gotta be bored. Come on." I can't believe I'm begging to play a game I don't even like that much, especially when my arm feels like it's gonna fall off, but I need something to go right today. Something to feel fixed. If we were home—together—I'd drag him outside to throw a ball around the yard, but right now this is the best I can do.

"Not bored enough to play with you because you feel bad for leaving and don't want me to be mad at you," Jason says sourly. "Thanks, but no thanks on the pity game."

"Jase! It's not a pity game!" God, I wanna tell him how much it would mean to me to hang out with someone who actually loves me, but I know he'll use it against me if I tell him how cruel the team is being. "I wanna play *Legends* with you. You think that's changed just because I moved?"

"I think everything's changed because you moved." His voice is flat and he gives me no chance to respond before he cuts off the connection.

As if on cue, a new bruise on my shin starts to throb, and I take it as my sign to go grab an ice pack and see if my mom wants to get subs from Publix for dinner.

I am grateful I am grateful I am so goddamn grateful.

- - - - -

I'm on edge all day Wednesday, waiting for Coach to pop his head into any one of my classes and tell me I need an extra session or whatever before our first game on Friday night at Lawndale High. It's still a huge issue that the guys don't wanna listen when I call plays, and while they're the ones being complete and total fucknuggets, I'm the one who's gonna suffer if we can't work shit out.

I let my gaze travel around my English class, drifting over Bro of All Bros Chase Hamill, overachiever to the stars Aisha Bates, and uber-preppy Austin Barrett, who is, as usual, pretending to listen while sneaking glances at Cheer Girl's legs every three seconds.

In fairness, they are extremely good legs. Strong legs. Strong legs that can do a split on command.

Strong legs that probably still want to kick my ass for being such a prick to her the other day.

It shouldn't bother me. She was just being fake and cheery

because it's literally her job. But I didn't realize it would be my one and only experience here with anyone being friendly. Even if she was faking it, that's still more than anyone else has done. Maybe I *should* apologize. Hell, it certainly wouldn't hurt for anyone to see me getting along with a cheerleader.

And then it hits me. What if she were willing to broker a little peace? Anyone that hot has definitely got at least one guy on the team willing to do anything she wants, and maybe, just maybe, I can talk her into getting that guy to see how much I have to offer. Maybe *he* talks to the other guys on the team about that. Maybe we stop wasting so much fucking time and finally get somewhere.

Of course, there's no reason she'd be willing to help me, but I'm desperate, and I'm already late to the season; I don't have any more time to let my skills earn my respect for me. I'm gonna have to kiss some miniskirted ass, and not in a fun way.

Whatever it takes, I tell myself as I let my gaze drift over to Amber again, (mostly) ignoring her legs in favor of scrutinizing what would be the best way to get her on my side. *Whatever it takes.*

- - - - -

I don't catch up with her after class, because if that first day was any indication, she'll be running right into cheerleaders who think I'm an abomination unto the Lord. But Amber proves to be a hard girl to track down privately. Every time I spot her in the hallways, she's with another cheerleader or Miguel Santiago, the one guy on the team who doesn't treat me like shit. (Not that he talks to me; he just doesn't glare at me or mutter about me like I personally killed Robbie Oakes.) I can't decide whether it's better or worse if Santiago's her boyfriend. He seems well-respected enough by the other guys, but he also never stirs the pot—something I'm guessing has to do with being one of the few players of color on a team whose assistant coach drives a truck with a huge-ass Stars and Bars decal on the back. He's probably not the guy to go to for making any waves.

Plus, for all I know, Cheer Girl is *already* why he's being as nice to me as he is. Maybe this is what he's like maxed out on Not Being a Dick.

If that's the case, I'm fucked.

But I can't try nothing, so I keep on keeping an eye out until I finally see her alone in the parking lot at the end of the day, standing at her car and tapping her foot as if she's impatiently waiting for someone. I've probably got a minute, and despite thinking about this all day, I still haven't come up with any script. Still, it's my one window, and I take it.

"Hey! Amber!"

She looks up, huge sunglasses obscuring most of her face, and I'm sort of glad for them. "You remembered my name this time. What's up, Jack?"

The little butterfly flitting around at the fact that she remembers *my* name needs to quit it right the fuck now. Of course she remembers my name; I'm the fucking quarterback.

It's her job to know, every bit as much as leading our atrocious offense is mine.

Also, I'm about to have to swallow a whole lot of pride.

"Listen, I'm really sorry I was such an asshole the other day. I'm still getting used to being an outcast here. You were the one person who was actually nice to me, and—"

"And now you want something."

Well. Girl cuts right to the point. Guess the least I can do is the same. "I do. Hoping you've got a little more kindness in you. I'm prepared to do whatever in order to find it."

Her eyebrows shoot up high enough that I can see them over the frames of her sunglasses, and I realize that sounded like a come-on that it absolutely was not. Great. The literal last thing I need is a cheerleader thinking I'm trying to get under her skirt.

Her whole body shifts then, and it hits me as she tilts her head that whomever she's waiting for is coming, and I only have a couple of seconds; I can't waste them on reassuring her that I'm not a perv. "I really, really need the guys on the team to listen to me, and I'm hoping you can somehow help. That's all."

"Me?" She sounds completely puzzled, but I have no time to get into it, because when she speaks again, it's to yell, "Cara, do you even *know* how late you are?" She turns back to me. "We have to run."

"No problem," I say, quickly stepping away before Cara— the tiniest of the cheerleaders, I recognize now—stomps on my foot in her rush to Amber's passenger seat.

I'm not nearly far enough away yet when I hear Cara say, "What the hell did *she* want?"

And I'm still close enough to hear Amber reply, "Just the English homework. Chill out." For the first time all day, I get to breathe a sigh of relief that someone somewhere is kind of listening to me, and hope that maybe, just maybe, there's a snowball's chance in hell something can actually change for the better.

Chapter Three

-AMBER-

Jack and I don't exchange a word the next day, but I'm still thinking about it over smoothies at Diana's pool with the rest of the squad after practice. It was just so sad. Like, *I'm* her best bet at getting taken seriously? We've barely exchanged five words, and they haven't exactly been nice ones. Does this mean she realizes I've been checking her out? Does she think I'm an easy mark because she's spotted me mentally licking her biceps in English?

Or is she serious that I'm literally the only one who's been nice to her for even point-five seconds?

It doesn't matter, the more responsible part of my brain, which doesn't get hung up on strong, sad girls with incredible arms, demands. I readjust the edges of my leopard-print bikini and shift on the chaise I'm sharing with Cara to take a long sip of strawberry-banana deliciousness. *Forget Jack Walsh. You are not friends. These are your friends.*

"I think you're starting to burn," Cara observes, lifting up her sunglasses an inch and poking at my shoulder. "Hand me the sunscreen. I'll do your back."

See? I think as I do exactly that. *Cara is my friend, who cares about protecting me from wrinkles and cancer. You, Jack Walsh, are just a girl I happen to find very attractive, and that is probably because I am queer-starved. And you are a freaking quarterback—you'll be fine. You don't need my help.*

As soon as Cara's done, I thank her (I'd reciprocate, but she's already wearing a caftan over her SPF 70) and lean back in the chair to watch Sara, Zoe, Claire, and Ella compete for who can stay in a handstand the longest while Virany judges. On the chaise to our right, Kelsey Coleman's leafing through the newest issue of *Megaphone* and flagging every page for stuff she's gonna beg her mom to get. On her other side, Taylor keeps texting someone and giggling as if no one can hear, which means Matt Devlin is definitely on the receiving end of some smut. In front of me, Crystal, Nia, and Diana are sitting with their legs in the water and discussing homecoming dresses and nail polish shades.

This is my happy place, with the girls I love and know like

the back of my hand. I don't have to think about Jack. I don't have to think about anything. I can close my eyes and let myself drift off, just a little bit . . .

I'm not sure how long I've been dozing when the sound of Jack's name brings me back to reality, but the handstand contest is definitely over. Everyone's gathered around our area of the pool now, and Cara's moved from our shared chaise to a wicker armchair with Kelsey behind her, braiding her hair. At first I think the mention of Jack was just in a dream, but then Cara says, "Come *on*," and I know I'm not about to hear anything good. "We can just skip her."

"Seriously," says Kelsey. "Who wants to sneak into *her* room at night?"

Everyone cracks up laughing, and that's when I realize the topic at hand is Midnight Breakfast, one of my favorite traditions, and yet another thing that looks like it's about to go sideways. It's always done the night before the first game, and it involves sneaking into the football players' houses at night, dragging them out of bed in whatever they're wearing, and bringing them to Maggie's Diner—an Atherton institution that also happens to be one of our squad's sponsors—for a carbo load.

I guess no one's fighting over who gets to creep into Jack Walsh's bedroom the way they do over Lamar Burke or Dan Sanchez.

"You're not really talking about leaving the quarterback out of Midnight Breakfast, are you? Come on, guys." I'm addressing everyone, but I keep my eyes fixed on Crystal, because if anyone else can put what's best for the squad over everything else, it's her.

"Look, I wish it weren't true that the team would probably be happier without her there, but . . ." Crystal shrugs like it's totally out of her hands. She doesn't look entirely comfortable about it, to be fair; she's Atherton's first Black cheer captain, which means she knows exactly what it's like to go through some shit on her way to the top. But that was from a few asshole alumni, not the squad itself, which voted for her unanimously. Having someone whose own people want them to fail is uncharted territory for all of us. "It's not being mean to say that no one wants her there. It's being honest. And we have to think about what the team wants."

"She's part of the team," I argue. My voice sounds feeble and I hate myself for it, but it sucks arguing with Crystal. It isn't that she's the type who's never open for debate—one of the reasons I most respect her as our fearless leader—but having fought her way to where she is means she doesn't like having her final decision questioned, either. Most of the time, that's fine; it's rare I disagree with her. But I sure as hell do now.

That said, how hard do I wanna fight for this? I need the squad to see me as a team player; they aren't gonna want a captain next year who isn't. But if I back down as a leader, is that any better?

I can't imagine shoving Jack to the side is the best thing for team unity, but maybe Crystal's right that including her isn't either. And it's not like I promised Jack I'd do what she asked; all I did was listen. I don't owe her anything.

But if that's true, why is guilt settling into my bones?

"Tell you what," Zoe says, a smug smile on her face as she stretches her right heel over her head. "You want her there so badly? *You* creep into her room at night and bring her."

Everyone else laughs and whistles, and oh my *God* the irony that seeing Jack in whatever she sleeps in (if anything at all—oh God, please let it be something or I am going to die) is supposed to be some sort of punishment. But I believe this is what they call a win-win scenario, and there's no way in hell I'm gonna pass up on that, even if I have to pretend this is somehow the nightmare everyone else thinks it should be.

"Oh, leave her alone," says Cara, shooting me a look that's somehow both sympathetic and a warning at the same time. "Ammo's just full of team spirit."

She's trying to come to my defense, and usually I appreciate it, but this time around, it irks me. Of course, I can't say or show that, so I just roll my eyes dramatically, complete with a little wrinkle of my nose. "No, you know what? I *will* do it. I want that Team Player trophy at the end-of-the-year banquet." I toss my hair to give it some extra drama, and there's more laughter. "But y'all are buying my breakfast if she sleeps naked."

Everyone cracks up, and I happily join in. Amber, 1. Jack, 1. Everyone else . . . who cares?

- - - - -

My heart thuds in my chest as I stand outside Jack's window that night, grateful she lives in a strip of single-story apartments, just like I do. Ordinarily I'd have another base with me, lifting me up, but tonight I'm the one member of the squad who's on her own.

Just leave, my heart pounds out. *Get out of this mess. No one will mind. Hell, they'll thank you. And the fact that you're wondering what she sleeps in is* not good.

Unfortunately, I'm too stubborn and stupid to listen, and I've got the stepladder I brought with me. All I need to do is climb it and knock.

So, I do.

There's a crashing sound and the flicker of a lamplight turning on in the window *next* to the one I knocked on, and then there's Jack, low light highlighting her sharp cheekbones and the curves of her biceps bared by her tank top. I can see her lips mouthing "What the hell?" through the window before she throws it open. "Cheer Girl?"

"At your service!" I wave imaginary pom-poms. "I'm here to get you for Midnight Breakfast."

She rubs her eyes and yawns. "What the hell is Midnight Breakfast? And stop knocking on my mom's window. She sleeps like the dead, but if you do wake her, she'll kill both of us."

Oops. I scurry down the ladder and move it to the right window, then climb back up until we're face-to-face. Behind her, there's a pull-out couch messily covered in boring sheets, so I guess she sleeps in the living room. As far as I can tell, the walls are completely bare, and there isn't much more to speak of, furniture-wise. It definitely does not look like a place a family has actually settled. "The varsity squad picks up the starting lineup the night before the first game and we all go to a diner to eat breakfast. At midnight. Hence the name. Didn't anyone tell—You know what? Never mind."

Her lips twist into a scowl-smile combo. "Yeah, so weird I didn't see that in the team newsletter Dan Sanchez gently places on my lunch tray each day. Anyway, I'm already asleep. Why would I want breakfast?" She fumbles for something else on the nightstand, then slips on a pair of glasses. "Don't you dare tell a soul I wear these."

I roll my eyes. "There's nothing to tell, precious; you're wearing 'em to breakfast. Come on. The whole idea is to go however we found you."

"But you get to be dressed and made up?"

I'm glad she can't see my blush in the darkness. My mom *did* point out that I was a little prettied up for something that takes place when most people are in their pajamas. That's what I get for asking to borrow her mascara, I guess, especially since she's one of the only people in the world who knows I'm not wearing it for Miguel. "Right. Because I'm a cheerleader and if anyone sees me looking like a mere mortal, they turn to stone."

She snorts and there's a genuine laugh in there and it

50

softens me a little despite myself. Maybe more than a little, or maybe it's the late hour, because I get a bit too stupid and say, "The glasses look cute. Seriously. Come on."

"Cute?"

I'm about to snap out a reminder that she's the one who asked me for a favor and maybe she should consider not teasing me, but when I catch her eye, it feels like there's a question in it, wanting to know exactly how I meant "cute," and my stomach tightens.

I know the queer girl dance. I'm pretty sure it just began. And maybe I'm projecting or maybe I'm stereotyping because she's built like a brick wall and exudes more masculinity than half the football team or maybe I'm not. And as a frequent hater of this dance, I can't help but want her to know that at least in this, we're on the same team. "Very fucking cute, okay? A little too cute, if I'm being honest. Don't make me say it again."

There's no more fight as she grabs a sweatshirt and follows me down the ladder and out to my car.

The ride to Maggie's is short, but Jack still finds a way to be an asshole for the length of it. "Do the other cheerleaders know that you're treating me like at least half a human? Is that gonna get you in trouble?"

It might, I bite my tongue to stop from saying. "They know I'm here," is all I offer.

"Funny how they were a whole lot friendlier when they thought Jack Walsh was a guy, decorating my locker and leaving me cookies like I was an actual member of the team. Doesn't that bother you?"

Oh no. This girl is not baiting me. "Maybe I'm just as disappointed," I say coolly.

She snorts. "Maybe you are. Somehow not one person in this school gives a shit that Sundstrom approached *me*, or are we all pretending we don't know that because, oh right, he'll get in deep shit if anyone calls him on recruiting? My stats make your last QB's look like a joke. It's the whole reason I'm here, and yet it doesn't seem to count for a damn thing."

Okay, number six might be a pain in my ass, but even so, I know it'd be cruel not to warn her to keep herself out of even hotter water. I pull up to a red light and turn to her. "Listen, I know being a badass is very important to you, but you can't say stuff like that about Robbie," I tell her. "It's only going to make them hate you more. Robbie's dead, so he's a saint. He's dead, so he's the greatest they ever had. And the fact that you make him look like a joke is a very big part of the problem."

She's quiet for so long, I'd wonder if she even heard me if not for the cold look in her deep brown eyes and the defiant set of her jaw, bared by her omnipresent tight blond topknot. Then the light turns green, and I'm forced to look away and concentrate on the road again. Which also makes me feel freer to keep talking.

"I know you wanna prove yourself, and I'm *not* telling you

to play any worse than your best. I just want you to get that if people are a little harsh right now, that's why. They'll chill out once the season starts and they're getting wins they've never seen before." *At least I hope they will.*

"If I were making him look like a joke but I were a guy, they'd be okay with it, though, right? It's only embarrassing because I'm doing it in a sports bra."

There's no point in lying about that. She's not stupid. "Correct."

She sighs. "So what am I supposed to do, then?"

"I don't know," I admit. "This kind of thing isn't in the cheer manual. But I think doing team-bonding stuff like Midnight Breakfast is a good idea."

"What if it isn't?"

"Then . . . I don't know. Pretend it went well even if it doesn't. Be a leader, because it's your job. Play like you came to play."

She's quiet again, and I think that'll be it for the rest of the short ride, but then she says, "Why do you even care? You didn't seem like you wanted to help me."

"Because I'm not an asshole," I say flatly. "But if I'm being honest, it's also because I'd like to be captain of the squad next year, and I'm betting on being able to make peace between you and the team to be proof that I know how to lead. And if it keeps being a shitshow, then the team is gonna pass over me to go with someone who hates you, and I'm gonna be pretty pissed."

"So, this is actually, like, ninety percent selfish."

"And? You approached *me* yesterday being one hundred percent selfish. We want the same things."

There's a pause, and I think she's about to lay into me, but instead she says, "Plus, you think I look very fucking cute in my glasses."

I groan, wishing I'd left my long waves down so I could hide behind them, but I'm stuck avoiding eye contact as I pull into the parking lot of Maggie's instead. "Please forget I said that. I am a terrible flirt and I wasn't thinking, okay?" And in a flash but still way too late, I realize what I've just said. "No, wait, forget I said *that*." Jesus fuck. I pull into a spot, park, and bury my face in my hands. "Just kill me."

For the first time in my life, I hear Jack Walsh truly laugh, and it's low in her throat and coated with honey and it sends pom-poms waving through my insides, or at least that's how it feels. Definitely less gentle than butterflies. "Actually, Cheer Girl, you're not that terrible at it. Now let's go get some pancakes."

I don't need to be told twice.

- - - - -

The look on Jack's face when we exit the car and she gets her first real viewing of Maggie's run-down exterior is skeptical, but she joins me anyway, tugging her hoodie tightly around her body as if it'll protect her from whatever lies ahead. I'm praying she's got nothing to worry about tonight, that one of our favorite traditions will remain delightful and celebratory no matter what, but truthfully, I'm almost as anxious as she is.

I just hope Miguel's already there.

Of course, there's no such luck, but most of the others aren't there yet either; they had more people to coordinate, and more stops to make. I nudge Jack forward and greet the group that's already seated—Lamar Burke, Matt Devlin, Zach Sawyer, Taylor Broussard, Ella and Virany Chow, and Claire Marlow—with big smiles as we slide in next to them. "Y'all are *fast*," I say, grabbing menus for me and Jack even though I've been dreaming of waffles with whipped cream and strawberries since the bell rang this afternoon.

"*Somebody* was awake, fully dressed, and playing video games when Virany and I walked in," says Ella, sticking her tongue out at Lamar. "Not exactly a super-fun surprise."

"Midnight's not that late! I don't know why y'all are asleep then." He takes an ice cube out of his glass and crunches it between his teeth. "Devlin was just faking it to get Taylor to see him sleeping naked."

"He was *not*," Ella squeals, and Matt grins.

"Man, stop ruining all my game."

"*What* game, Devlin?" More guys and girls roll in, teasing and laughing, and when I see Miguel among them, I yank him into the seat next to me.

"Someone's excited to see me," he teases, kissing the top of my head. "Seems only right, since you sent other girls to pick me up."

He knows full well why Cara and Kelsey had to get him instead of me, but Diana saves me the trouble of responding. "Y'all are too cute." She looks like she's gonna puke.

From across the table, I see Jack's eyebrow shoot up, undoubtedly wondering why the hell I was flirting in my car if I'm already tied to the strapping young lad next to me. I'm not sure how to react to that, so I just tear my eyes away from her and focus on Diana.

"Your sincerity overwhelms me, D. And someday you, too, can get the biggest nerd on an athletic team, I'm sure."

"Aw, mi amor." Miguel swings an arm around my shoulders and squeezes tight. "Your pride in me and our magical romance means everything to me."

I can't help shifting my eyes back to Jack, but the look on her face is unreadable now. Everyone else jumps in on the teasing as usual—making fun of each other is our little "couple gag" and pretty much the only way we stay sane through the bullshit—and I'm happy to draw more of it if it means keeping heat off Jack. But I know she must think I'm playing one or both of them, and I wish I could tell her the truth.

Conversation flows light and easy as the tables fill up with everyone's arrivals, and while no one actively greets Jack the way they do the guys, they don't say anything nasty to her either. Which I guess is . . . something.

"Lemme know if you need some menu guidance," Miguel

says to Jack, the first person to speak to her all night, and I think I fall even more deeply into platonic love with him in that moment. "Not everything is as safe as it sounds."

"Do tell." She leans forward, eyes glittering, and a little ache forms in my chest at how alive she is from just being acknowledged here. "Is Maggie's Super Combo Breakfast Platter not super after all?"

"I'm so glad you asked," he responds in his booming announcer voice, then drops to a quieter tone so it won't carry to the kitchen. "You see, while Maggie is excellent at pancakes and waffles, and no one can really screw up bacon—"

"That's a dirty lie," Zach pipes up. "Devlin's mom may be super hot, but her bacon is god-awful."

"That's because it's vegan, you fucknugget," Matt replies, smacking Zach on the back of his head. "And stop talking about my mom being hot."

"Is his mom hot?" Jack murmurs to me.

"Very," I mouth, and she smothers a laugh behind her hands, disguising it as a cough.

"And no one can really screw up bacon," Miguel repeats firmly, never one to allow his life lessons to be interrupted, "Maggie's hash browns are always underseasoned and somehow manage to be both burnt and raw at the same time."

He's not wrong, and it truly is a mystery of science. But before anyone else can confirm or deny, Cara somberly says, "Robbie used to get the Super Combo Breakfast Platter," and it shuts everyone's laughing right up.

"Oh man, yeah, he did," Dan Sanchez murmurs, and the rest of the table nods.

Jack's eyes widen as she looks to me for help. "Guess it's truly the breakfast of Alligator champions," I say cheerfully. "Even if Maggie has not mastered hash browns."

No one laughs except Miguel, and a couple of people toss glares at Jack. I claw my fingers into Miguel's sweatpants-covered thigh, and he squeezes my hand. At least one person here knows everyone's being utterly ridiculous. "Really, you should try the Western omelet," Miguel suggests to Jack, as if changing her order will somehow sufficiently preserve Robbie's memory. "That's really good here."

It's not. Maggie puts in too many tomatoes and it always ends up a little watery. But Jack nods, and that's the order she gives to the waitress.

"I'm gonna have the Super Combo Breakfast Platter," Dan declares. "In honor of Robbie."

"Me too," says Lamar, and Matt agrees, and so forth down the line until every football player's doing it except for Jack, and Miguel, who hasn't ordered yet. But he mumbles that he'll have it too, even though he hates Maggie's hash browns and thinks her cheese grits are a microaggression against all people of color and anyone else with working taste buds. I feel mildly betrayed on Jack's behalf, but if she feels the same, it's impossible to tell, because you can't meet someone's eyes who refuses to lift them from the table.

Talk shifts to Robbie then, and though Miguel easily joins

in—or at least he makes it look easy, though it's probably killing him—I can't even bring myself to fake interest. It's bad enough that I brought Jack here; to skip out on "Remember that time Robbie" and "It was hilarious when Robbie" Hour would be a sin worse than dropping a top girl on her butt. I do my best to give context to Jack every now and again, but it's clear as she pushes food around on her plate while barely eating any that she's checked out.

Finally, once I've shoveled my food down my throat without really tasting it, I declare I've gotta go home.

"It's not even one thirty!" Cara whines, as if her parents wouldn't absolutely flip if they knew she was out right now. No one sneaks out of the house with the agility of our best flyer. "Don't be a party pooper. Your mom never cares when you stay out late."

"My mom might not, but my trig homework does," I reply with a sad face. "I gotta get up early to do some makeup work."

Now it's Miguel's turn to dig into my thigh. I'm stealing one of his best patented excuses for when he needs to get away for a date he doesn't want anyone to know about. I don't say anything to him, though—just leave money on the table and ask Jack if she wants a ride, like she's not obviously dying to get out of here. She agrees as if the idea only just occurred to her, and we head out even while Cara yells, "Boo, you whore," at my back.

This time, we don't exchange any words on the ride home,

but when I pull up in front of her building, I say, "Okay, that did kind of suck. I'm sorry."

She shrugs. "I should've known it'd be as bad as I thought. Or I guess maybe it wasn't *as* bad—nobody spit in my food."

"Progress!" I cheer, and she snorts. "Though I couldn't help but notice you ate ketchup with your eggs, which is so much worse than spit."

"Don't you dare blaspheme my favorite vegetable."

"Ketchup?"

"Salad of champions," she declares solemnly, and I don't know whether to laugh or hurl. "And hey, thanks for trying tonight, even if it was kind of a bust. And, uh, thank your boyfriend, too. He's the only guy on the team who's been halfway decent to me."

It's the first time in a year that the truth about me and Miguel has danced on my tongue. There was nothing to tell Veronica, since we knew absolutely nothing about each other outside of cheer world and had no plans to change that. But whether it's Jack's rare laugh, or her strength and drive, or the shyness so at odds with this massive thing she's doing here, somewhere along the line the name "Cheer Girl" went from pissing me off to curling my toes. And now I just . . . feel like I want to know more. And for her to maybe really know me, a little.

But I swallow it down, because as much as I hate this, Miguel's secret is wrapped up in the lie too, and I can't break his trust like that.

"I will," I force out, wishing I could apologize for what must seem like messing with her head.

I expect her to let herself out of the car then, but after a few beats of awkward silence, she speaks again. "I know you're doing your best at this whole 'cheer' thing, and I appreciate it. Guess I'm just beyond help."

"You are *not* beyond help, four-eyes," I say. "It's gonna get better. You'll see."

"If you say so."

"It'll make a difference when you start winning. I know I sound like a broken record, but I really do believe that." I think. I'm pretty sure I believe it, anyway.

"Except that winning could also make it worse, right? I see what you were saying now about the sanctification of Robbie Oakes. Maybe it's just not possible for me to replace a dead guy. Sorry if that sounds insensitive," she adds quickly. "I hadn't realized he was a friend of yours, too."

"He wasn't," I say, glad there's at least one secret I *can* safely tell her tonight. "I mean, that's between you and me—and Miguel—but . . . yeah. You don't ever have to worry about Robbie love coming from this direction."

"Good to know." She unbuckles her seat belt, and I don't know why, but it feels like the end of the world's worst date. "Thanks for the ride and everything."

Again, all the things I shouldn't say rise to the tip of my tongue, and I bite it. But biting my tongue doesn't stop me from taking her phone from the center console and putting in my number before handing it over. "In case you find yourself needing a personal pep rally," I say in as platonic a voice as I can muster.

"And here I thought you were planning to use my window for all your communication needs," she says with a slight smile as she slips the phone into the kangaroo pocket of her hoodie.

"Well, I don't have *your* number," I point out, "so I still might."

Her smile widens a little, and she bites her lip as if to tamp it down. "Duly noted."

Okay, we're flirting. I am a horrible person. But at least I'm not yanking her across the seat by the drawstring of her sweatshirt like I desperately want to, so I guess this counts as self-control.

And then, while my stomach is already fluttering like leaves in the late-summer breeze, she says, "G'night, Cheer Girl," and lets herself out of my car.

If I don't crash on my way home, it'll be a fucking miracle.

-JACK-

Getting back to sleep is not happening.

I can blame being dragged out of my house in the middle of the night, or Maggie's overbaked biscuit sitting in my stomach like lead, but it's four thirty in the morning and every time I close my eyes, all I see is the cheerleader putting her number in my phone.

Why would you, an obviously queer girl, put your number in the phone of another obviously queer girl, if you already have a boyfriend?

Or is Amber McCloud actually *so* heterosexual that we were having entirely different conversations tonight? Am I conjuring rainbow dreams out of nothing?

I don't know.

Maybe.

Probably.

I wish I could just knock on my mom's bedroom door to plague her with my girl troubles, but while I never really had to come out—everything from my clothing to my hobbies kinda did that for me—my sexuality still isn't something we acknowledge beyond the bare minimum. Open queerness isn't something she grew up around in Niceville, and she's not exactly the kind of mom who gives the Talk, either.

No, what I really need is for Sage and Morgan to wake up, because I cannot figure this shit out alone.

Say Cheer Girl was flirting—and she *did* say she was flirting. Would it matter? I'm not hooking up with a girl who has a boyfriend, especially if that boyfriend is my teammate, and my only decent one at that. Besides, Amber's the closest thing I've got to a friend here, and I don't wanna fuck that up either.

But.

I could really use a personal pep rally.

Especially if that's a euphemism.

Fuck it. I slip my hand under the covers and find the relief I desperately need as quietly as humanly possible. Personal pep rally indeed.

I've got plenty of time to hate myself for this in the morning.

- - - - -

Turns out, I hate whoever came up with the idea of doing Midnight Breakfast the night before our first game waaaay more than I hate myself for a little ill-advised self-love. Every single one of us—cheerleader and football player—spends the entire day yawning, and the neon Gatorade we're all pounding isn't nearly as energizing as I need it to be.

The only physical activity I'm up for today is hiding from Cheer Girl, which is made easier by the fact that she's doing the same thing.

Sage and Morgan agree that she was flirting but are torn on whether that means I should run in the other direction. (Sage is forever on team "Go get some!" while Morgan says "I do not understand allosexuals at all" at least once a week.) All I know is that I have to get all thoughts about Amber and last night out of my head because there is *no* coming back from fucking up tonight. Not for me.

When the bell finally signals the end of third period, I bolt out of my seat and head to the coach's office, where he walks me through the same video he already has at least twice, pointing out weak spots in the Lawndale lineup and quizzing me on different plays. If anything goes wrong tonight, it isn't gonna be because of me, and he knows it, because I ace that shit.

The game is at seven, which only gives me a few hours before the pep rally. The whole idea of prancing around in front of everyone at this unsupportive school makes me wanna hurl, but Coach made it clear that pep rallies are not optional to anyone who wants to play that day. Part of me may wanna hide out in some corner anyway, but mostly, I can't believe that tonight I actually

Get

To

Play.

Nothing else matters.

I barely get through the rest of my classes, spending the time mentally running through the playbook and drawing the number six over and over like the self-absorbed bastard I am.

Finally, it's time.

The cheerleaders have been wearing their uniforms all day, so I have the locker room to myself to change and spend an extra minute marveling at the sight of myself in my game-day jersey. Damn, I really do make this look good. I send a selfie to Sage and Morgan, smoothing down my tightly pulled hair one last time, and then . . . wait.

I don't have a coach telling me when to go in. I'm not there for the locker room shit. I hear cheering sound off in the gym, but I have no idea if anyone's coming to get me, or if I'm just supposed to *know* when it's my turn to storm in.

I know every single play by heart, but I don't know when to enter a fucking pep rally.

Superstar!!! Morgan texts back with a bunch of different emojis, and I've never felt less like one. Thank Jesus they cannot see me right now.

The cheers get louder, so the football players must've started jogging in. Every fifteen seconds or so they rise up a little extra, suggesting one of the more popular guys—Devlin or Sawyer or whoever—has run in. It makes sense for me to be last, I think, being the QB. But how do I know when they're done? Are they just gonna forget about me, or—

Fierce banging on the locker room door jolts me out of my thoughts, so fucking terrifying it makes my heart race. But I guess that's my cue. I'm not sure whether I'm supposed to wear my helmet or not—yet another thing no one's told me—so I carry it, and figure I can put it on if I see the other guys wearing theirs. At least the cheering's still going on, so it's not like I've missed everything.

Except that when I run in to the fog-and-flashing-light-filled room, it's like I somehow pulled out the plug. The effects keep going, but the room goes quiet. For a second I think maybe "Number six, your quarterback, Jack Walsh!" was all in my head, but I know better.

The emcee—whoever it is—definitely said it out loud, and it sucked all the pep out of the room.

At that instant, if someone straight-up asked me, I would give this up. I would tell my brothers I was wrong, tell my parents I want to go home, tell Morgan and Sage I'm a loser, and tell little kid Jack, who never even dreamed she'd get this shot, to trust me, she doesn't want it.

If I had a sword I could fall on out of shame, I would.

Before I can look for the nearest sharp object, I hear what I'm pretty sure is a muttered "For fuck's sake," and then Miguel Santiago emerges from the blob of players and holds out his arms. Amber neatly flies into his hands and the crowd goes wild as they do this vomitously adorable little dance routine that I think was somehow a favor to me but might make me feel even worse.

The next fifteen minutes of cheers and marching band tunes go off without a hitch while I mentally disappear into the only thing that matters: the game. I let the plays fill my brain, the scouting report of Lawndale flood my memory, and the adrenaline course through my veins all through the rally, the shuffling onto the bus, and the pregame meal. While I shovel chicken and mashed potatoes into my mouth, barely tasting anything, I think about Sanchez's blind spot, Burke's tendency to look down at the ball too often, and every single one of our other flaws that got picked apart on film at practice earlier this week.

Let the guys fuck around and use this time to talk about

"kicking Lawndale ass" (with nothing to back it up) and which cheerleaders are looking particularly good this year, which involves a lot of elbowing Miguel.

Let the guys take me for granted, even if those same films showed me playing with near-flawless form and accuracy.

Let my brothers stay home, refusing to show up with my parents and support me.

Let the entire school stay silent at the sound of my name.

Let everyone underestimate me. Because they have no idea what I can do.

But they're about to.

- - - - -

Channeling immense amounts of negative energy does epic things for my arm, as it turns out.

By halftime, I've thrown for two TDs and run one in, and even the most hard-core of Robbie's worship squad have stopped trying to crowd me as if I can't aim more than ten feet in front of me. They may not wanna acknowledge to my face that I'm good, but it's just embarrassing for them if they can't acknowledge it to the crowd. We're up 20–7, and we'd be up by more if they'd trusted me sooner. But two of those touchdowns have come in the last ten minutes, and there's a frisson of electricity passing through the entire team at the certainty there will be more.

I chug my Gatorade as we huddle up and Coach Sundstrom lays out plays for the second half, but I can't help my gaze drifting over to the cheerleaders setting up in the middle of the field. There's no special chant for me the way there is for Devlin, Burke, Santiago, and Sanchez—the way I'm sure there was for Robbie—but they have no choice but to kick and shout with every first down and every score, and the crowd's energy is soaring now as the girls form an impressive pyramid.

I really need to stop staring at Amber McCloud's pompoms.

She's dating one of my teammates. It doesn't matter if she was flirting with me or why. It doesn't matter if she came to my rescue at the pep rally, or got me to Midnight Breakfast, or thinks I look cute in my glasses. If I'm not letting all the other shit distract me, I'm *certainly* not letting a pair of legs do it.

Not even really good legs that can do absolutely mind-blowing things.

"You're doing great, Walsh," Sundstrom says, bringing my attention back to the huddle. A couple of the guys grunt in agreement. I can't look around to see who without being obvious, but my money's on Santiago and Burke, the only two guys who ever give me so much as a nod. "This is our game to lose, and we get to slow things down now." He turns to me. "You ready to run again? Or you need a rest?"

"No, Coach," I say automatically. And I don't. I feel great. Physically, anyway. "I'm good. Lemme run."

I get a gruff nod, and then he turns to say something to Devlin, so I let my gaze travel back to the field. Amber and the cheerleaders are doing a bunch of complicated jumps and yelling and, God, the way her entire face lights up when she's doing this. She looks like I feel, like she can't believe she gets to do this thing she was absolutely born for. I'm pretty sure I'm not the only one on the team specifically checking her out either. But I *am* the one who can't get caught doing it, so I put my full focus on the huddle, let Coach pep-talk us a little more, and then shout and break.

And okay, maybe I glance in her direction one more time, just to make sure she's watching.

She is.

Not only do I throw fifteen yards in the most beautifully perfect spiral for our third touchdown, but I end up running in another one in the fourth quarter. A 33–7 win is a wider spread than the Alligators have seen in a long time, even in their luckiest wins, and it feels so damn good, especially when I catch my parents waving and hollering in the crowd. My dad drove four hours to get here, and I'm so fucking happy I made it worth his while. I won't even dwell on how my brothers opted to stay back and be babysat by my grandma rather than join.

All around me, the guys are leaping on one another and slapping each other's asses, pouring Gatorade on Sundstrom that splashes far enough to hit the assistant coaches, too. I let myself wait for two minutes for congratulations that never come, and I know that somehow, even this win is being attributed to the ghost of Robbie fucking Oakes.

That gets made perfectly clear when Devlin grabs the mic and quiets everyone down. "I think we all know who to thank for this win." He looks up at the sky, and I'm not sure whether those are genuine tears in his eyes or he's just blinded by the lights. "Robbie, brother, we miss you, man. I can't believe you're not here. But we know you're watching out for us, guiding our hands, and that you delivered this win. Number one forever."

My gut twists into knots as I watch the cheerleaders, Amber included, get into formation and do what must've been the standard Robbie cheer. It's somehow rowdy and somber at the same time, something they must've practiced, and it's followed by the marching band's equally confusing rendition of "When the Saints Go Marching In."

Whatever. My parents seeing this win is what matters. They know they didn't move me here for nothing. And hopefully, one day, the right person to move me forward somehow will join them in the stands, but if not—even if it's always "just a game"—playing under the lights tonight felt like pure magic.

That's why I'm here. That's why I'm tolerating teammates who ignore me and cheerleaders who hate me and Amber McCloud's stupid cute ass. Because the field is where I most feel like myself, and this could make my future. The chance is tiny, I know. There's certainly no future ahead playing QB in the NFL. But that doesn't mean I couldn't be a sports reporter like Holly Rowe, or a coach like Katie Sowers.

I just have to get through the fucking season.

Even if my parents are literally the only people cheering me on.

(*Are they?* I wonder, thinking of the number in my phone, the hotline to a "personal pep rally." But that way lies dangerous thinking. Dangerous, stupid thinking.)

I push that dangerous, stupid thinking aside and pick my way over to the field house, where I stop short, realizing there's only one visitors' locker room and it's currently being filled by a mass of wretched, sweaty boys. This is what I get for spending halftime on the bench, paralyzed by the irrational fear that they'd find a way to start without me if I disappeared to the locker room that apparently doesn't exist for me.

"Tough luck, Walsh," Sanchez says with a smirk as the guys watch me try to figure out where the hell I could possibly take off this stinking uniform, and laugh their asses off at my helplessness.

I set my jaw and ignore them, looking to see where the cheerleaders are heading, but none of them seem to be doing anything other than chatting with each other and flirting with the boys who pass by. For all the work they did tonight, somehow none of them look like they even broke a sweat.

How nice for them.

Desperate, I yank out my phone and pull up Amber's

number. *Where do we go to change?* Then I remember she doesn't have my number. *It's Jack btw.*

I don't see her anywhere, but my phone lights up with a message thirty seconds later. *Go around front. Someone will let you in and point you to the bathroom.*

I do what she says and strip off my jersey and pads the second the door closes behind me. I'm filthy, but a shower won't be happening until I get home, no matter how much my muscles are screaming for one. The baby wipes I brought will have to do. I'm swiping one down the center of my sports bra when the door opens and I freeze like a deer in headlights.

Chapter Four

-AMBER-

I should stay away from her for so many reasons, but between the pep rally and no one bothering to tell her where to go after the game, I can't help but check on Jack to make sure everything's okay. I tell Cara I'm going to the "locker room," knowing not one single girl will follow me in there because we never change at other schools, and then follow the exact instructions I gave Jack, gingerly pushing open the bathroom door and keeping my eyes on the floor just in case. "Jack?"

No answer, but I can hear her breathing. I step in, letting

the door close behind me. "Jack? It's Amber. *Just* Amber," I clarify.

"Lucky me," she mutters.

I follow the sound of her voice, despite how harsh and unwelcoming it is, but as soon as I see her, I freeze in my tracks. She's taken off the top half of her uniform, and as cute as she is in that, seeing her in nothing but a sports bra and football pants makes my mouth go dry. I quickly look away to give her some privacy, and it takes a few pathetic attempts to get my next words out. "What's wrong?"

"Nothing." I hear a yank on what must be her hair elastic, and it occurs to me I've never seen her hair down. I can't even picture it, and don't think she'd like me to. "I just played football. I'm sweaty."

Me too, I think, rubbing my palms on my cheer skirt. "I'd think you'd be a little happier-sounding that you just won your first game."

"Yeah, well, guess you don't know me very well." A snap of the hair elastic on the skin of her wrist echoes in the bathroom, and then the sink turns on.

"Ooookay." I lean against the wall and cross my arms as I listen to her splash water on her face, then wind her hair back up into its usual knot with another snap. "I was just coming to check on you. I can go. But are you gonna tell me why you're mad at me after I just cheered you on for hours?" I usually avoid conflict like the Whelans avoid PG-13 movies, but I just spent hours watching Jack kick some major ass out on the field. While I knew my congratulations fantasies were just that—fantasies—she felt comfortable enough to text me, so I expected a slightly warmer reception than this. "And spare me pretending you're not. You're way better at sports than you are at acting."

"Yeah, well, I'm sorry we can't all win Emmys for playing the role of 'single girl flirting' when we actually have boyfriends," she snaps, and my gaze flies to hers without even registering that she's still not dressed. It's clear from the way she immediately winces that she did *not* mean to say that out loud.

But she did, and now it's out there, and I have to either explain and apologize or deny, deny, deny.

Before I can make a choice, her voice gets even more acidic as she says, "Let me guess—you were *not* flirting."

Now's the time to say, "Of course I wasn't *flirting*." But even with her being a sweaty mess, cheeks burning so red that I'm not sure if it's from exertion or embarrassment, I don't think I've ever wanted to touch someone this badly.

She was amazing out there. *Amazing.* She was fearless and strong and defiant and just thinking about it makes me stupid enough to say, "No, I definitely was."

Her milk-chocolate eyes light on me, something between anger and surprise in them. I have an actual effect on this girl. This girl who just led a terrible football team to victory, who played her heart out even though no one gave her a second look, who's probably strong enough to break me in two—she has a weak spot.

And it might be me.

She is *definitely* mine.

Fuck it.

"It's complicated," I say, stepping closer. I can't tell her the whole truth, because it isn't just mine, but I hope this will be enough. "Miguel and I. It's complicated. But he knows I like girls; he's good with it."

"Congrats on having a boyfriend who manages the basic task of not being biphobic." Her face is returning to its normal tan, and she throws on a tank top from her bag, which helps sharpen my focus a little bit—enough to realize I haven't been clear enough.

"No, I mean, we're not . . . *exclusive*, I guess, is the word. Not that anyone else knows that, but." Jesus, I sound like a creep.

"Oh wow, okay, so he's cool with you having a sidepiece as long as he gets to watch, or something? Got it. So glad we had this conversation. Can you please get out now so I can finish changing?"

It's my turn to wince, feeling every ounce of the implication that she won't change in front of me. I know she's queer herself and *my* queerness isn't why she's talking like I'm some kind of predator, but somehow, in a locker room context, the fear you'll be called out for watching a girl change never quite goes away, even if you would never in a million years.

She must get it too, because for a second, her face softens, but no apology comes, and I can't blame her.

But I also can't leave, not while she thinks this about me and Miguel. "Our relationship is fake," I blurt out, even though it's far more information than I want to give. "I got tired of constantly making stuff up to turn down guys, and Miguel . . ." I fumble for a second, then pull something out of my ass, uttering a silent apology to Miguel's extremely cool mother, Dania, whom I love dearly and who makes me the most delicious flan this side of the gulf for my birthday. "His parents are really strict, and they don't want him screwing around. Having a serious girlfriend keeps their eyes off him, so this was our solution. And it works. Except . . ."

"Except?"

I don't even realize how much closer I've moved until I inhale the scent of grass and earth mingled with baby wipes. "Except that I cannot stop thinking about how cute you look in glasses."

Finally, *finally*, her defenses fall away and the shoulders she'd been tensing up to her earlobes relax. "Oh."

"And I mean, you know what they say about cheerleaders and quarterbacks."

Her lips curve in the slightest of smiles. "You know, somehow I don't think that's something they're saying at Atherton these days."

Well, maybe they should, I think but don't say.

I am thinking a lot of things I'm not saying right now, most of which revolve around her mouth.

I definitely should not say any of those things.

Right?

I'm still contemplating *what* to say when she gives a little awkward laugh and says, "Sorry, I really do need to change. I don't trust them not to leave without me. Plus, I'm gross."

"You're not gross," I say automatically. "Well, you kinda are, but in a tough way. Very sporty."

She grins. "You should probably go too, but . . . maybe I'll see you later?"

"That window of yours still open?"

"Might be."

I match her smile with one of my own. "Well, then, you 'might' see me later."

- - - - -

It feels extremely wrong to go from the game straight to a victory party that doesn't include the obvious MVP, who also happens to be the girl I was just thinking about maybe kissing. But if I learned anything from Midnight Breakfast, it's that forcing it won't do anyone any favors. Still, when I show up to Zach Sawyer's house with my brain still buzzing a bus ride and a quick change at home later, I expect the team to have turned a corner on Jack, seeing as she's glaringly responsible for their huge win. But once again, I was expecting too much.

"Did you hear Coach? 'Great job, Walsh.' Like she could've done shit without Sawyer and Woods on everyone's asses to make sure she didn't break a nail." Dan's already mid-tirade—and mid-Heineken—when I show up. "Pathetic."

What's pathetic is you acting like that's not their literal jobs on the field, I wait for someone to say. But nobody does. Definitely not me.

I should say it.

But I don't.

"Man, this victory would've been so much sweeter with Robbie," Zach says mournfully. Everyone murmurs in agreement, no one pointing out that the victory wouldn't have *happened* with Robbie.

"We should pour one out for him," Lamar says somberly.

"If you pour one out on my mom's fucking rug, I will fucking kill you," Zach snaps, which of course sets the guys off. They all take turns pretending to pour their beers out, pulling them up at the last minute, while Zach's girlfriend, Mia, squeals and he glowers.

"Even community college guys are gonna be better than this, right?" Cara rests her head on my shoulder with a sigh, the smell of her vanilla body spray strong in my nostrils.

"Here's hoping," Not that it's a guy occupying my brain, but I link pinkies with Cara in our traditional "make a wish" move anyway. Game nights are the only Friday nights Cara's exempt from spending with her family, and it's strictly because football players and cheerleaders are so revered in this town that Pastor Whelan's congregation loves that his daughter is on the squad, skimpy skirt and all. I know full well he'll rope blessing the Alligators into his donation collection on Sunday, and Cara will be there in one of her church-perfect pink or white or yellow or baby-blue dresses.

But right here, right now, she's the version of herself that gets just as high on flying through the air and being cheered on under the lights as I do, the version who sang along to Camila Cabello with me on the way here, who sneaked me a pouch of her little sister's fruit snacks that she knows I love, and who's helping bring me back to myself after one of the most confusing weeks I can ever remember.

Speaking of friends who help me feel normal. "Miggy!" the guys yell as Miguel lets himself in, having dropped off his parents and sister before taking the family car. Miguel is a permanent designated driver—alcohol gives him migraines—which is actually how we became friends. I got stupid drunk at a party as a freshman who had no idea what she could hold, and he was the valiant and newly licensed sophomore who drove me home. It was only because he thought I was passed out plastered in his back seat that he had a brief conversation with his secret then-boyfriend on speakerphone, and I was so relieved to find another queer kid at Atherton that I drunkenly blurted out that I was gay too. (No one had introduced me to the sexuality spectrum yet. I had, however, been introduced to Diana's cousin Mariana's lips in the coatroom at Diana's quinceañera.)

We didn't talk much that night—mostly he focused on making me drink water and getting me safely to bed without my mom noticing (he failed miserably, getting me grounded from everything but cheerleading for a month). But we started chatting in the hallways, developing secret codes to discuss crushes. Then, once my grounding was lifted, we started hanging out for real. I learned the wonders of his mother Dania's ropa vieja, Silvio Rodríguez's music, and how to properly make Café Cubano, and he got introduced to my mom's small but excellent queer lit collection, the glory of nail polish (which we always meticulously removed before he left), and homemade hash browns that are far superior to Maggie's (even if he does insist on bringing his own hot sauce to eat them). When people started assuming we were a couple, we ran with it; it was the perfect cover. He's been my rock ever since.

And as my rock, I really want him to stand up for the girl I was just thinking about kissing.

But he doesn't know that I thought about kissing her. And while he's very Team Get Amber Laid, I don't think hooking up with the new QB and threatening to blow our cover is what he had in mind. As badly as I wanna tell him what went down tonight, part of me is nervous he'll be pissed, and I don't know what to do with that.

But, bless him, as if he could read my mind, he asks, "Where's Walsh?"

The guys laugh. "Whoops," Zach says with exaggerated slowness. "Guess her invite must've gotten lost."

Don't laugh with them, I pray in Miguel's direction, wishing Cara wasn't lying on me so I could reach over and squeeze his hand or something. *Please be a decent human being and don't laugh with them.*

He does laugh, but only after he says, "Y'all are such dicks," and I decide I'll have to be satisfied with that.

He glances at me, as if waiting for me to build on his statement, and I'm embarrassed to realize I was expecting him to do more on Jack's behalf than I've been willing to do myself. "Not very team building," I manage, though I let it sound like a joke.

"Please, like you fine ladies wanna cheer for a girl." Matt flexes his biceps, which are, admittedly, nice and sizable. "Not when you could be cheering for this."

"You weren't exactly next in line for QB1, Devlin," Miguel says wryly, and I could kiss him, even while other guys throw chips in his direction, booing.

"That isn't the point," Matt says, just as Zach says, "It should've stayed Robbie."

"It's *Robbie's* fault it wasn't Robbie," someone blurts out, and oh crap, that was me. "Y'all keep acting like Jack stole something from him, but—"

Cool air rushes to my skin as Cara shoves away from me,

and Miguel immediately swoops in. "Clearly someone's had enough to drink," he says as he pulls me to my feet. "Just how I like 'em," he adds with a wink.

Thank God, his gross humor actually works and a few people laugh, failing to notice I haven't even opened the can in my hand, while a few others—including Cara—stare at me in horror. I've taken their lord's name in vain, apparently. Which is ridiculous, because I haven't said a single word that isn't true, but no one's ready to talk about that yet. And Jack being quarterback has given them yet another excuse to avoid it. Because it's so much easier to channel their anger at her than it is to get pissed at their friend for drinking and driving.

This is the Atherton Alligators' grieving process, and God help anyone who tries to disrupt it.

Miguel's hand on my back steers me into Zach's yard, and he automatically drapes his varsity jacket over my shoulders as soon as we find a quiet corner. "Loud—"

"I know." I blow air into the cool wind through pursed lips, wishing it were chilly enough outside for it to curl into smoky vapor and let me feel like I'm setting something free. "They're still in their state of Robbie delusion. I know."

"We have to let them have this," he says quietly, holding my hands as if to keep them warm. But I feel the truth of his grip in his shaking fingers. "No matter how much it hurts."

We're both quiet for a moment, and finally I let *our* truth into the air. "He was a homophobic asshole."

Miguel nods stiffly. "He was."

"And he can't blackmail you anymore."

"No, he can't."

"And he can't hurt you anymore."

Miguel lets go of my hands and slides his arms around me instead, and I hug him fiercely to calm his entire body's shuddering. "No, he can't. That fucker is dead." He smiles into my hair. "And he was replaced by a girl."

"Mig . . ."

"A girl who's ten times the quarterback he ever was."

"A girl whose window I'd like to climb through again," I murmur, keeping my voice too low for him to hear but wishing it would somehow penetrate anyway, just to clear the air.

It doesn't.

"Mami taught me better than to wish someone was burning in hell."

"Dania would've sent him to hell herself if she knew what he put you through."

He laughs. "Nah, she'd just lecture him on basic human decency for *hours*, like she did when she caught Roberto stealing that Snickers when we were kids."

"That wasn't hell?"

"Fair point." He sighs and releases me, still holding me at arm's length. "Are you gonna go back inside, or head home?"

Neither. But he can't know where I'm going, so I lie and say, "Home, I guess."

"You okay to drive?"

"On zero alcohol, because you whisked me out of the room before I could even crack this open?" I hold up the can of Natty Light. "Yeah, I'll be okay." I rise on my toes and kiss his cheek. "Te quiero."

"Te quiero," he murmurs, and then he gives me another quick squeeze before releasing me for the rest of the night.

-JACK-

It's pathetic, lying around in your pajamas on a Friday night, eating sliced turkey out of the package and watching old episodes of *Schitt's Creek* while the rest of your team is at a party celebrating a fucking win *they could not have gotten without you.* I put on a happy face and told my parents I was exhausted and needed to chill at home with an ice bath and they should go to Pensacola and celebrate without me. With how little they'll be seeing each other now, I want them to have a real date night, especially since my brothers opted to stay at my grandma's rather than show up for me. But now I'm having regrets about not just letting them toast me with fried mullet and hush puppies or whatever so that I could get *some* acknowledgment that I did a great thing tonight.

I'd hoped the win would do it, but with every minute the team celebrates without me, another ounce of joy from the victory gets sapped away. Especially knowing a certain cheer-leader is at that very victory party.

Part of me is mad at her for going. And it's a *big* part, even though I know that turning her back on the team isn't going to help her be my advocate. It doesn't help things that she's deeper in the closet than her last-season wardrobe, but then, I'm not exactly wearing a rainbow-striped uniform my-self, so.

On the screen, David and Alexis are sniping at each other and I'm staring at my phone, willing it to light up with any-thing to prove that Cheer Girl hasn't already forgotten about me. Which is pathetic. But I guess that whole "watched pot never boils" thing applies to staring at your phone, too. I shove it down between the couch cushions while fixing my eyes on the screen as if watching people who've always sucked at rela-tionships will somehow provide all the answers I need about mine.

Orrrr maybe they should be reminding me that I should be paying attention to my own friends, rather than fixating on the Cheerleader. I slip my phone back out and open the group text with Morgan and Sage that we've had running since the dawn of time. At least *they* were interested in my opening game; the texts from tonight are rows of question marks followed by rows of celebratory emojis.

I am having the world's saddest solo victory party, I type, but I don't send it. I don't want to sound pathetic to the last re-maining people on Earth who actually think I'm cool. Plus,

I'd already lied and said I was hanging out with my parents tonight; it seemed the easiest way to dodge both Morgan's inevitable "You have to celebrate yourself!!!!" and Sage's predictable "Go get some and tell us evvvvvverything."

I delete my text and stare at the screen. I've already asked how the movie they went to tonight was and seen a hundred pictures of Sage's newest cake creation and Morgan's latest cosplay. Sage has already told us about her crush on a guy she met at her dad's hardware store. For the first time in as long as I can remember, I don't know what else to say to them. Especially since I don't want to say a word about Amber in case the chemistry crackling in the Lawndale High bathroom tonight was entirely in my head.

Then my screen lights up with another message, and my brain goes blank. It's a selfie of Amber standing under my window, holding up a can of Natty Light, and the text underneath says, *To today's champion.*

I don't know what makes my skin heat faster, that she looks fucking adorable in the picture, with a braided pigtail swung over her shoulder, or that there's actually someone at Atherton who's acknowledging the awesome thing I did tonight, but I do know this: I have a fucking terrible crush on a cheerleader. Who's waiting just a few feet away for me to let her in my window.

Fuck, I smell like deli meat. I run to the kitchen to scrub my hands and rinse out my mouth, then yank open every drawer until I find a pack of gum. I'd only broken into the turkey after talking myself into the idea that she wasn't gonna show, and now I'm cursing myself for it.

But any regrets fall away when I slide up the window and see her there, wearing little overall shorts and a tank top, sitting on the grass and ruffling it with her fingers.

I wish taking a picture of her wouldn't be a creepy move, but it would, so I settle for a mental one.

"How was the party?"

She glances over her shoulder and pushes herself to standing. "Oof, you scared me. Where have you been?"

"Not literally waiting at the window for you to show up," I say, wishing I could reach out and flick one of her braids.

"I see that. Well, anyway, not to shock you, but victory parties without the person who led us to victory are tremendously stupid, actually."

God, I could kiss her right now. "You don't say."

"I did, however, steal a beer for you, just in case. Figured we could toast your victory, and there wasn't any champagne."

"Do you actually like beer?"

"Not even a little bit," she says with a laugh that lights up her face. "You?"

"Not even a little bit. But I do like cute girls who bring me beer."

"Whew, that's good to know." She wipes imaginary sweat from her forehead and takes a couple of steps in my direction. "What else do you like? Just, you know, for the next time I have to decorate your locker."

"I will never complain about Famous Amos cookies," I assure her, resting my head on my arms atop the sill, "but if you're baking, I happen to be very into those peanut butter cookies with the fork marks on top."

"The fork marks are an important part of this recipe?"

"Probably the most important part. Something to do with physics."

"Makes sense." She's close enough now that I can smell her floral shampoo and spicy cinnamon gum, but neither of us makes a move to touch the other. "So, can I come in or what?"

"Oh, right." I was digging the *Romeo and Juliet* feel of the window so much, I almost forgot I had a front door. I gesture for her to walk around to it, then let her in and show her to the couch while I head into our small kitchen. "Something to drink?"

"Nah, I'm good." She curls up on the couch I haven't yet pulled out for sleep, tucking her feet under her. "So, I have to know. Sexist political bullshit aside, how'd it feel?"

I sigh and run a hand over my hair, pulled tight as always. It's not exactly the sexiest question, but it does feel good to be able to tell the truth to someone instead of having to keep playing happy. "Honestly? Harder to separate from the sexist political bullshit than I thought it would be. On the field, though . . ." I don't even realize my hands are cradling an imaginary football until I'm about to pull it back to throw a perfect nonexistent spiral. "Fuck, that felt good. Seeing my parents cheer felt good. Getting to play felt *so* fucking good. And running one in . . . God, there is nothing like it. But."

Her face falls. "I'm sorry. I was cheering for you. I wish I could've done a whole run for you. Watching you was really incredible."

"You can make up for it now." I cross my arms over my chest and watch her gaze follow. I have absolutely no boobs to speak of, which means my biceps might be proving to be good for something other than throwing fifteen-yard passes. "It's never too late for a personal cheer."

She waggles her eyebrows. "You may be testing me, QB1, but I *always* rise to a cheer challenge." Her eyes dart to the bedroom door, which is wide open.

"They're out celebrating me," I confirm. "My mom and I moved here by ourselves while my dad stayed back with my brothers, so it's usually just me and her, but he came out tonight to see my first game."

"You didn't want to go with them?" she asks. "Or . . . were you not invited? Don't worry," she says quickly. "I can empathize with the latter. My dad sucks."

"No, no, I sent them off on their own. I didn't feel like going out." I don't wanna get all sad sack about it, but from the way Amber nods, she gets it. "Anyway, thought they should have a nice date or whatever, since they haven't seen each other all week. But I'm sorry your dad sucks. How sucky are we talking? I'll come with you to egg his house right the fuck now, if you want."

She laughs, lifting all the tiny hairs on my arms. "He sucks hard enough to deserve that, but his house isn't close enough to egg, anyway. He was completely obsessed with the Blue Angels as a kid and decided that having a family would hold him back from his dream of flying, so he ditched me and my mom when I was still tiny to join the Air Force. He just left divorce papers on the counter, periodically checked in from around the world, and stopped doing even that when he got remarried. I did see him for my sixteenth birthday, so he could offload his old car onto me as a gift, but now he's up in North Carolina. Probably not gonna see him again for at least a few years, if that."

It's so much more than I expected her to say, and so much shittier than I imagined, which makes it all the more shocking to me that this girl makes the choice to get out of bed every day and *cheer*. I feel like I should say something monumental, something that acknowledges what she's trusting me with, but all I can manage is, "Wow, what a dick."

She shrugs, like it's no big deal, like she isn't strong as hell for not just pushing through that but becoming a person whose *job* it is to exude joy. "The bright side is that *his* mom was so appalled by his shittiness that she writes me a big check every birthday, though that'll probably stop now that he and his wife are expecting their second kid. So, you know. Fingers crossed for a winning lottery ticket or a miracle scholarship. Not sure which is more likely at this point."

It takes me a few seconds to realize the stinging in my

palms is the result of me digging my nails into them, making fists I wish I could take to this dude I've never even met. I loosen them, shake out my hands, and say, "You're gonna get it. I know it. You're the best one out there."

"Oh yeah?" She grins, and there's the tiniest dimple in her left cheek. "How closely were you watching the other girls?"

"What other girls?"

Now she laughs for real, and I wonder if she feels the same unraveling in her chest that I do. "Good answer."

"I've been known to be mildly smooth in my time. And I mean, if you wanted to practice with, say, a cheer for a certain quarterback, I would be happy to offer some notes."

"Oh, would you now?" Her blue-green eyes twinkle, and suddenly, she morphs right in front of me, adopting a perfect ramrod-straight cheer stance, lightly closed fists grasping fake pom-poms. "J-A-C-K Jack Jack Jack! She's our favorite quarterback! Watch her throw and watch her score, then watch her come right back for more! Goooooo Jack!"

My jaw is on the floor as I watch her leap and jump and split and shout, for *me*, and good God this is the hottest thing anyone has ever done for me in my entire life. She finishes with her arms thrust in a V in the air and a huge smile on her face, and when she winks, it's all I can do not to melt into the floor, leaving my black T-shirt and cutoff sweats behind.

"So, what'd you think?" she asks.

I can barely get words out, but I manage a few. "I think we should make out immediately."

Her smile grows even wider, and she waves her fake pom-poms. "Go team!"

"Jesus H," I mutter, but then my hands are grabbing for her overall straps and her cinnamon mouth finds mine and we somehow land in a pile on the couch.

Best.

Victory party.

Ever.

- - - - -

The high of spending Friday night fooling around with Amber lasts a whole lot longer than the high of the game did, especially when I let the memory of her cheer replace the ones of the quiet pep rally and the missing party invitation. In fact, it lasts right up until Monday afternoon's practice, when all the usual anger, annoyance, and general shittiness comes flowing back. If I'd thought a win would be the ticket to a change, I know now that was a stupid, pointless hope. And even though Coach tells me I did a good job, the fact that he waits until everyone else is gone just makes me angry.

He's such a damn coward.

The difference the blessing of his shoulder pat would make if the team actually saw it is huge. I know it and he knows it.

But.

This whole fucking school is full of cowards.

I'm trying to get where everyone's coming from. I am. When we were catching our breath the other night, Amber gave me a lot more background, and I gather that Robbie was well-liked and the guys are taking his death really hard. But why they're taking it out on *me* is still something I don't get—not when I'm helping them win.

Whatthefuckever. Homecoming is coming up, and given that this isn't my home, I couldn't give a shit about making Atherton alumni proud, but these guys should.

I knew they were gonna be weird about playing with a girl. Coach even warned me it might take the guys some time to warm up. But I throw a hundred and sixty yards a game, rush for sixty-five, and had every single play memorized before I even started here. I haven't asked them to change a damn thing about the way they act or talk around me that might offend my feminine sensibilities. (Not that I have any, but if I *did*.) Hell, I'm even fooling around with a cheerleader like most of them are, or at least have at some point, if the shit they shoot around practice is to be believed. What more can I do to get the message across that I'm here to stay and that it's a good thing I am?

It's hard to hold on to my rage when I think about Amber, even if she's pretending to be just as hard-core Team Robbie as the rest of them. Hours of talking and making out kinda dulled that edge. Even now, I'm half pissed about Coach keeping his praise on the DL and letting the rest of the team continue to treat me like crap, and half pissed that I missed out on riding home with her for the privilege of being their punching bag.

Even now, I'm thinking about texting her, seeing if she's up for company. Is that pathetic? It might be pathetic. Besides, I have to keep up my GPA to hold my spot on the team, and I'm thinking Cheer Princess and I aren't gonna get much studying done if I hightail it over there now.

Fucking responsibilities.

I give my shoulders a few rotations to help loosen the frustration that's been building for the last hour and get behind the wheel. I'm about to pull out of the lot when I spot a familiar figure standing a few feet off in the distance, alternately looking down at his phone and looking up for a ride that seems to be very, very late.

If it were anyone on the football team other than Miguel Santiago, I'd probably floor it out of there, but he still seems like my best shot at getting a little human decency on the field. And so, I stick my head out the window. "Santiago! Need a lift?"

He startles, I guess too absorbed in his phone to realize there was still a car in the lot. Judging by his muttered "mierda," he's not too pleased to discover that he's not alone, and even less pleased to discover I'm the person talking to him. He walks over slowly, still darting glances at the entrance to the parking lot. "Hey, Walsh. I'm, uh—no. Someone's coming to get me, thanks."

Judging from his frown when he glances back at his phone,

he's not feeling too confident about that, and there's a layer of subtle agony there that suggests he's being stood up. "You sure? You can always text them and tell them you've got a ride."

He's still hesitating, and I'm starting to get antsy to pull away from the building. "How late are they?" I press gently.

"It's just some traffic," he grunts. "Don't worry about it. You can go. You should go."

"Cool, so, even the one guy on the team who hasn't been a complete asshole to me won't get in my car when he's been stranded. Good to know." The words roll out of my mouth before I can give them a second thought and land with a splat on the pavement between us. "Go Alligators."

I rev the engine and back out of my spot, but reluctantly stop shy of pulling out of the lot when I see Miguel vehemently shaking his head. "It's not that," I hear when the sound of the engine dies down. "I swear. It's—it's not that."

My "okay, whatever" drowns in the sound of another car pulling right up to us, and then a new male voice says, "Shit, I'm so sorry. I was running low on gas and the closest gas station was the one with the skinhead, so I had to drive another ten minutes out of the way. I tried to text but it's a total dead zone—"

"It's fine," Miguel bites out, yanking open the passenger door to the silver Malibu. "See?" he says to me. "Cousin's here. I'm good. But thanks."

The driver whirls in his seat to look at me, clearly not having noticed anyone else was in the lot. Slighter and darker than

Miguel, with eyelashes so long they fan his cheekbones when he blinks and a face that's softly rounded everywhere Miguel's could cut glass, it's hard to imagine the two of them share an ounce of DNA.

Of course, some cousins don't. But the way they both eye me before they peel out of the lot is . . . something.

I think back to what Amber said about how their relationship isn't real, and looking at Miguel now, I know it's true.

But as to *why* they have this arrangement . . . I'm starting to think there might be more to it.

Chapter Five

-AMBER-

"Ammo! Where is your focus today?"

I groan as I pick myself up from the grass, rubbing my bruised dignity as I wither under Crystal's glare. "Sorry, Crys. I'm here, I swear."

It's kind of a lie—my brain has been stuck in Jack Walsh's "bedroom" for days—but Crystal's right to yell at me; I *have* to do better than this. I just can't stop thinking about how we're sneaking around, how I'm keeping the truth about Miguel from Jack and the truth about Jack from Miguel, and all I want is to be able to enjoy finally sharing the halls with someone who gives me butterflies.

"You okay?" Cara asks, passing me my bottle of water. "I mean, thank you for stopping just short of dropping me, but this isn't like you."

She's definitely right about that, but I gratefully take the drink to avoid answering and down a huge swig. I wish a million times over that I could ask Cara for advice, the same way I've asked her for advice on everything from my campaign for captain to outfit choices for dances and parties. But I can't tell her about Jack or Miguel either. . . .

Maybe there's a way I can get her advice without using specifics, though, because Lord knows I need to talk to *somebody*.

"Just . . . having some relationship thoughts. I—"

"Trouble in paradise?" she cuts in, sounding way too gleeful about the possibility of a rift between me and Miguel, which is weird because not only does she like Miguel (as far as I know), she thinks it looks good for cheerleaders and football players to date. She'd be allll over the team if her parents hadn't strictly forbidden dating until she's eighteen. Then again, maybe this is her jealousy talking.

"Not exactly," I say, not wanting to give rise to this weird false hope she's showing. "It's just, Miguel and I don't, uh, see eye to eye on everything." *Like, for example, being attracted to girls.*

"Oh, thank the Lord," Cara says on a sigh. "He was being so nice to her at Maggie's, and it was driving me nuts. I was wondering if it was bothering you, too. Honestly, I'm relieved that it was, because I feel like you've been a little soft, especially at the pep rally."

I'm sorry, *what*? "Her who? Jack?" I mean, Cara's not wrong that this is about her, but wowwww, it is not in the way she thinks.

"Of course Jack. Everything's about Jack now!" she says bitterly, as if she weren't the one who just *made* this about Jack. "I can't wait to take her down."

It's like watching my best friend transform before my very eyes. I'm surprised I don't see foam gathering at the corners of her mouth. But there are no changes to her outsides as far as I can see, and I know them almost as well as I do my own—the ears she was finally allowed to pierce with basic gold studs for her sixteenth birthday, the reddish-brown hair that always smells like the two-in-one her mom buys in bulk, the scar of two parallel lines on her knee from when we gave up trying to get one of our parents to teach us how to ride a bike and struck out by ourselves. . . . I *know* that girl. And yeah, she can be petty like we all can, especially when her little siblings are making her world feel too small, but this is a level of wrath that exceeds even the time her brother Christopher and his friends ate every one of the cinnamon buns we spent an entire Saturday making for a bake sale fundraiser.

I don't know where all this anger is coming from, but that's only one of my many questions here. "What do you mean, 'take her down'? How much further down can she go? She hasn't gotten her own cheer, she was iced out at the pep rally, and she wasn't invited to the victory party." Just listing the slights makes me sick to my stomach, thinking of how cruel it all is, for what? For Jack's daring to be a girl? Even if I *weren't* into her, I'd recognize that this was tremendously shitty.

So why doesn't Cara? And why don't the others?

Am I being soft because I have a crush on Jack? Or is this group of girls I'm supposed to be closer with than anyone actually being as horrible as I think they are?

"Oh please—that's nothing. She couldn't have expected we were just gonna act like she and Robbie are the same. But she doesn't seem to be getting the hint that we don't want her here, and homecoming is the perfect time to make that clear."

Homecoming. Shit. Of course. The team is away again this weekend, but the week after that is one of the biggest weeks at Atherton; we've already been doing lots of planning for the game, the dance, and various school spirit events that'll be happening the week leading up to it.

I just hadn't factored "ruin Jack's life" into the already packed calendar.

"So, are you in, or what?"

I look down at Cara, who's striking a fierce pose with her hands on her hips and her hair in a tight bun. I don't have to glance around the room to realize it's quieted down. People are watching us, and what's more, no one's asking what's going on, which means this isn't a new conversation for Cara—she's been peddling a plan around.

A plan everyone must be on board with.

A plan that's going to make her look like a leader.

A captain, even.

You don't have to help them, I tell myself. *You just need to know what's going on so you can get everyone to chill out. It's helping Jack to agree to take part in whatever shit they have planned. This is not just about keeping an eye on the race for captain.*

When I put it that way, I can pretty much believe it.

"Of course I'm in," I say casually, giving my arm a good stretch. "Let's talk after practice, okay?"

For the first time since she approached me, the hard set to her jaw lifts and she finally looks like the girl I used to spend endless afternoons with making up new choreography for Ariana Grande and Beyoncé.

It's a good face to see again.

And all I had to do was agree to destroy the girl I like.

- - - - -

Apparently, I'm not doing a great job hiding my angst, because my mom calls me out as soon as I get home from practice and crankily slam the front door behind me. She's back on the night shift, which means we've got a couple of hours of overlap before she leaves for the hospital.

"You seem . . . less than cheery, dear daughter."

"I feel less than cheery," I grumble, taking a banana from

the bowl on the little peninsula in our kitchen and yanking down the peel as if Cara would be able to vicariously feel my wrath.

"Do you want to talk about it?"

I take a huge bite. "No," I lie as I chew.

"Let me rephrase. Let's talk about it! What's going on, sweetheart?" She hops up on one of the two stools that line the breakfast bar, which serves as our dining set, and smooths her hand over the top of my head.

The banana is soft, but swallowing feels like choking down a rock anyway. "Have you ever dated someone all your friends hated?"

She snorts. "You mean your father?"

"That doesn't count," I say, although I guess it sort of does. My parents were high school sweethearts, but as I got older, my mom confided more and more that it wasn't all that sweet a romance. Not that I couldn't guess considering he abandoned us a couple of years later.

"There was a woman, for a little while, when you were still in day care and I'd gone back to school. Aunt Lily despised her, because she was always insisting I get a babysitter so we could go on dates. I obviously couldn't afford that, so I'd beg Lily or my mom to watch you, constantly."

"Hey, I thought they loved watching me."

"They did! Of course they did. But they also thought if this woman—Rowena was her name—was going to be in my life for real, she needed to accept that my beautiful daughter was going to be a significant and constant presence. It hit me when Lily said that Ro really didn't get that, how she was picking out the parts of my life—of me—she wanted to enjoy. And if she couldn't appreciate that, or appreciate *you*, then she wasn't the one for me. Especially since things were only going to get more complicated once we finished school and weren't surrounded by quite as liberal an environment."

"So Lily was right not to like her."

"In that case, yes. But she also disliked that guy Jeff I went on three dates with a few years ago because she thought his sideburns were too long, so she's a bit of a mixed bag." She takes a clementine from the bowl, and I watch her dig in with her stubby purple nails. "Is this about Miguel?"

My mom is the only person in the world besides Miguel's mom and his boyfriend, Malcolm, who knows that Miguel and I are both queer. But she's worried throughout this entire fake relationship that I was going to catch feelings Miguel couldn't reciprocate, and since talking to my mom about my hookups has always felt like a step too far into awkward, she doesn't know about anyone else I've been with.

"Sort of? I mean, not about him, but it does involve him. And also someone else." I break off another piece of banana and roll it gently between the tips of my thumb and forefinger, even though I know it's gonna leave that gross banana residue.

"Can I have a little more detail, please?"

I smile wryly. "I'm living the dream, Ma. Cheerleader snagged the quarterback."

"What a wonderful cliché you are," she says, handing me a clementine segment. I pluck it between my pinkie and ring finger, my other fingers still holding the piece of banana, and admire the little fruit cocktail in my hand before shoving it all into my mouth. "A well-mannered, classy cliché."

"Or am I?" I pull out my phone with my fruit-residue-free hand and show her a selfie Jack and I took on the couch. "That's the new quarterback."

"Okay, this just got very interesting." My mom puts down the fruit and dusts off her hands before plucking my phone away. "First of all, very cute. *Very* cute."

Sometimes it's really nice to have a bi mom. "Isn't she?"

"I meant the two of you together," she says, giving me a smirk. "I've never seen you look so couple-y. How is she as a quarterback? I imagine she's gotta be pretty great for Atherton to have given her a shot."

"Incredible. You should've seen that first game. Robbie *never* ran in plays or threw for over one-twenty in a single game. She's *really* good, but everyone treats her like dirt because she's not him."

"Even your friends?"

"Especially my friends," I mutter, grabbing my phone back and dropping my chin into my hands. "Cara *hates* her. Like, is actively plotting against her. And I don't know how to handle that, especially since I haven't come out to anyone and Miguel and I are still supposedly dating and everything is . . . you know. Complicated."

"Honey, if your friends have a problem with you because you're—"

"It's not a queer thing. Not really," I amend, thinking of Cara. The others might not be marching in any Pride parades soon, but Cara was the only one to look at me any differently after news of me and Veronica spread around camp faster than the wave for any reason other than concern I was "cheating" on Miguel. "I mean, I don't know how they would take it, and I don't want any of that 'Oh my God, is she checking me out in the locker room??' crap, and I probably wouldn't have a shot in hell at captain if everyone knew. But it's a more immediate problem that people just . . . hate her. No matter how good she is and how much she wins for us, people can't get past the idea that the memory of Robbie has been desecrated by a girl getting his spot."

"Robbie being the treasure who found out Miguel's gay and blackmailed him for months?"

"The very one." God, it feels nice to be able to speak ill of the dead, and with someone who knows these darkest secrets. "But obviously no one knows that. And the coach won't budge on this, so the only way everyone can deal with it is by taking their feelings out on her."

"And where do you stand on this? Publicly, I mean."

"I've tried to get them to back off," I offer, but it sounds as weak as my efforts have been, and I can tell by her frown that she sees right through it. "You know how badly I need to be captain next year. I can't risk having the whole team hating me or wondering why I keep going to bat for her. What's it even gonna do?"

"You tell me," she counters. "How would you feel if the situation were reversed and your girlfriend didn't stick up for you?"

"She's not my girlfriend" slips out before I can think better of it, and I know as soon as I hear the words come out of my mouth that I'm being a coward. We talked and made out for hours the other night, right up until her parents sent her a text that they were on their way back from dinner and I bolted out of her apartment like I was being chased by a coyote. I can't even imagine Jack rolling over like I have. When I told her about my dad, she looked like she wanted to go to Fayettville herself to rip him to pieces. She'd fight for me if she had to—I know it—and here I am, backing down at the first sight of the wolves.

But Jack's the first female football player in the entire county. She's got her thing that makes her a safe bet for college. She's got her thing that makes her special, even if people don't wanna acknowledge it. And she can handle herself; if push came to shove, she could snap the entire squad in half, and a good portion of the football team, too.

What do I have?

"Amber—"

"I know. God, I know it's bad, okay? But cheerleading is my entire life. All my friends are on the squad or the football team. You've watched me work my ass off at this basically since I could walk and now you're telling me to give all that up for a girl I've known for, like, five minutes because she's a good kisser."

My mother narrows her eyes. "Well, if that's all she is." And because my mother is the queen at making you feel like dirt when she wants to, she turns away and walks out of the kitchen.

-JACK-

Even after taking a long, hot shower at home, I'm still feeling completely wiped from practice, but nothing is going to keep me from chatting with Sage and Morgan tonight. I haven't seen their faces since the game, and I'm excited to finally have hopeful, fun, and, most importantly, true things to share.

The second the screen opens up and I see the windows with their faces, I feel a knot loosen in my chest. It doesn't even matter that they don't look the same as I left them—Morgan's purple-streaked hair is now spiky and green all over, and Sage has already scrubbed off her trademark shiny red lips and washed out her huge curls for the night. I'm just so glad to see friendly, excited faces.

"Oh man, Jack, you look so happy," Sage says immediately, breaking into that familiar huge smile that could bring even a jackass like Dan Sanchez to his knees.

"I told you we had nothing to be nervous about," Morgan adds, sticking their tongue out.

"You were worried about me?" The knot loosens a little bit further, just knowing they didn't really expect it to be sunshine and roses from day one. "You both seemed so optimistic."

"Yeah, because we believe *you* can do anything," says Sage. "But we all know how cis boys can be when they feel threatened by a girl. We've been so glad you're not dealing with that shit over there, but we were a little afraid that maybe you were downplaying stuff, being brave and all that. But you look really happy."

"Well . . ." I debate whether to tell them the truth, that I'm dealing with it from not just the boys but the girls, but they look so relieved at whatever my face seems to have confirmed for them that I let it go. That things between us haven't been quite as dishonest as I thought is enough for now, and I'm determined to focus on the positive tonight. "The win certainly helped. But also, remember when you told me to go get some? I may have done that, too."

The squealing noises that erupt from my monitor force me to cover my ears, but I can't help laughing. "God, Sage, take it down."

"Okay, but tell us *everything*." There's a crinkling sound and I realize Sage is literally digging into a bag of popcorn, probably sprinkled with the spiced powdered cheese she calls her "proprietary blend." I can practically smell the garlic and crushed bacon bits from here. "Who is she?"

"Is this the cheerleader?" Morgan demands. "What happened to the boyfriend?"

"The boyfriend is apparently not a real boyfriend. It's a fake-dating arrangement, and she actually likes girls, and by girls I mean me. She came over after that victory party the other night and we, uh, hung out for a while."

I expect more squealing from Sage, but both she and Morgan look way too serious for my liking. "Is she *still* pretending to date this guy?" Morgan asks.

Sage adds, "And does the guy know about you?"

"And how do you know she's actually telling the truth about the relationship being fake? I mean, what's in it for him?"

"He's trying to keep his parents off his back, so . . ." I trail off as I realize how ridiculous this sounds. More and more, I'm thinking my instinct from the parking lot—that Miguel is hiding just as much as Amber—is correct.

I certainly hope it is, anyway, because if she was just straight-up lying, this is bad.

"Anyway, she and I aren't anything official," I finish, before this conversation veers into sexuality-speculating territory. "We're just having fun."

"Oh okay," Morgan says slowly. "Well, I'm glad it's fun. We just don't want you to get hurt. Remember—"

"I remember," I snap. I couldn't forget if I tried, and I definitely try. Pretty sure no one at my old high school will be forgetting Amy Jelinsky publicly declaring that she was tired of dating a wannabe football player, or Jenna Pressley saying no one should date me because I had gross callused hands, or Iva Kellerman hooking up with me for weeks until we got caught and she spread some lesbian predator shit about me rather than admit that she literally begged me to get her off in the back seat of her car. Yes, there were things I loved about being there, especially the two people I'm talking to right now, but coming to Atherton wasn't exactly leaving one Garden of Eden for another.

Every high school has its people who just fucking suck, especially when you're queer.

"It's not like that," I add flatly, but I don't have proof it isn't and they know it and this conversation is over before it even began. (Why was I so excited for this virtual friend date again?) "But anyway, I should go. I rolled my ankle at practice and I need to go ice it some more."

We all know it's a lie—they've seen me ice my various injured body parts plenty in the small tub I keep in my room—but the awkwardness and discomfort are palpable, so they take the excuse and we say goodbye.

And once again, I'm alone and wondering what the hell is

wrong with me that I keep making choices that everyone but me thinks suck.

- - - - -

When I get to practice the next day, I'm feeling up for a fight, and my timing is perfect, because it looks like the entire team feels the same way. Fucking great. While I was suiting up in the empty girls' locker room, they were turning into a single-minded force, just waiting for me in a semicircle on the grass, arms folded and eyes blazing.

Coach is nowhere to be found.

Dan Sanchez steps forward, apparently the appointed spokesman for the team. "Duggan wants his spot back," he says without preamble.

Jesus H. Christ. Who has time for this shit? "Oh really?" I turn to Tim, whose biceps in his cutoff T are proof he hasn't been hitting the weight room beyond our required biweekly sessions. I could take this kid in my sleep. "You want 'your' spot back, Duggan?"

Everything in his shaky nod tells me what I need to know.

"Okay, so, you want to be QB1 again—a spot that's yours, not mine, apparently—despite the fact that I threw more yards in my first game than you did all summer? That you fumbled your first snap in every fucking game? Yeah, I've seen the videos. Or that I've run in two TDs—something you've never even done once? You want back the hours you sit in ice baths because you don't spend half the time on conditioning I do? And I assume you've run this by Coach, who very specifically put me where I am."

"Someone's on her period," Zach Sawyer spits. "Way to be a fucking bitch."

I wheel on him. "These are facts and stats, asshole. And the only one being a little bitch is you, trying to shove your friend back into a position he doesn't even want because you all can't fucking stand that the first time in your entire careers you have a winning season, it's thanks to your quarterback who happens to be a girl. Grow the fuck up."

"*You* grow the fuck up," Sanchez snarls. "Just because we happen to be winning while you keep Duggan's spot warm doesn't mean it has shit to do with you."

I blink. "What does it have to do with, then? You think the spirit of Robbie is nudging the ball into your hands? Or do you maybe finally have a QB who's found your sweet spot and actually has the accuracy to hit it? You're welcome for helping you suck less, by the way."

There's a low whistle from somewhere in the crowd and maybe no one is coming to my side, but no one's coming to Sanchez's, either. No one says a word at all, including Duggan, who's suddenly a little less determined to put QB1 back on his résumé.

"You're so fucking lucky I can't hit a girl," Sanchez spits, and I knew—I *knew*, the way I knew a stupid comment about

114

my period was coming, the way every girl who ever stands up for herself knows—it was only a matter of time till he pulled that one out. My brothers try that shit all the time, like if only they could swing a punch at me, they'd win every argument, even if they were being complete dumbshits. Whereas with my brothers I'd fight back with words, here I honestly feel done talking. Finally standing up for myself has adrenaline coursing through my veins, and I want the fight just as much as Sanchez does.

"Let's just say today you can. Go on." I put up my fists. One thing I'll say in favor of my brothers—they definitely made sure I knew how to throw a punch. "Give it your best shot. Let's see if your arm is as weak off the field as it is on it."

"Oh, you think I won't?" Spit flies from Sanchez's mouth and he rears back, but his swing is predictable enough to catch in my right fist and my left returns the favor straight into his gut.

"Y'all, *stop*." I'm not sure who yells it. Santiago, maybe. But I'm not taking my eyes off Dan to look and I'm definitely not stopping.

Neither is Sanchez, even though my punch knocked the wind out of him for a second. "Fucking bitch," he growls, diving for me, but at least two sets of hands hold him back.

"Sanchez, she's *not* worth it," Devlin declares, which makes me want to take a swing at him, too. But none of the guys are coming near now, and in fact, they start backing up.

That's when I realize Coach has arrived.

"What the *hell* is going on here?" he roars, taking in the

guys grabbing at Dan and how we're all locked in some grand standoff. "Walsh?"

Because of course, the sole girl on the team, currently staring down ten other guys, is the one in the position to answer this question. Sure. I clearly started it.

"Nothing's going on, Coach," I say coldly, my eyes flitting from Sanchez to Devlin before briefly landing on Miguel Santiago, hoping I'll find some confirmation there that I'm doing the right thing. But his face is impossible to read, and it's all a little too ridiculous, the lone hope for sympathy on the team being the guy whose "girlfriend" I've been making out with. "Just a pre-practice chat."

My knuckles flex and crack, wishing we could make this chat a little longer.

"There a problem, Sanchez?"

"No, sir," he grunts, and then it's over as quickly as it began, everyone shifting into place as if it were a perfectly normal, threat-free afternoon. Of course, Sanchez flubs catches left and right during passing drills as if that'll disprove my commentary and make *me* look bad, but Coach just tells him to get his shit together.

I'm guessing that's not gonna make me any more friends. And what kind of cheer do they create for a girl who socked her own teammate? I'm sure it's a doozy.

Of course, thinking of cheerleaders just makes me think of Amber, which feels like taking one more bite of a shit sandwich. Homecoming is up in less than two weeks, and what do I have to show for it? Not a coach who supports me. Not a team who appreciates me. Not a girl I can go to the dance with. Not a school that gives a shit about me. Not friends who can hold a candle to Sage and Morgan, both of whom think I'm being a lousy home-wrecker right now.

In that moment, I feel done. And since I'm done, I don't really need to go to class tomorrow, right?

The second I'm back in my school clothes, I head for my car and peel out of the lot.

Chapter Six

-AMBER-

I know it's not a good sign when "Walsh, Jack" goes unanswered in first period. It's certainly not good when I don't spot her by her locker afterward. And the rumors that are hitting my ears . . . Yeah, somebody's having a bad morning, and judging by the way my stomach's felt filled with lead since that conversation with my mother, that somebody is more to me than just a good kisser.

I finally catch up with Miguel and yank him aside for details, putting aside that I'm showing my hand by caring way too much about somebody I'm not supposed to. "What the hell happened at practice yesterday? Was Jack in a fight?"

"Hard to even call it a fight," Miguel says with a snort. "She got ambushed by Sanchez and the rest of the guys, and he threw a weak-ass punch. She would've kicked his ass if Coach hadn't shown up. She got a good swing in anyway. But yeah, it was a mess."

Oh God. I knew it was bad, but not physical-fight bad. That is fucked-up. That is *fucked-up*.

"Yeah, it is," says Miguel, which is how I realize I've said it out loud. "I guess you're still on your thing about creating unity or whatever? You seem pretty upset. Everything okay?"

The truth is on the tip of my tongue—about Jack, about Cara, about everything—but I can't force it out. Not here. And not before I talk to Jack. "Where is she?"

He shrugs. "Stayed home, I guess."

"Okay, thank you. Do me a favor and take notes in physics for me?"

"Why?" He narrows his eyes, but I'm already turning away, pulling out my phone to see if I have any messages from Jack. Nothing. "Where are you going?"

"I'll fill you in later!" I call back over my shoulder, meaning it. "Just take the notes!"

I am not a girl who cuts school, especially because it means getting benched if I miss practice, but I jump into my car and floor it to Jack's, perfect attendance record be damned.

- - - - -

The second Jack opens her front door, my hands are on her face, checking for bruises. Only when I'm satisfied that Dan hasn't chipped a tooth or broken her nose do I finally speak. "What the hell happened, Jack? Miguel just told me you threw down with the entire football team. Are you okay?"

She laughs bitterly. "Come on, Cheer Girl. Do you really give a shit if I'm okay? Because not a single one of your friends does."

"What the hell are you talking about? Of course I care. I'm here."

"You're here now, yeah. But what's the point? You can't actually be there when I need someone to stick up for me and say that I belong here. And you won't be there the next time someone comes at me." She looks so tired, it makes me want to pull her into my arms and just hold her. "I'm not in the mood to fool around right now, so maybe go find somewhere else to cheer."

She starts to close the door in my face, but I catch it with a firm hand, even though I don't know what to say. She's right. I haven't been there. But I wanna be. I want to be able to stick up for her and hold her hand and kiss her and keep my friends and become captain and why is that too many things to want?

"Jack. I care. Please let me in."

She doesn't swing the door open in welcome, but she

doesn't finish shoving it in my face, either. Instead, her hand limply drops to her side and she walks away, which I take as an invitation to come in.

"What happened?" I ask, closing the door gently behind me.

"I don't know. An ambush. It was barely even a fight. Anyway, it doesn't matter. I'm done with it." She stalks to the couch, currently in its folded-up position with a pile of sheets neatly stacked on the end, and I have no choice but to follow.

I'm done with it. The words could mean anything, but it sounds a lot more final than just having pushed the fight out of her mind. Besides, if she truly had, she wouldn't be hiding at home instead of facing those assholes in school. "Done with what?"

"With football and with this place. I came home to pack. I'm not staying here." She gestures down the hall. "My brothers hate me for taking my mom away, my parents only get to see each other once a week, nobody wants to be in Atherton, and I'm tired of going through this shit for a team that doesn't want me."

"But *I* want you" slips out of my mouth before I can stop it.

"Yeah, you do," she says with the slightest hint of a smile that she immediately bites her lip to suppress. "But your libido is not a reason for me to stay."

"It's more than my libido," I protest, even though I know I haven't shown that. Even though we haven't *been* more than that. But I want to be; I understand at least that much since my mom called me out, since I stayed up half that night thinking about it, since my immediate reaction to finding out Jack had been hurt was to run out of school and right to her doorstep. "I'm not in your house right now because I thought I'd get a hookup out of it."

"Yeah, I'm not really clear *why* you're in my house," she says flatly.

And it's officially time to let it out. "Because I care about you, okay? I like you, even though you're prickly as hell and looking at me like you wish I would vaporize and you think ketchup is a vegetable."

She snorts, but at least it sounds like there's a little genuine laughter in it. Progress. "It's not enough, Cheer Girl. We barely even know each other."

"But you like me, I bet."

She crosses those glorious arms, which have deeply bronzed from all that practice on the field. "I like making out with you, sure."

"And that's it? That's the only thing?" *Please don't let it be the only thing.*

"Well, no." She strokes her chin thoughtfully. "I also like your legs."

"Okay, fuck you, quarterback." I turn to go, but I don't get more than a step toward the door before a hand on my wrist pulls me back and then her mouth is on mine.

"You make me laugh occasionally," she says, a whisper against my lips. "And I know you probably had to take some shit about getting me for Midnight Breakfast. I appreciate it."

"And?" I'm pushing my luck, but my heart is pounding and I need to buy a few seconds to catch my breath.

"And I like how hard you push—both yourself and other people. Even me, occasionally. And that you don't even blink before scaling the wall of an apartment building. And maybe we don't know each other so well yet, but maybe it wouldn't be the worst thing if we changed that."

The pounding is easing up, trading itself for some intense fluttering in my stomach. This is where I would ask her on an actual date, but.

Miguel.

The squad.

The team.

"But we have to do that in secret, I'm guessing," she fills in, and I realize my face must not be holding anything back. "Is that because of Miguel, or because of everyone else?"

"Both?" I say quietly, missing the warmth of her immediately when her arms slip off my waist. "But not the way you think. I promise I'm not cheating on Miguel."

The lips I was just kissing twist into a little smirk. "You know, on that I actually believe you."

"You do?" I mean, *I* know I'm telling the truth, but I get that it sounds shady.

"I do. For one handsome, long-lashed, silver-Malibu-driving reason."

Oh. Well, hell. "You know."

"I thought," she admits. "Now I know."

Crap, crap, crap, crap, crap. "Miguel is going to kill me."

"I saw them," she clarifies, putting a calming hand on my arm. "I mean, he said the guy was his cousin, but. Either way, it's not your fault, and I hope you know I would *never* out him. Or you."

Even if I didn't know, the serious look on her face gives me confidence, and I want—I *need*—Miguel to see it too. It's time to get at least one part of this right. Even if Miguel might want to kill me for other reasons. "Okay. So now that you know, I want him to know too. And I want you to get to know each other. What do you think of a double date? We can spend time together, you can make a friend on the team, Miguel and Malcolm can actually hang out with other people. . . ."

"Somehow I don't think anyone on the Alligators wants to hang out with me socially, whether I'm dating his friend or not." Her voice is dry, but the drop of hurt that seeps through goes right to my heart.

"This isn't about football and cheerleading, or the Alligators, or anyone else," I assure her, knotting my fingers with hers. "Four people, out having fun, getting to know each other. You want to get to know me, right? Miguel is a part of me. Besides, you want an ally on the team? He's your best bet."

"And you think he'll be down for a double date?"

No. Yes. I don't know. "The only thing I'm better at than

cheerleading and kissing is wearing down Miguel Santiago."
That part, at least, I'm confident about. "Leave it to me."

- - - - -

Even though all we wanna do is skip the rest of the day and
spend it at Jack's house, we manage to convince ourselves to
get our asses off the couch and head back to school, separate
cars and all. We're just in time for lunch, where I manage to
tug Miguel into a corner of the courtyard where we can speak
privately.

"Okay, I have to ask you a favor, but I have to break a few
things to you first," I say before I can lose my nerve.

Miguel eyes me suspiciously, his deeply tanned skin crinkling at the corners of his dark eyes. "Well, considering the
way you ran out of here earlier, I'm guessing it has something
to do with Walsh. I'm trying not to run wild with what that
might mean because I know my best friend and *loyal girlfriend*
wouldn't be cheating on me without a heads-up."

Ouch. Okay, I deserve that. And because I have zero poker
face, I wince. Miguel visibly tenses up. "It's not what you think,"
I say, because apparently that's my mantra lately. "I didn't tell
Jack about Mal; she saw you together."

Miguel mutters something under his breath that he definitely wouldn't say within a hundred feet of his mother. "But
the two of you?"

"Have maybe fooled around a little bit. Just a couple of times," I add sheepishly, like that makes a difference.

"I cannot *believe* you didn't tell me."

"I didn't want you to freak out! And I didn't know how to handle"—I wave my hand back and forth between us—"this. There are reasons I don't usually mess with Atherton girls, as you know."

"But you like her."

"I do, yeah. And I want you to like her too. She could use a friend on the team. And I know you and Malcolm could use some relationship normalcy. So, I was thinking . . . double date?"

I suppose I should be grateful to finally see an expression on Miguel's face other than anger, but him cracking up at my proposal isn't what I had in mind. "You're joking."

"Oh, come on—it'll be fun!"

"And where exactly do you want to go on this magical date?"

The ride to school gave me exactly enough time to plan this, in fact. "Gutter Kittens. You know no one from school would be caught dead there." For good reason—the decrepit bowling alley is ridiculous and cheesy and somehow looks like a Victorian disco. But my mom and Aunt Lily used to love taking me there when I was little. It's been years now—Aunt Lily got married and moved to Hilton Head, and now she and my mom drink over video chats rather than bowling lanes, Cyndi Lauper, and watching me struggling to lift a hot-pink glittery ball—but I know it's still around because I took Miguel once when he needed an extreme injection of goofy fun. "You can't tell me Mal wouldn't love it."

"Of course he would," Miguel mutters, affection bleeding into his voice. "That dork."

"So? Saturday night? Eight o'clock?" I don't even care that I sound too eager; this is far too win-win for everybody for me to have an ounce of shame about it.

He sighs heavily, and I know there's a yes buried inside that obnoxiously loud breath. "Fabulous!" I say without waiting for him to vocalize it out loud. "Now, let's go shake on it with some tater tots."

-JACK-

I can't believe I'm doing this. I can't believe I'm going on a date. With a cheerleader. And a teammate. And his boyfriend.

I can't believe how much I'm looking forward to it.

My leg jiggles in my cutoffs as I wait in the car for Amber to emerge from her apartment, my fingers fiddling with everything they can reach. She told me not to bother coming to the door, to just text her when I was outside, but it still feels wrong, like I gotta prove chivalry isn't dead.

Then the door opens, and suddenly I'm glad to be where

I am because she steps out looking so cute, I know my knees would've weakened if I'd been standing in wait.

It doesn't hurt that she practically dances to the car I begged my mom to borrow so I could do this properly, every bit as excited for tonight as I am. She's curled her hair and she's wearing one of those one-piece things that's shorts on the bottom and shows off her incredible legs, and her lip gloss makes me ache to know how it tastes.

Fuck, our date has been three seconds long and I'm already a goner.

I at least have the presence of mind to lean over and push open her door, and when she slides in with a sultry "Hi, there," it's all I can do not to leap over the center console. Sage and Morgan would be laughing so fucking hard if they could see me now, smitten by a walking Barbie doll. We talked again last night, though we replaced real conversation with bingeing *Love, Victor*, completely avoiding talk of Amber. I haven't even told them about this date, just in case it turns out to be as big a disaster as everything else has since moving to Atherton, though I did—with Miguel's blessing—clarify the other stuff.

"Hi, yourself," I say, because clever words have escaped me. "So, where are we going?"

"Somewhere you can show off all that athletic prowess." She holds up her phone, then puts it in the little bracket thing that sticks out of the air-conditioner vent. "Don't worry. I put the address in here. Just follow the directions."

Being as new to town as I am, I had no choice but to let Cheer Girl pick the spot; the only remotely cool place I've been outside of school and that one shitty night at the diner is the batting cage I went to with my dad when he visited last weekend. I didn't think Amber would be quite as into it, not to mention that there's no way we wouldn't run into anyone from school there.

I shudder to think where we might be going that won't have a single Atherton teen there on a Saturday night.

But let's be real—I'd follow this girl anywhere.

Still, I can't help teasing. "I'm not sure you can be trusted. Promise me there'll be no clowns?"

"Oh, come on. Give me a little credit." Her phone declares a left turn and I follow. "But good to know your feelings about clowns."

"Aren't those everyone's feelings about clowns?"

"I for one happen to find clowns extremely sexy," she says, and it's so deadpan and unexpected that I laugh hard enough to miss the next turn. Eventually I get back on the right path, and Amber promises to stop distracting me, only to sing along to the radio in the most tone-deaf fashion possible.

"For some reason, I thought you had to at least be able to carry a tune to lead a cheer. I'm really learning a lot about you on this ride."

"There is a difference between chanting and singing, thank you very much. And it's not my fault you listen to weird emo shit."

"You're the one pretending to know the words!" I point out.

"I didn't say I don't also listen to weird emo shit!" She turns up the dial, and then we're both singing along, anxiety and inhibitions forgotten as we continue toward our mystery destination.

- - - - -

When we arrive, I have to blink three times to make sure I'm actually seeing what I think I'm seeing. "We're going bowling?" I ask, only vaguely aware I've already asked this at least twice.

"Okay, please stop being 'too cool' for this and at least give it a shot," Amber says with a roll of her blue-green eyes. "First of all, it's fun. Second of all, no one else from school ever comes here. And third of all, if you're afraid I'm going to embarrass you by bowling you under the table, you're right, I will. But it's still fun. Maybe more for me than for you."

"You know I'm the quarterback of the football team, right?" I can't help returning, even though she has it all wrong. I'm charmed as fuck that this is where a cool, sexy cheerleader brought me on a date; it's a whole dorky side I didn't even know she had, and it's a-fucking-dorable. And yeah, we're here because no one else at Atherton would be caught dead at—I squint at the half-burned-out neon sign—Gutter Kittens, but she also clearly likes it here.

And if she thinks I'm going to let her beat me just so I can see her do a cute little victory dance . . . Okay, she might be right.

"You know I'm a cheerleader, right?" she counters. "I lift and throw girls in the air, do stunts that would make you weep, and I'm waaaay more limber." She lets the words stretch out in the most infuriatingly teasing way that makes all my clothing feel too tight. "Prepare to eat dirt, QB."

"Prepare to eat those words, Cheer Girl," I shoot back as we get out of the car, but I still hold out my arm for her to take with her dainty little hands, because I am nothing if not a gentlewoman.

Miguel and his boyfriend are already inside when we enter the wonderland of sensory overload that is Gutter Kittens, looking adorably couple-y as they crack up over some joke I'm guessing from their gestures revolves around the fascinatingly glittery collection of bowling balls, which emerge from creepy-ass returns designed to look like gaping mouths. It's by far the lightest I've ever seen Miguel, who usually requires heavy machinery to pull his lips into a smile. Next to me, Amber radiates a sort of warm joy at the sight. It's clear she really cares about him, more than I even realized, and I wonder how tonight is going to balance between Miguel My Cautious Teammate and Miguel My Maybe-Future-Girlfriend's Best Friend.

If the latter is as impossible to impress as the former, this may end up being Cheer Girl's and my only date.

My concerns are confirmed when Miguel spots us, and it's like someone dimmed all the brightly colored lights in the room. (And there are a *lot* of brightly colored lights, weirdly placed in Gothic chandeliers and reflecting off the shiny harlequin wallpaper.) For a moment, I worry that somehow they got their lines crossed, and Amber was never supposed to bring me here. All the "Intruder! Intruder!" feelings I get from practice and weight-lifting class and even just wearing the uniform come rushing back. But then Miguel smiles and Amber squeezes my arm as she gently pulls me over and I see that they've already input our names—right below "Better M" and "Best M" are "Loud McCloud" and "QB1."

I let out the breath I'd been holding tight. Okay. We are in the right place, right time. Okay.

Amber skips over to the boys and I follow, trudging on the dusky paisley carpet like I forgot how to move like a normal person. Miguel's smile widens a few notches when Amber ignores him completely to give Malcolm a hug, and I have to dig my nails into my palms to stop myself from biting them.

"Malcolm, this is the one and only Jack Walsh. Jack, this is Miguel's extremely better half, Malcolm."

"I like her better and better every day," Malcolm says to Miguel before extending a hand to me. "And you're the famous Jack! It's great to meet you. Thank you for making it one hundred percent less embarrassing to be an Atherton football fan."

"I like *him* better than both of you," I inform Amber and

Miguel, and the genuine laughter that follows feels like slipping into a warm bath after a game.

"So how does your bowling arm compare to your throwing arm?" Miguel asks, and there are so many snarky things I want to say in response, things about how it doesn't matter because they'll probably all treat me like I suck anyway. It's not exactly fair—Miguel doesn't treat me like shit the way the other guys do. He's just neutral. But neutral hasn't helped me, and it's hard to hang out with him like we're friends when he hasn't been a friend to me at all.

This is for Amber, I force myself to remember. *Amber, the only person who talked to you like a person that first day, and the only person who went out of her way to welcome you to events. Amber, the only person who came to check on you after the fight. Amber, who's right next to you subtly hopping from foot to foot because despite being gorgeous and popular and basically a high school cliché, she's nervous. Because she thinks you look fucking cute in glasses even Morgan and Sage don't get to see, and she wants to be more than two people who make out and she hopes you do too.*

And that's all I need.

"Might be the only thing better," I say smoothly, "but I should warn you that Cheer Girl seems to think she's got this all wrapped up."

"Did 'Cheer Girl' tell you about the time she dented a fucking *table*—"

"Hush, Santiago," Amber demands with a huff. "Just

because you're embarrassed that I got *double* your score last time we came—"

"We came to cheer me up because I'd gotten my wisdom teeth out! I was high on painkillers!"

Amber rolls her eyes at me. "He always has excuses. What's it gonna be this time, Migs? Achy fingers from practice?"

"Empty stomach, maybe." He nods at the snack counter. "Nachos, yes?"

"*Yes,*" we chorus emphatically, and I realize I like a cheerleader who isn't afraid of a little neon cheese sauce. I slip Miguel some cash and he and Malcolm head off to stock up on salty provisions while Amber and I trade in our footwear for super-chic bowling shoes.

"I have to admit, I thought you might put up a fight about the bowling shoes," Amber says as she pulls a pair of tiny socks out of her purse and slides off her sandals. She's so freaking delicate and feminine, right down to her perfectly pink-polished toes, and I feel like such a cliché for finding that so hot.

And then she brings me bowling, at this absurdly ridiculous place that has lamps designed to look like fishnet-stocking-covered legs at every alley, and somehow that's even hotter.

"Bowling shoes are rad," I say, showing off my feet, because I pull the shoes off quite nicely. "I've never worn ones with glittery laces before, but I think I'm rocking 'em like a champ."

"That you are." Her grin lights up her face, and she is just so fucking cute, I have to look away.

I know this isn't going anywhere good. I'd have to be

completely deluded to think this is ever going past the occa-sional secret hangout somewhere absolutely no one she cares about other than Miguel will ever see us. I know that even though I'm here with them now, I'm going to be alone again on the field come next Friday.

I know, I know, I know.

But she has that fucking smile.

And she brought me to a bowling alley with vintage post-ers of *Rocky Horror* on the walls.

And I've actually found some queer kids to hang out with again.

And I don't know what I'm gonna do when this blows up spectacularly and I lose everything.

"Ooh, nachos!" She grabs my wrist to pull me to the table, springing me back out of my misery, at least for one night.

- - - - -

"So, when is all that domination gonna start?" I can't help teas-ing Amber as she knocks down exactly one pin. For the third time in a row.

She flips her long brown hair. "I'm just getting warmed up," she sniffs. "It takes me a little while to hit my stride, but *then*."

"Then comes total domination," Miguel says dryly, his lips curving into a smile around his straw before he takes a noisy sip of Coke and ice. "Just wait—by the tenth frame, she'll be knocking down *two*."

"Screw you, Splitter." She makes like she's going to throw a chip at him, but chomps on it instead. Malcolm and I snort with laughter at the nickname, because yeah, Miguel does have a weird tendency to get a 7–10 split every single turn, and no, he's not one of those masters who can turn that into a spare.

"You're up, champ," Malcolm says with a toothy grin. He's taking a lot of pleasure in the fact that I'm kicking everyone else's asses, and normally, I would be too, but historically my athletic successes have not exactly been welcome in this town.

Then again, Amber and Miguel are too busy being competitive twerps with each other to notice, which is probably for the best.

I *never* see them interact like this in school—playful and snarky and so clearly more like brother and sister than anything romantic. It's weird to imagine I ever worried about them dating. Plus, Miguel and Malcolm are aspirationally a-fucking-dorable.

Of course, now that Malcolm's drawn attention, both Amber's and Miguel's eyes fly up to the scoreboard. "Jesus, Walsh," Miguel groans. "Is there any sport you don't dominate?"

I brace myself for the wave of resentment, the kind I've become very attune to in the last few weeks, but don't catch any. However he feels about me as a teammate, here we're having fun. And it's going to stay fun. I can breathe. "Badminton," I assure him as I go up and hunt for the sparkly blue-green ball that's become my fast favorite. "I am terrible at badminton."

"Makes sense you wouldn't be into the shuttlecock," Malcolm says seriously, and I laugh so hard, I almost drop the ball on my toe.

"Malcolm!" Amber whispers fiercely. "Behave! This is a bowling alley! There are children present!"

"First of all, we're the youngest people here by at least three decades," Miguel points out, "and second of all—"

"This place is filled with glittery balls!" Miguel, Malcolm, and I all chorus, and we crack up again.

Then I throw a strike, and the laughter turns into hoots and claps.

"J-A-C-K!" Amber cheers, jumping up from her seat and waving and rolling her arms. "Knock those pins down all the way! Gooooo Jack!"

"Did I just get a personal cheer from future head cheerleader Amber McCloud?" I widen my eyes and flutter my hand over my chest.

"You did!" She flounces over and places a big smack on my cheek, and Miguel and Malcolm cheer as my face undoubtedly goes red. "I am very proud of my star athlete."

My star athlete. Fuck. I am a five-foot-nine puddle on the sticky floor.

When I finish the final frame with a strike followed by a spare, Amber does a full-on cartwheel in the middle of the room, just narrowly missing the decrepit air hockey table. I'm sure someone's going to yell at us, but instead they just whistle and urge her on. Turns out being an extremely hot girl with long, bendy legs helps you get away with a lot. Who knew?

"You're ridiculous," I tell her, but even as I say it I'm pulling her close, an uncharacteristically affectionate tone coming out of my mouth that I don't think I've ever used in my life. This girl is turning me into something different and I don't hate it. "But I can't say I mind having my own personal cheerleader."

"I can't say I mind having a future pro athlete on my arm either," she says with a wink, and I laugh even though we both know the future options for female football players are not exactly Tim Tebow possibilities.

Tonight it's kinda feeling like anything is possible.

We play one more game, and it's true that Amber hits her stride at some point, though I'm mostly just watching her form. (It is very good form. Especially in that outfit.) Miguel and Malcolm take turns giving each other bowling instructions, like "roll it underhand like you're three years old" and "do this one with your eyes closed," and though we obviously won't be posting them anywhere, we even take a few selfies. I make a mental note to send one to Morgan and Sage later.

With the nachos gone, we get spicy fries—the food is surprisingly decent for a six-lane bowling alley decorated like the home of someone's grandma on acid—and Malcolm gets fried calamari, which the rest of us refuse to try. "I cannot put squid in my mouth," says Amber. "I just can't."

"That's what she said," Miguel and I say together, and I swear to God it almost feels like I'm becoming friends with one of my teammates.

"Et tu, QB?" Malcolm asks, holding out the red plastic basket. "These two are cowards, but I expected more from you."

"Them's fightin' words. Fine, I'll try the damn thing." The truth is, it smells amazing, but Malcolm doesn't need to know that my mouth has been watering and full of regret since I initially squirmed at the idea of eating slices of tentacled sea creatures. I push up my flannel sleeves and watch Amber's face twist in horror.

"You know, this may threaten your chances at a good-night kiss," she warns me.

"Ohhhh," Miguel says as I immediately drop my hand like it's been burned. "The magic words."

They sure are. Even though we've made out a few times now, somehow the mythical good-night kiss feels like a way bigger step, and I wouldn't assume it was guaranteed, or even on her mind. But apparently . . . "Sorry, man," I say to Malcolm. "I'm happy to be a weenie if that's what it gets me."

"Well, I don't know if I wanna date a weenie." Amber taps her cheek thoughtfully, and I stick out my tongue at her.

"You're cruel, Loud McCloud." Miguel ruffles her hair, and she laughs. "And for the record," he says to Malcolm, "I will absolutely still kiss you goodnight."

"Awww," Malcolm and I chorus, while Amber pretends to vomit. If we were in another town, here's where the boys would probably kiss, but they settle for a quick hand squeeze on the table that makes them both smile.

We stick around for a while, finishing our food and playing on the ancient arcade games, until finally Malcolm announces his curfew is approaching, and he and Miguel go return their shoes while I finish letting Amber beat me at air hockey just because she looks so cute when she does a victory dance after each goal.

We don't leave until almost an hour after the boys do. There's just too much to play with, too many ridiculous pictures to take, and no parents waiting for us at home—Amber's mom is on the night shift, and my parents are on another date. They decided to end this one at the Atherton Inn for the night. When you only see each other once a week at best, I guess sharing a small one-bedroom with your daughter sleeping on the other side of the wall isn't ideal.

I'm trying not to think about it.

"It's nice to see kids back in here," the big mustached guy behind the counter says as he takes our bowling shoes. I haven't seen him before; a skinny redhead, no older than college-age, gave us our shoes earlier. But this guy is maybe fifty, a bunch of salt in the pepper of his hair, and has an air of "I was born in this alley and I will die here." The manager, maybe, or the owner. "It's been a few months since we had anyone from the high school."

A few months? Amber seemed confident no one from

Atherton ever came here. Judging from the look on her face, she's just as surprised.

"Other Atherton kids came here?" she asks, keeping her voice casual.

"Cute couple," he says, returning the bowling shoes to their cubbies and producing my Docs and Amber's sandals. "Wouldn't say they were a *nice* couple," he says with a snort, "but they came every week for a while and stayed glued to each other's faces every time. Maybe they broke up." The redhead calls from another corner of the alley with a question, and Mustache yells back before returning his attention to us. "She was so little, I thought she was maybe twelve at first. But they had their high school IDs, tried to use them to get discounts, which we don't offer."

"A cute couple with a girl who looks twelve?" Amber mumbles, and I can practically see her brain whirring through her hair. "Were they freshmen?"

"I don't think so. He had a varsity jacket."

I watch as Amber racks her brain, then shakes her head. "There aren't any couples I'd describe like that. The only girl on the team who looks *that* young is Cara, but she definitely hasn't dated anyone."

"No, that's it. Cara." He scratches his mustache. "I knew I'd know it if I heard it."

Amber blinks slowly. "Are you telling me Cara Whelan came here every week with a guy, and I had no idea? We're talking four-foot-eleven, reddish-brown hair, freckles, always wears a gold cross around her neck?"

"I don't know about the necklace, but the rest sounds right."

"With a varsity player? Any idea what sport?"

The guy squints at her. "I may have overstated my investment here. I really didn't take notes, and I don't follow sports other than . . ." He gestures at the bowling lanes.

"Right." Amber tries to smile, but it comes out shaky. I don't understand her friendship with Cara, who's been nothing but cold to me, but I do know it goes way back and it's clear Amber doesn't know her nearly as well as she thought she did. "Well, sorry I don't know what happened to them, then, but yeah, I guess they broke up."

"It's a shame," he says, dusting off the counter. "They were really into each other. She even did a cheer for him." A look of understanding dawns over his face. "Ah, your cartwheel. Guessing you're on some sort of squad together." He looks at me. "And I guess she wasn't cheering for either of the fellas," he adds, jerking a thumb at Amber.

My skin prickles as I wait for a comment that's lewd, homophobic, or both to hit my ears, but nothing comes. I guess you can't run a place that looks like Liza Minnelli's dressing room without expecting some queer presence. "Nope, sir. I kicked all their asses tonight."

"Nice." He reaches over the counter and gives me a high five. "I do remember this about them—they were both shitty bowlers. He used to get cranky about it, argued with her the one time she beat him, even though it didn't take much. Said his throwing arm was off after a game." Mustache snaps his fingers. "Football! I remember now. He said something 'bout being the QB. Musta been before they got that girl I been hearin' about."

"That's me," I say before I can think better of it, earning me a bemused look from our new friend. "I'm the QB."

"But you weren't a few months ago," Amber says quietly. "And neither was Tim. Which means the guy Cara was dating on the sly was Robbie Oakes."

Chapter Seven

-AMBER-

Cara.

And Robbie.

Cara—my best friend since childhood, the person I know better than anyone on the planet—had a secret boyfriend. They went to Gutter Kittens. They dated for months. How did she even pull this off? And *why*?

Well, the "why" is easy in the greater sense—her parents would've gone ballistic if they knew she had a boyfriend. But keeping it from the squad? From *me*? That's a little harder to comprehend.

But I get it now, why she's coming so hard for Jack. The very fact that Jack's here must be a painful reminder of who isn't. Cara'd be horrified if she knew where I am now, who I'm with.

My first instinct, as usual, is to tell Miguel, but I can't tell him this. He already thinks I should've dropped Cara like a hot potato years ago, ever since her father appointed himself conductor of the homophobia train. Any more ammunition and I worry I'm looking at being forced to choose between them. Especially if Cara knew about the blackmail.

Did Cara know about the blackmail?

God, I hope not. If there's one sliver of light I can hope for in this entire shitty revelation, it's that she had no idea she was dating a complete asshole. And if she did know . . . No, I can't even go there. She couldn't have. Cara might be Pastor Whelan's daughter, but there's a difference between "I don't approve of your 'lifestyle'" and "I will help someone ruin your life because of your sexual orientation."

It isn't a *big* difference, but Cara's the girl who stayed up all night trying to help me fix my hair when I decided to cut my own bangs. She's probably the only reason I passed freshman algebra. She made and sold friendship bracelets and cookies with me when I overheard my mom panicking on the phone about how she was going to pay the dentist's bill for my first and only cavity, and she's still the person I run summer cheer clinics with for kids in the area. So yeah, I'll cling to that tiny difference and pray to her god that I'm never proven wrong.

I certainly can't *confront* her. How would I explain why I was at Gutter Kittens to start with? And really, what's the point? To rub salt into the wound of his death? Yes, Robbie was an asshole, but clearly Cara didn't feel that way.

Maybe she even loved him.

Which means the only person I can really talk about this with is—

"Hey, you okay?"

I blink up at Jack, who's sitting patiently in the driver's seat, watching me stare at my front door without getting out of the car. Now is when we should be having an epic good-night kiss, not sitting in silence while I contemplate what it means that one of my best friends had a secret romance with the guy who tried to ruin my other best friend's life.

I should keep my mouth shut, probably. Miguel never wanted anyone to know what Robbie was doing, and Cara . . . But I'm not the one who spilled Cara's secret to Jack, and if she already knows that half, and she already knows Miguel is gay. . . .

If I don't talk to someone, I am going to explode.

"I'm sorry for ruining our date" is what comes out of my mouth, though. "I was having a really good time. I *am*, I mean. I like sitting here with you." All of that is so true, it hurts.

"Hey, Cheer Girl." She takes my hand in her rough one, her calluses lightly scraping my skin and making me shiver in the warm Florida night. "You haven't ruined anything. I'm just worried about you. You seemed to take that news pretty hard. Were you and Cara, uh—"

"No!" The idea is so ridiculous, I almost laugh in her face. "God, no. Cara comes from a super-religious family that is *not* down with the rainbow. Honestly, she's the number one reason I'm not out at school. She's not even allowed to date boys, which I guess is why Robbie was a secret. Her parents would ground her for life if they knew, or send her to live with her aunt in Winter Springs. Cheerleading would *definitely* be off the table."

"Oh. Yikes. No wonder she seems so uptight. And you weren't exactly tight with Robbie either, right?"

"Understatement of the year," I mutter. I look her square in the eyes, trying to decide exactly how much I can trust her, and nothing in the warm brown waiting there suggests anything other than that she's patiently listening. "Robbie made life hell for Miguel. He was the only person at school other than me who knew Miguel was gay, and he used it to his advantage constantly—blackmailing Miguel to vote on his side anytime there was any sort of team conflict, treating him like an errand boy, demanding money all the time, and just generally being a dick. It's true that Miguel and I are dating in part to keep other guys away from me, but the biggest reason was to discredit Robbie if he ever tried to out Migs. Except Robbie was such a fucking asshole that he took pictures as backup."

Jack's jaw drops so low, I can see a filling in one of her back molars. "*That's* the guy people are so pissed I replaced? That's the guy I've been trying to live up to? Are you fucking kidding me?"

"Trust me, it's killing me and Miguel, but as far as I know, not a single soul at AHS knows about the blackmail other than the two of us and now you. And you absolutely cannot tell a soul."

"You really wanna keep that a secret? Seeing how much everyone idolizes him? Seeing what hell I'm going through *because* of how much everyone idolizes him?" Fire flashes in her eyes and I worry I made a terrible mistake and shared too much. "They should know who they're putting on a pedestal. Those guys are Santiago's friends too—wouldn't they be pissed on his behalf?"

I'm not sure which of us let go, but I'm suddenly very aware we're no longer holding hands. "I'm pretty sure they'd be more focused on that he's gay, Jack. He made a choice not to come out to them, and we're not outing him on the chance it might make them let up on you. I'm really sorry they're being shitty, but—"

"*Amber.*" Her voice is fierce enough to shut me up mid-sentence. "Of course I'm not talking about outing Miguel. Jesus fuck, who do you think I am?"

I don't know, I think, because even though I want to, we're still so new. This is still so new. And right now, I'm learning I can't trust anything, and I don't know whether or not that includes this thing between us.

She sighs. "Okay, fair enough. I get how tonight has been a lesson that you never know anyone as well as you think you do. But listen to me, okay? I would never, ever out somebody, not even the devil Robbie himself."

I swallow hard. It's the absolute lowest bar of humanity, but the truth is, I'm not sure how many people at Atherton would clear it, and I'm just so relieved Jack is one of them.

"I know we can't tell them this specifically," she continues, and her hand finds mine again. "And yeah, I know it's a dream at this point that they'll stop sanctifying him for any reason. It's just . . . not fair, you know? I almost think I could take it all if he were a really great guy, but this . . . Or maybe I just want to think that. Maybe I'd crack under the pressure no matter what."

"Hey," I tell her, lifting up her chin. "You're not cracking. You are kicking ass. You are the best thing that's ever happened to the team and that's true regardless of who Robbie was. They may act like they don't know who's to credit for their first winning season, but believe me, they know. And someday they'll be grateful for it. Even if they're, like, forty by the time that happens. But they aren't the point—you are. And you're a star."

Her gaze drops, and my heart does a double back handspring at the sight of this powerful athlete going shy on me. "A star, huh?"

"Let's be real—I wouldn't bother sneaking around with anyone who wasn't."

She snorts, but it doesn't make her look any less kissable. And kiss her is exactly what I do.

- - - - -

Of course, the day after I find out about Cara's secret is a day I have to be trapped in a room with her and the rest of the squad for hours. It's Spirit Week, which means for the next seven days, our entire lives are dedicated to amping the school up for homecoming this weekend. Thankfully, because athletics rule Atherton, even despite our pre-Jack losing record, that means homework this week is a joke. Unfortunately, Spirit Week prep is *not*.

Tomorrow is Gator Day—which means tail-shaped cookies in the cafeteria, "snapping" your friends and lovahs (i.e., clipping festive clothespins to their shirts, which results in a schoolwide popularity contest), and a group of twelve cheerleaders sprawled on the floor of Diana Rivera's palatial living room the day before, threading garlands of fake alligator teeth and making glittery "Atherton Rules!" signs on oak tag designed to look like gator skin.

"What *are* these creepy things?" Zoe asks, holding up one of the plastic fang-like teeth. "Who just *has* fake alligator teeth lying around?"

"Girl, you are so clearly not originally from Florida." Claire tosses a green paper scale at her, but it drifts to the floor between them like a leaf. "Take that Ohio energy out of Gator Day."

"You're just jealous of my tan." Zoe flips her sun-streaked bottle-blond hair over one orangey shoulder.

"Your tan that comes straight out of the Spray Garden?" Claire counters, sparking a lot more throwing of décor.

Cara turns to me and rolls her eyes. "How's your garland coming along?" Her light blue eyes drop down to the pile of nothing in my lap. "Ammo, you know you're supposed to be stringing this stuff *on*, right?"

Whoops. Guess my brain is elsewhere. I wonder why.

"I've never been good at sewing," I say sheepishly, putting the string down. "I think I'll go help Crystal and Nia with the posters."

"You sure?" She furrows her brow. "I thought after last year you didn't wanna go within twenty feet of Gator-green glitter."

Ugh, it's true. I was washing it out of my hair and clothes for weeks. But sitting this close to Cara and not being able to ask about her and Robbie is slowly killing me. "I guess I have even more negative feelings about fake alligator teeth," I offer, wishing for the millionth time that I wasn't the world's worst liar.

Today was supposed to be a Step Up and Lead Day, one in a long line of planned ones where I came up with brilliant ideas and proved that I deserved the captain spot. But between Cara and the drama with Jack and, well, all the making out with Jack, I've barely given Spirit Week any attention. Any thoughts I may have had about streaming sequined ribbons from our uniforms or showing up with a perfectly manicured C-U-L-8-R on one hand and G-A-T-O-R on the other has flown out the window, along with my sanity.

"You sure you're okay?" Cara's eyebrows have even more incredible gymnastic capabilities than she does, and she's our best flyer. "You've been a little off all day."

And then, because I am incredibly stupid and I cannot help myself, I say, "I'm fine—just thinking about who I wanna snap tomorrow."

Maybe I only notice because I'm looking for it, but Cara's shoulders sink, like she was reminded she has no one to snap. Suddenly, I feel like crap. It's not her fault Robbie was a dick, especially if she didn't know he was blackmailing Miguel.

Which we've already established she didn't.

Right?

The possibility is there, I know, even if I don't want to think about it. It's not like she's particularly rainbow friendly. And maybe that's why she always seems to be looking for the cracks in our foundation. Maybe she thinks I have no idea, that I'm an innocent bystander in Miguel's grand queer plan. But then why wouldn't *she* tell me?

God, I wish I'd never found out about them. I feel like I'm going nuts.

"Not just giving them all to Miguel?" she asks, and I know she intends for it to sound innocent, but it absolutely does not.

"Obviously I've got to spread some love around the squad, too," I reply lightly, though I'm thinking about what it would be like to clip one to Jack's shirt, to claim her in front of everyone, to get a kiss and my own snap—maybe all three of her snaps—in return. "What about you? Who's going to be the lucky beneficiary of Cara Whelan's gator bites?"

Okay, maybe my question doesn't sound quite as innocent as I want it to either.

Her face pinches tight. "You know my parents' rules—squad only. If you're lucky, you might get one."

"I would be honored." It's definitely time to change the subject, but before I can ask if she's picked out a nail color for our Saturday afternoon pre-homecoming dance mani-pedis or whether her adventurous coworker at the Bean Counter has actually come up with an idea for a seasonal flavor that isn't disgusting yet (I do *not* recommend trying his attempt at Turkey Roast), Diana picks up the conversation.

"You're an upperclassman now, Whelan. Live a little!" She shakes a couple of capped containers of green glitter like maracas. "Surely there's gotta be someone you'd like to snap like a twig."

"Someone you like to cheer a little extra hard for?" Zoe adds with a glint in her eye.

"Someone you'd like to sink your teeth into?" Sara shakes one of the gator-tooth garlands to illustrate her pun.

Cara pastes a smile on her face, but my eyes drop to her hands because I know her moves, and she's digging her nails into her skin to keep from crying, just like she used to when her parents yelled if we were being too loud during a sleepover. Suddenly, I don't care why she kept Robbie a secret or how much I hate him; I just want to sweep my friend into a hug. So I cut in and do my best to save her.

"Hey, you heard her—those snaps are mine. Stop trying to draw her attention away from me." I wrap an arm around Cara, the closest I can come to offering her the shoulder I want to, and place a loud smack on her cheek. "Snap that, ladies."

The girls laugh and tease us, but all I care about is that Cara's easing up on her wrists, the crescent moons left by her nails slowly regaining their color and losing their shape.

Whatever happened between her and Robbie, it was something real. Her loss was real. And there's nothing I can do to make it better.

Nothing except make it clear I'm in her corner no matter what, and that Robbie will never be replaced. Which means joining her anti-Jack crusade.

So, what's it gonna be: Her heart, or mine?

-JACK-

There is a hell, and it is Gator Day.

I knew it would be a drain, but it's made so much worse by how everyone has clearly taken it upon themselves to turn this into a "Make Jack Feel Extra Shitty Day."

Example number one? The football players are covered in those stupid clothespins everyone's been snapping onto each other all day.

Guess whose shirt has nothing, not even from the girl she made out with Saturday night?

Example number two? In what has got to be the cheesiest move known to man, the varsity athletes are wearing not our uniforms today, but Lacoste shirts—you know, the overpriced polos with the little green gators on them. It's so fucking stupid and elitist, not to mention classist—I can't be the only one who can't drop that kind of cash on a single article of clothing—but what's really special is being literally the only athlete in the school who isn't doing it.

I, of course, am wearing my jersey, exactly as the apparently bullshit team email sent out by Dan Sanchez last night reminded us to do.

At least I look good in the jersey, which is extremely cold comfort as everyone points and snickers at me everywhere I go.

It's not fair to be mad at Amber. She's been working toward becoming captain for years, and the only thing that might kill that dream faster than coming out is for everyone to know who she's really been making out with. And it's not fair to be mad at Miguel, who has his own shit to deal with.

But I'm so fucking sick of being alone, and those stupid little clothespins and stitched-on alligators are pushing me toward the edge.

"You know it's Gator Day, not game day, right?" some girl I don't even know calls at me. "I know you're excited, but jeez."

"Careful," a dorky-looking boy I'm confident I could rip limb from limb stage-whispers back at her. "You might forget for two seconds that she's the quarterback. We can't have that."

Oh yes, because I wear this jersey with so much pride. Try harder, loser.

Still, I'm this close to chucking it into my locker after next period and just walking around in my sports bra. It'd probably be less embarrassing.

You know what? Fuck it. That's exactly what I'm doing.

I whip off my jersey before I can give it another thought, and stuff it into my locker. It's not like my sports bra is much more revealing than half the crop tops girls wear to school here, or even the cheerleaders' uniforms. And if they're gonna whisper about me anyway, let them do it about something on my terms, not a stupid prank my supposed teammates pushed me into.

I put all my irritation into the satisfying slam of my locker door, but the catharsis is short-lived when I turn around to find Vice Principal Foster standing a few feet away, a deep frown wrinkling her face. "Ms. Walsh. A minute?"

I resist the urge to shudder off the "Ms." and square my shoulders as I walk over, which is maybe not the wisest move, since it pushes out my chest. "Yes?"

"A hallway is not the place to change your clothes, as I'm sure you are aware."

"Oh, I'm not changing," I clarify, gesturing at my closed clocker. "I'm dressed."

If possible, her expression turns even stonier. "Undergarments are not appropriate school attire, Ms. Walsh."

"You can really just call me Jack," I tell her, because if I hear "Ms. Walsh" one more time, I'm going to scream. "And I'm pretty sure I'm every bit as covered as they are." I gesture to two girls pretending not to watch us from behind a notebook, one of whom is wearing a top short enough to show off a belly chain (ew). The other one's neckline is so low, there's almost as much of her bra showing as there is of mine, and hers isn't exactly plain black cotton from Target.

Foster refuses to turn her head, though; we both know she won't like what she sees. "The point stands that you are not wearing clothing, M—"

I cut her off before she throws out the M word again. "How about we say I'm wearing a crop top without a bra underneath? There—everybody wins."

Somewhere in the corner of my mind I think about how Morgan would melt into the floor if they heard me now. The thought makes me smile.

It is a very bad time to smile.

"That's enough," Foster snaps. "You football players all think you can get away with—" She breaks off, even though it's obvious to both of us what she was going to say. I guess accusing a team of murder, even if it's just a saying, is maybe a little classless when one of them died.

Now we're just at an awkward standoff with everyone watching, which is exactly when Cheer Girl shows up, the clothespins on her stupid alligator shirt clacking in time with her steps. "Hi, Ms. Foster!" she says brightly, smiling to show her perfect teeth. There's something different about her, and I realize it's the first time I've ever seen her outside of class without at least one other cheerleader around. I wonder what excuse she made to free herself from the pack and come over here. "I was just coming to pick up Jack to bring her to the locker room to get her special QB gator polo."

If ever there were four words that made no sense together, it's "special QB gator polo," and from the expression on Foster's face, she's aware of it. But Amber is Amber, and she's impossible to say no to or even question, especially when she has the Cheer Girl Charm turned all the way up—I should know. Foster is gonna crack.

But not without putting up a fight first. "Is that so?" Her thin eyebrows shoot skyward. "Because I was just informed she was wearing 'a crop top without a bra underneath.'"

Amber rolls her eyes in a way that suggests she and Foster are having a laugh at my expense. "I keep telling her she's not half as funny as she thinks she is, but you know football players. . . ."

"Mm-hmm. Get her dressed, Ms. McCloud," commands Foster, and then she heaves a heavy sigh like we might be *the* most annoying children she has ever encountered, and continues on down the hall to find her next lucky delinquent.

"You really—" *Shouldn't have*, I start to say to Amber, even though I can't ignore that part of me likes how she came to my "rescue," but she doesn't let me get a word out.

"Come on." She yanks me toward the locker room, muttering under her breath. I can make out "wearing a fucking bra in the fucking hallway," but it all gets unintelligible from there.

"You seriously have an extra one of those shirts in there?" I ask as she literally shoves me inside.

"No, I don't," she snaps. "And we're not exactly the same size, so I can't just give you mine. You're welcome for buying you some time to figure out a solution rather than letting Foster bench you for homecoming."

"She would never." I feel mostly confident about this, but Amber's giving me a "You're not as smart as you think you are" glare.

So now I'm not as funny *or* as smart. Yikes.

I'll just have to look good in this bra.

"You really wanna take that chance considering you don't exactly have the support of the team?" Amber says coldly. "If I'm remembering right, Tim Duggan would be happy to take your spot Friday night."

Actually, it's everyone but *Duggan who'd be happy for him to take my spot Friday night*, I think but don't say. God, if even Foster knows she could pull me out with no resistance from the team despite the school finally having a winning record, that's just sad. "So now what?" I ask through gritted teeth.

She sighs. "I don't know. Let me text Miguel."

Ten minutes later we're all late for class and I'm wearing a spare polo of Santiago's disguised beyond recognition with extra tinsel and crap Amber yanked off a poster. It's not even one of those gator polos, but it's done up too festively for anyone to notice. I look absolutely ridiculous.

But two people at this school actually helped me out. So I'll wear it with pride.

"You look extremely festive," says Amber, smirking with satisfaction at her work. "Even Foster would approve."

"Well, you know how much I crave Foster's approval."

She folds her arms over her chest. "You crave mine, don't you?"

Grudgingly, I concede that maybe, a little bit, I do.

"Good." Finally, there's a hint of a real smile, and it makes something inside me flutter.

Fuck, I really like this girl.

"Don't let it go to your head," I growl, because I can see that it is, and I hate that it's so cute.

"I would never." And then she reaches into her bag and produces a plain, unadorned clothespin, gives it a quick kiss, and clips it to the hem of my new shirt. "Now get your ass to class."

I resolve to stay on my best behavior for the rest of the day. After all, there's a whole week of this shit—Spirit Day (which sounds celebratory but is apparently a day we all just dress up like ghosts?), Atherton Pride Day (which is, sadly, not the kind of Pride I was hoping for, but a day to celebrate the things we love about our fair city), Pajama Day (which I can definitely do), and Books and Balls Day (when we're *definitely* supposed to wear our uniforms, Amber confirmed)—and I'm sure I'll find plenty more ways to get in trouble.

When the bell finally sounds, it's a momentary relief, until I remember I have to face the stupid assholes who pranked me at practice. But no one says a word, and no one seems to know Miguel had any part in saving me, and at the end, I have an offer of a ride home from Amber, so actually, it ends up being a pretty good day.

I take my time changing back into my clothes, waiting until I hear the guys emptying out of the school. Finally, when the coast is clear, I duck out and into Amber's car.

"Hi, troublemaker," she says, her eyes sparkling.

I can't help it. I have to lean over and kiss her immediately. "Hi, savior. Can we please get the fuck out of here?"

"Don't need to ask me twice." We drive away from the

building, and Amber suggests we take the long way back to my place.

"How about we go to *your* house for once?" I suggest as casually as I can. And okay, maybe I'm curious about going beyond her front door and seeing what her room looks like, maybe even what her mom's like. Hooking up in the back seat of her car isn't a relationship, and if I learned anything from going on an actual date with her, it's that I want to go on more of them. I want to know this girl who rescues me with tinsel and takes me to bizarre bowling alleys and loves to put on a short skirt and wave pom-poms. I want to get that last part, to understand what makes her tick.

I want a lot more than I should, especially from someone who's keeping me a secret.

And yes, I've seen what happens when you want something you shouldn't. But even though getting my last dream turned out to be half nightmare, I still get to play, to wear the uniform, to watch the ball soar from my hands under the lights.

I know that getting what you want can be both heaven and hell.

And I'll take it, if she'll let me.

"My house? It's really nothing special."

It's special because you live in it. "No offense, but does anyone in Atherton live in anything special? That's not the point."

"Well, it's not exactly spacious or full of privacy, and my

mom is home tonight, so, maybe another time would be better."

I shrug, words coming out of my mouth I can't seem to stop. "Or maybe we hang out with your mom. Y'all get along, right?"

Amber snorts. "Yeah, we get along great, but—" She stops at a red light and turns to me. "You're serious? You wanna come over and meet my mom?"

So help me God, I do.

And that's how I know I'm in deep.

- - - - -

Heidi McCloud just might be my favorite adult on the planet.

First of all, she says, "So *this* is the girl," with a wink at me that makes Amber blush to the heavens, which is just about my favorite thing that's happened since I moved to Atherton.

Second of all, she's queer. Her *mom* is queer. When we somehow get onto the topic of haircuts, she laughs and says something about how she has the stereotypical "bisexual bob" like it's nothing, like I must've met so many openly queer adults before, like it's no big deal to live in Northwest Florida and have a job and a kid and just *be bi.*

It must be weird for Amber, being out at home but completely in the closet at school. Not that I'm super out at school either, but I don't exactly pass for straight unless you're determined to be clueless as hell; even my grandparents have finally stopped asking when I'll meet a nice boy. Nothing about her gives off vibes until she wants to, though, and turning it on and off frankly sounds exhausting.

"You sure you don't want any more?" Heidi asks, tipping the pint of mint chocolate chip ice cream we've all been sharing in my direction. It's the green kind, for Gator Day, which was a little horrifying until Amber rolled her eyes and told me her mom has a different flavor for every day of Spirit Week and calls it her "favorite excuse of the year."

"I'm good, but thank you." Truth is, I don't really like ice cream, but she was so excited to serve it to us and I loved the idea of being doted on by a girlfriend's mom so much that I swallowed it down anyway. I feel like I've just drunk icy mouthwash. Amber shakes her head, though it's obvious she wants more. From several references at Gutter Kittens and tonight, I'm guessing homecoming and the accompanying dress have something to do with cutting herself off.

We haven't actually talked about the dance, but there isn't really anything to say—she and Miguel mentioned going together the other night at bowling, Malcolm pretended (?) to be sad about missing out, and I didn't say a word, because it's a dance and those are extremely not my thing. Technically, my presence would be required as quarterback, but oh right, no one gives a shit about me, so I get to stay home and watch ESPN Classic while everyone else squeezes into dresses and uncomfortable suits and ties.

I definitely don't want to be doing that.

I definitely haven't pictured rocking my own suit, Amber on my arm in a dress that shows off lots of glowing skin, swaying against me at slow dances. Maybe sneaking kisses in the corner. Maybe taking some pictures to send to Sage and Morgan or even post online. Maybe hanging out with Miguel and Malcolm and having as good a time as we had the other night. Maybe having the room stop and toast to our win the night before and the quarterback who led them to victory. Maybe sneaking into her room together afterward and leaving that suit on the floor.

Whew, good thing I have not imagined that at *all*.

"We have to go strategize for the rest of Spirit Week," Amber says apologetically to Heidi, tugging me out of the tall seat at their breakfast bar. "Thanks for the ice cream, Mom."

"Ah yes, strategizing for Spirit Week," Heidi says dryly. "I believe that's how you were conceived."

"Oh my *God*, Mom." Amber's cheeks flame as she yanks me toward her room. "You are not allowed to talk to any of my friends ever again!" she calls over her shoulder.

"Leave the door open, honey!" Heidi calls back sunnily.

"We can't even get pregnant!" Amber slams the door behind us, but it's more for punctuation than anything else. She cracks it open a second later, and her mom makes a satisfied noise from the kitchen before retiring to her own bedroom with the door fully closed.

"Sorry, she's the world's most embarrassing human." Amber rubs her hands over her face. "Just ignore everything she ever says, ever."

"So you didn't bring me here to get me pregnant?"

"Oh shut up." She grabs a pillow from her bed and whacks me with it. It's one of many—her bed is one of those froufy things with big pillows and smaller pillows and smallest pillows, and it looks very, very comfortable and uncomfortable at the same time. But even with her mom's door closed, it's impossible not to be hyperaware that she's all of fifteen feet away; their apartment isn't that much bigger than ours. "There— you've met my mom and seen my house. Is it everything you dreamed it would be?"

"Kind of, yeah," I admit, taking myself on a little self-guided tour of her room. It makes me miss having my own space at home—my trophy shelves and posters and sketches from before Jason decided it wasn't cool to want to be an artist.

Amber's room is as peppy as she is in the halls, full of pictures from cheer camp and games, selfies with Miguel, Cara, and other girls from the squad, and one sweet, framed, slightly faded photo that's clearly of her and Heidi when Amber was a little kid.

"That was my grandma's favorite picture," says Amber, watching me pick it up. "She died just before I started high school. She and my mom didn't get along that well, so I didn't see her much. But that picture always made her smile, so I took the frame from her house when we went to clear it out."

"That's sweet."

"Don't get used to it."

I snort and keep browsing. Everything is just as it should be in a cheerleader's room—pom-poms hanging from the slatted closet doors and a fresh mint color on the walls that's not unlike the ice cream we just ate. A couple of YA books on her shelves that have cheerleaders on the cover, one of which looks super gay that I may have to ask to borrow later. Her desk is a mess of everything but homework and her floor is neat as a pin. It's exactly what I would've guessed her room looked like based on our first meeting, but not what I would've imagined now that we've spent time together.

"It's brutally extra, I know."

Yes feels like the wrong response, but it's true. Where's the girl who likes the ridiculous décor of Gutter Kittens? Where's the fierceness of the girl who lied to Foster just a few hours ago? Where does she fit in to the feather boa artfully wrapped around the bulletin board covered with Gator paraphernalia?

"It both is and isn't exactly what I imagined," I say, which feels like the truest response I can give.

She laughs. "That's very diplomatic of you. My other grandmother—my dad's mom—used to come over every Sunday, and she loved this room. She bought just about everything in it."

"The one who writes a big check every birthday?"

"That's the one. She used to come by a lot, until my dad had his first new kid. Now I see her maybe once a year, but redecorating is expensive, and anyway, she's helped me with so much, and I like knowing that my room would still make her happy." She fiddles with a stuffed alligator, or maybe it's a crocodile—its teeth are showing. "Hell, even the polo shirt I wore today was a Christmas present from her. I should probably make some changes, especially since she moved up to Myrtle Beach. I don't know if I'll see her this year at all. But it's not like I hate it." She shrugs. "I got to choose this wall color instead of the pink she wanted, and the black-and-white sheets instead of florals. And I do love cheerleading and my friends."

"Okay, but if you were decorating it from scratch instead of pleasing someone else," I ask, settling into her desk chair, "what would it have been?"

"Probably something stupid," she says in a voice that lets me know she's definitely thought about this a hundred times. "More travel-themed stuff, maybe. Miguel and I have talked a million times about going to Havana one day to see where his grandfather grew up, but honestly, I'm happy to go anywhere that's farther than Georgia. I've never gone beyond this little corner of the US."

"What else?"

She hugs her knees to her chest. "Okay, so, there's this really funky artist who does pop art—you know, like Andy Warhol stuff—of celebrities, and not that I'm a starfucker or anything, but there's this one print she has of Lizzo that's amazing. I'm obsessed. It'd go right over there." She points at a spot on the far wall. "And I would definitely have a more modern desk, maybe one made of, like, smoky glass or something. I saw one on a show once and I thought it was the coolest thing."

"This is turning into a very eclectic room."

"Oh, I know. I have no cohesive taste. That's why it's probably for the best that a sixty-five-year-old woman designed this one. If it were up to me, and I could afford anything, I'd replace that light fixture with one of those little chandeliers from the bathroom at Gutter Kittens. You know, the ones with the purple glass beads? God, it would be so ugly."

"Why stop at the chandeliers? Why not just decorate the whole thing like the inside of your favorite bowling alley?"

"Yes!" Her smile lights up the entire room. "Who needs wheat-colored carpet when you could have an aubergine-and-forest-green paisley? And these walls would definitely benefit from stripes."

"And there's your design for shoe storage," I point out. "Right under your Lizzo art, you can have those wooden cubes and fill them with all the bowling shoes you can dream of."

"Gosh, that sounds beautiful," Amber says dreamily.

"Doesn't it? And you already have a trophy case." I gesture to the small one on her wall, full of gold-tone cheerleaders and medals. "This place practically *is* Gutter Kittens already."

"Okay, I think this is starting to depress me," she says, but she's laughing.

I glance at the door, which is still cracked open, and decide to take my chances and crook my finger in her direction. She hops off the bed and sits her tiny butt on my lap, and our lips meet for a kiss.

"What about cheerleading?" I ask when we part, fiddling with the ends of her hair. "Was that grandmother-influenced too?"

"Nope, that was all me. I know you think it's silly, but it's not just, like, a bunch of girls jumping around in short skirts."

"Hey, I know it's not," I say, and I do, but also, isn't it, kind of?

The look she gives me suggests the combination of my words and expression are every bit as predictable (with the same edge of disappointment) to her as her room initially was to me. "You know we have the exact same weight-training class as you, right? Same frequency, too?"

I didn't actually know that, but I've definitely noticed the cheerleaders are in killer shape. "Amber, you lift humans and throw them in the air. And nobody watches you more closely when you do it than I do. I promise, I know you're not just a girl jumping around in a short skirt. Although I do very much like the short skirt."

When her eyes narrow, I wish I could take back the joke at the end, erase any doubt that I see her as first and foremost a peppy pair of legs. "I love cheerleading," she says evenly. "My entire family is basically my mom, who works nights half the time, and still, I'm never lonely because I have an entire squad full of sisters. I practically lived at Cara's growing up. Ella and Virany's family took me on vacation with them to Disney when we were kids and I was the only kid on the squad who'd never been. And I get to be athletic and make people happy and have fun with my friends and show off amazing skills, and I'm *good* at it. Cheerleading was my choice. It will always be my choice."

Then she presses her lips shut, and I know there's more she's not saying. "What?" I nudge, trying to keep my voice gentle.

She huffs out a breath. "Cheerleading is *also* something I need. I need something that makes me stand out. I need something that makes people give a shit about me, because let's face it, half my DNA-givers sure don't. And I need something to put on my college applications so I can get the hell out of here. It's so much pressure, and I'm not sure you get how hard it is for me and what it means that I'm risking it on you."

"You think *I* don't get how hard it is?" Of all the bullshit. "It's been hell here for me; you know that better than anybody. And I wouldn't say you're taking a huge risk when we're Atherton's best-kept secret." Well, third-best secret, after the Cara/Robbie revelation and, of course, AHS's most beloved couple: her and Miguel. But I'm not looking to get into an even bigger argument right now, so I keep that to myself. "It took you worrying I might get tossed out of school to clip one of those stupid things on my shirt, and don't think I noticed you chose one that couldn't possibly get traced back to you. I know you decorated yours with the squad. Everyone could tell the clips on Miguel's shirt were yours."

"I still came to your rescue. You didn't have to throw a shit fit like that so I'd have no choice but to help you."

"The team *lied* to me about what to wear today. The entire school was looking at me like I'm a fucking idiot who's obsessed with being quarterback."

"Who cares?" She throws her hands in the air. "You think anyone would like you better if you'd gone ahead and worn a pristine Lacoste shirt? News flash, Jack: nothing is going to make it okay to them that you replaced Robbie. If you haven't noticed that by now, you're . . ."

She trails off, but I won't let her. "I'm what?" I demand. "You *know* I notice that particular fact every fucking day, so what is it you think I am?"

"A *problem!*" she blurts out. "You are a problem, Jack. I was doing just fine before, on my way to becoming captain and enjoying life as a popular cheerleader, and now I'm lying to my friends and hiding out in locker rooms and having secret dates. I had a whole plan for getting out of here and finally getting to be myself—*all* of myself—in college, and all I had to do was stay the fuck away from Atherton girls. This isn't the junior year I had planned."

"You think this is the junior year *I* had planned?" I can't help it—the low blow slips out. "You think this is the junior year Cara had planned? Things change. I'm sorry life has gotten harder in the closet, but I didn't pull you in here with me. You climbed into *my* window."

"I—" She stops. I'm right, and she knows it. I don't know why we're having this fight, or if it really even is a fight and not both of us just desperately needing to vent, but there's something under the surface here. I'm not sure what it is yet, but it's simmering there, biding its time, a gator with its eyes peeping out of the swamp. "I shouldn't have. I'm sorry."

Never have the words *I'm sorry* landed like a punch to the gut the way they do now, but I want her to take them back. "Are you?"

"Yes." She tugs on the hem of her shirt. "No. I don't know."

"Okay." It's not okay. "Okay. Can we start again?"

She looks so tired all of a sudden. "What's the point?"

I sigh and sink back into her chair. "Look, I know you had a simpler life before I came along, but you are the *only* good thing for me here outside of the game. I broke my family apart. I left my best friends behind. I play with guys who hate me for a school that hates me. But you literally send me, like, one stupid smiley-face emoji and it turns my entire day around. I don't want to put something huge on you that you don't want, but I think you might be the only reason I can stick it out here. I'm not sure sheer stubbornness is enough anymore."

"That is so sad."

"So it is." And I guess that's it. I start to walk past her toward the door and out of her room, her house, her life, but a hand grabs my sleeve and pulls me back.

"What I mean is, it shouldn't be that way, for a million reasons. But also, honestly? It's not that simple for me. I can't date *anyone* because everyone thinks I'm taken. I've pinned so much on this captainship, this one thing, and part of it is because I have nothing else to fight for. Amazing grades are out of my grasp, and until now, a real relationship has been too. And yeah, it's hard to see all that work go off track, but it's . . . not the worst that it's because I've found something else I actually *want* to focus on."

"Not the worst, huh?" My fingers lace with hers.

"Uh-uh." She strokes the rough skin of my palm with her thumb. "But I don't want to give up what I've worked so hard on, either. Which means I need you to respect it, and at least try to understand it."

"That's fair."

She pulls me over to the bed and sits back against the carved white headboard, then waits until I join her before curling up in my arms. I love how small she feels, wrapped up in me like this. "I could've done sports too, you know. I thought about cross country."

"Well, maybe we should start running together." I trail my fingertips over her knee. "Maybe you can kick my butt into high gear."

"If you're lucky," she says, and I feel her lips curl into a smile against my arm. "Anyway, I just . . . didn't like the constant competitive part of it. Cheerleading lets me be just as athletic without constantly looking over at the person next to me to compare stats or trash-talk another team. Obviously we have competitions and stuff, but most of the time, we just get to be positive together. And trust me, I *know* that is the cheesiest-sounding thing of all time, but like I said, it's not a tiny thing for me to have what I have in the squad."

"That makes plenty of sense to me." Her hair is so soft. I can't believe I'm allowed to just lie here and stroke it. Despite our maybe-fight, this might be the most at peace I've felt in a while. Maybe *because* we were fighting, because we care enough about each other to fight. "Frankly, I'm jealous you have that. Do you know how ridiculous it feels that I traded in my entire life to be on a team and now that I'm finally on one, it's . . . well, you know."

"I know," she says softly. "But hey, I guess we're a team now too, right?"

She says it lightly, a little jokingly, but as soon as I hear the words, I want them to be true so, so badly. "A very secret team," I reply. I don't mean it to come out as sarcastic as it does, but I can't hide how it would make a world of difference to me if everyone at Atherton knew that I did in fact have someone on my side. "I'm not sure that quite counts in the same way."

She shifts out of my grasp, the softness of her hair brushing my fingers before it disappears. "You know I can't change that, right? Even if I could come out to the team, there's still Miguel, and—"

"I know," I assure her. "You've been clear. And I don't want to hurt Miguel in any way, or make anything unsafe for him.

I promise, you're not in any danger of my blowing our secret. Either of you."

Her face softens, and her hand finds mine again. "Thank you."

I nod, and then we're out of words to say, and soon our mouths become too busy to say them anyway.

Chapter Eight

-AMBER-

Spirit Day is probably the goofiest day of the entire week, but it's kind of great to roam the halls without really knowing who anyone is for a day. We all wear sheets with holes cut in them for our eyes, like the most low-rent of kids' Halloween costumes, and while we're supposed to take them off for class, not every teacher makes us.

I could probably get away with holding Jack's hand right in the middle of the hallway and no one would know it was us.

Not that I want to do that, except that I really, really want to do that. I'm not sure what set me off last night, but I do know that when I dropped her off afterward, it felt like something had changed, in a good way. Like I could stop questioning whether we were Something and just think of her as my girl-friend. And yeah, we haven't had any sort of label conversation yet—what would be the point when there's nowhere to use it?—but I'm pretty sure she feels the same way.

And okay, maybe I do know why I blew up. Maybe I care what she thinks in a way I haven't cared about anyone . . . ever. I want her to know that this athletic drive, this strength—it's not just something she has because she's our first female quarter-back, badass as that is; it's something we share.

And maybe I wanted to feel certain, too, that we had something significant in common, that this isn't some goofy "opposites attract" mess that isn't going anywhere. I want it to go somewhere.

I just don't know where.

"Hey!" A tiny little ghost pops up at my locker after first period, and even if it weren't obvious from her build and voice that it was Cara, the plain white sheet—the kind on every bed in her house—is a dead giveaway. Over time, the rest of us have realized that it makes the day a lot more fun to wear sheets with cartoon characters or pro sports logos, but Cara goes classic. "You mixed it up this year."

"My mom was so upset about spilling nail polish on her good sheets, I promised her I'd make good use of them," I explain, holding out the red splatter design for closer investigation. "We did the whole thing Jackson Pollock style with some paint to cover it up and voilà."

"Very industrious of you. Maybe you should be in charge of the signs for Friday's pep rally," she says with a twirl of her sheet.

"I'm always happy to take on anything and everything," I remind her lightly, because that's been my mantra for the past two years as I try to push my way into everyone's brains as the obvious choice for captain. I haven't exactly been showing it lately—leaving practice as soon as it's over in the hopes of catching Jack to drive her home, letting Sara Copeley take charge of the signage this Friday—but I still mean it when I say I'll do anything for this team.

They don't even know how much I'm proving it by staying in the closet.

"You've seemed a little preoccupied lately," she says, not for the first time in the past few weeks. "Are you stressed about the game?"

Of all the things I could be stressed about, the game is dead last. We have PSATs around the corner, I'm way behind on my campaign for captain, I have a secret girlfriend, I know *Cara's* unsettling secret, I'm in a fake romance with my gay best friend . . . whether or not the Alligators can win a game they haven't won in at least a decade isn't exactly at the top of my concern list.

She doesn't wait for me to respond, though. "I am too,

honestly. It's, like, we're supposed to be cheering and wanting the guys to win, but, like, nobody wants to win this way. It's bad enough she's getting credit for their wins this year when everyone knows they're just upping their game to make Robbie proud." She stands a little taller when she says this, and I don't know whether I'm gladder I can't see her face or that she can't see mine. "But now the alumni are gonna come back and buy that same bull if we win. I'd rather they see how much she sucks."

But she doesn't suck. There's no reason to state the obvious here, especially now that I know about Cara and Robbie. There's nothing I could say to make her accept that Jack's the hero here if she's determined to believe that somehow Robbie's "magic" is at play, the driving force behind the team's newly winning record.

I can't bring myself to say anything really shitty about Jack, so I go with the safest bet: "Considering how long it's been since we've won a homecoming game, I wouldn't worry too much about it."

She snorts. "Yeah, right?" She leans against the lockers. "What is it then? Are you nervous about performing in front of the old squad? I know Jamie will be back. I bet if you impress her, she'll put in a good word to Crystal."

Jamie Rhodes was last year's captain and she would've done a fifth year of high school to do it again if she could. Cheerleading was her entire life, and it paid off—she got a partial scholarship to the University of Central Florida. She threw a party when the news came in that probably ate up a good portion of the money, but it wasn't about the thousand bucks for her; she loved the prestige that came with it.

I need the freaking money.

"Well, I *wasn't* nervous about that, but now I am." I'm not sure if I'm kidding or not, but Cara laughs anyway.

"You're gonna be great. We always are." She gives me an air-kiss from beneath her sheet. "See you at lunch?"

The very idea of eating with one more thing added to my anxiety plate makes me want to puke. But I cheerfully say, "Yep!"

It only occurs to me that she can't see my flutter-wave goodbye when she's already out of sight.

- - - - -

Turns out to be a good thing I'm not in charge of pep rally signage, because before we can even pack the signs up into Sara's car that night, my phone beeps with a text from Miguel. *Drip?* Another text quickly follows. *Please.*

The use of actual words instead of emoji-code gets me, and *please* is the icing on the cake. Miguel never says please.

I'm so not in the mood to do anything but crash on the couch, but that *please* will not be ignored. *K,* I text back with all the energy I can muster, and then I make my apologies about slipping out and get in my car to make the drive.

Nausea creeps up my throat with every passing minute, a

feeling in my bones that this has to do with Malcolm, that Miguel's just had his heart broken. Malcolm's his third boyfriend—first was some guy he met on the internet in eighth grade but never met in person, and then there was Stephen, the guy he was dating when we met—but Malcolm is the first one Miguel's felt really serious about, and he'll be shattered. Hell, *I* really like Malcolm; we had a great time with him on our double date. Not that this is about me.

I practice the sweet, comforting things I'm gonna say for the length of the ride, but when I step into Drip and see Miguel waiting, he doesn't look sad; he looks . . . nervous? His foot is frantically tapping on the floor and his hands are already doing that straw-fiddling thing. And yes, there's a drink waiting for me, too.

He has to tell me something bad.

Jack.

Fuck.

All the platitudes I'd been ready to say to him fly out of my head and I take the other empty seat, ignoring the drink and dropping my bag like a stone. "Did she get into another fight?"

"Did who what?" He knits his thick brows. "Oh, Jack? No, no—just the usual stone silence today. This isn't about Jack. Or, I guess maybe it is."

"You're starting to seriously stress me out, Santiago."

His eyes dart around the coffee shop and he exhales deeply before saying, "I want to take Malcolm to homecoming."

"Huh." That was the last thing I expected him to say. "Okay.

And you want me to ask Jack to bring him as her date? I don't think she was planning on going at all, but—"

"No." He wraps his hands even tighter around his drink, until his knuckles go white. "I . . . I want to bring him as my date."

Okay, *that* was the last thing I expected him to say. Lowering my voice to a whisper seems silly, given that we're literally talking about him being out in the open, but judging by the way he glanced furtively around the room a moment ago, he's still not totally comfortable. Besides, it's too ingrained a habit for us both at this point. "You want to come out at homecoming, of all places?"

He sighs. "It's not that I want to come out at the dance. Honestly, that sounds like a fucking nightmare. But I don't wanna keep missing out on shit. Nothing about this year has been normal. If I'm being real, nothing's felt normal since Robbie first started blackmailing me."

"Yeah, and he was able to blackmail you because you wanted to keep your sexuality a secret," I say carefully, "so what changed?"

He sets the drink down and puts his foot up, then drops it back down, like he's still trying to figure out just how comfortable he can get. "I guess I'm just finding it harder and harder to give a shit what the guys think. I see them around Jack, and the way they talk about Saint Robbie, and it feels like I'm watching some surreal-as-shit movie. They're deranged. They don't feel like my friends. And I'm a little tired of trying to hide from them. What's the worst that could happen? They'll want me off the team? Honestly, being on it kind of sucks this year anyway."

"Even though you're finally winning?"

"Especially because we're finally winning," he says with a snort. "Like, if we can stop sucking and there's *still* no joy in it— even less than before, really—then what the fuck am I doing? My mom would kill for me to spend that time on something else. I could get a job, save up for college, actually spend time with Malcolm. . . ."

"And what if 'the worst that could happen' is worse than that?" I ask, because I have to, because this isn't exactly a town where people fly rainbow flags and vote in a blue wave.

"I don't know. I've never known. But I know I can get through shit better with him than without him."

"Dude. That is the most effing romantic thing I've ever heard." I hold out my arm. "Chills, a little."

"Oh, shut up," he says, but he laughs. Then he grows serious. "Listen, though. Are you okay with this?"

"Am I okay?" I lean back in my chair and finally take my first sip of the drink. Mmm, caramel macchiato. Which will probably keep me up half the night, but whatever, it's worth it. "I mean, I'm not gonna lie—I'm nervous for you. But if you feel this is what you want, of course I support you."

He coughs into his fist. "No, um. I mean, if I bring him to homecoming . . ."

That's when it finally hits me—why he's brought me here

and why he's paying for my drink and what he's trying to say. "Oh. If you bring him to homecoming, everyone knows our relationship has been a sham."

"I mean, I guess we can say you had no idea. . . ."

"But then everyone will think you're an asshole," I fill in, "and I'm not exactly gonna look like the brightest bulb in the chandelier."

"Unless maybe . . . you wanna take Jack?"

His voice is so hopeful, and for the briefest of moments, I consider it—the ultimate in solidarity. The four of us riding there together. A night dancing with the person I actually wanna have my arms around.

But just as quickly, I push the idea out of my head. "I can't. I know you're burned out on the team, but I still need the squad. I need a shot at becoming captain. I can't destroy that by coming out, and definitely not by coming out with Jack Walsh on my arm." I hate asking him to do this, but we had a deal, and if I didn't break it when I got my first girlfriend, he shouldn't be able to break it now. "We can have Jack bring Malcolm. He'll still be there. But I can't come out. And I definitely can't force Jack out. This is a chain reaction, Migs, and on, like, five seconds' notice. I'm sorry, but I can't just . . ."

"Yeah, yeah, I get it." He's trying to hide the sourness in his voice, and he's failing. "Fine. Maybe Jack will bring him. Then at least we get to be in the same room. Though that'll probably make it even harder for me to talk to him."

I hate how true that is, but yeah, talking to Jack Walsh in

public isn't exactly the key to winning a popularity crown. And speaking of which: "Hey, remember that we've got decent shots at king and queen. That's not nothing."

I haven't forgotten for a second; it's yet another part of my plan to get cheer captain. Because cheerleaders and football players take the titles so often, it's Atherton tradition to crown the king and queen at the dance, rather than do a whole halftime thing when we can't exactly don our finest royal attire. Our nominations to the upperclassmen court were announced at last Friday's pep rally, so now all I need to do is win the actual title. How can you not want a captain who's been celebrated by the whole school and gotten to wave like a beauty queen with a pretty little tiara on her perfectly coiffed head?

"Yep, great," he says with a weak-ass smile, holding up his drink in a mock toast.

I pretend I don't see that he's absolutely faking it, and clink my plastic cup to his.

-JACK-

"Soda?"

No hesitation there. "Mountain Dew."

Amber's face takes on the disgust of someone who's just

stepped in roadkill. "*That's* your favorite soda? How are you not radioactive?"

"It's not like I drink it that often! But it's good! And the radioactive look is part of the fun." I poke her with my foot under the blanket we're sharing on her bed, careful not to tip over our bowl of popcorn. Coach called me a couple of hours ago to casually mention that one of the alumni who'll be returning for homecoming happens to be a scout—a fucking *DIII scout*—and he's excited to see me play. And I know it isn't anything, that he's not there to actively recruit, but still. Just the idea of being on a scout's radar feels massive, and of course, the first thing I did was call Amber, and the first thing *she* did was invite me over to celebrate. "Why, what's yours?"

"Fresca," she says, like it's obvious. "It's the perfect soda. Refreshing and calorie-free."

"My grandparents would definitely agree with you."

"Oh, shut up." She pokes me back, far less gently. "You don't even know what you're missing."

"Which I'm okay with, if what I'm missing is grapefruit soda. That sounds like an oxymoron."

"*You* sound like an oxymoron."

"You kiss girls with that mouth?"

"Not when they taste like Mountain Dew."

Cracking up, I can't resist pulling her toward me and planting a kiss right on that snarky smile. "Good thing I taste like popcorn, then."

"Very good thing," she murmurs, wrapping her arms loosely around my neck.

We fall into a full-on make-out for I don't know how long, broken up only by the sound of Amber's phone ringing. At this point, I recognize her mom's ringtone, so I pull back and let Amber pick it up, smoothing down my rumpled clothes and hair as if her mom's about to walk through the door even though she has hours left on her shift.

By the time she hangs up a couple minutes later, we've both cooled off, and we shift back into the same easy conversation we were having before—our favorite things. "I've got one," she says. "What's your pump-up music?"

"My pump-up music?"

"You know what I mean." She gets up on her knees and does a little rah-rah with her fists. "What's the song or album or whatever that kicks your ass into gear?"

"How do you know I have a pump-up song? What's yours?"

"I don't have just one song." Her voice drips with bewildered insult. "I have a whole playlist."

"Okay, so what's on the playlist?"

She ticks off her fingers. "Britney Spears's 'Work, Bitch,' Doja Cat's 'Boss Bitch'—"

I hold up my hand. "I think I'm seeing the theme here."

"I make no apologies," she says with a smirk.

"I wouldn't want you to."

"So? Are you gonna tell me what's on yours?"

Am I? The answer is mildly embarrassing, but I do want her to know me, so. "It's, uh, *Hamilton*."

"*Hamilton*, like, the musical?" I nod. "Wow, that is . . . surprisingly nerdy. And also kind of cool? But mostly nerdy."

"Oh, come on. You've never listened to it?"

She snorts. "Of course I have."

"And it doesn't make you wanna jump up and start a revolution?" The words tumble out of my mouth before I can even think about how vulnerable I'm making myself in this moment. "That's what I thought I'd be doing here, you know. I thought people were gonna think it was badass that there's a female quarterback. I had a whole vision of my brothers' friends asking to meet their awesome sister, and the team being stunned by my arm, and all that shit. What a sucker I was."

"Jack." Her voice is uncharacteristically soft as her face falls.

"It's childish. Whatever." My eyes are stinging and I quickly back away from her before this can get any more intense. "Anyway, the point is, I can rap the hell out of 'Guns and Ships,' and you're jealous."

I see the shift in her expression as she realizes it's time to drop it and follow my conversational lead; we aren't gonna be talking about broken dreams any more tonight. "You cannot."

It doesn't escape me that she knows the show well enough to know exactly which song I'm referring to. Why is a secret nerdy side so damn hot? "Oh, but I can!" And I can, in my embarrassingly white girl way. No one's ever heard me do it other than Sage and Morgan—Morgan is a huuuuge nerd for the show and Lin-Manuel Miranda in general—but I have an inexplicable urge to perform it right now.

I stand up straight and give her a nod, and she laughs as she yells, "Lafayette!"

Boom—I'm off, and watching her jaw drop is so damn gratifying, I sail right through the rapid-fire verses, even letting my limbs dance a little, all thoughts of shame and shyness forgotten. When I'm done, I give a sweeping bow, and she rises up on her knees and gives me a round of hollering applause. Morgan would be so proud.

I have kind of a ridiculous thought, then—what if we FaceTimed with Sage and Morgan? It sucks that Amber's image of me here is as someone with no friends. It'd be cool to actually get to introduce her to some.

But . . . as what? Is she my girlfriend? Are we technically dating if we can't even go on dates by ourselves? If I'm sitting at home on Saturday while she goes to the dance without me on another guy's arm? A gay guy with a boyfriend, yeah, but a guy nevertheless. Besides, everyone else is sure they're boning, so thinking of her as mine feels even more ridiculous.

"Earth to Jack. What are you spacing about?"

Do I tell her? I look at her, sitting back on her heels on the bed, perfect brown waves disheveled from rolling around with me, blue-green eyes tinged with concern, freckles dusting her little ski jump of a nose. She's not meant to be an outcast. She's not *going* to risk being an outcast, for me or anyone else, and *I'm* not going to risk losing the one good thing I have here.

Time to go back to playing games.

"So, are you gay or bi or . . . what?"

She purses her lips. "Why?"

"Just curious," I assure her. "Not a judgment. Promise. It doesn't matter to me."

She scrutinizes my face as if trying to see whether there's a lie behind it, but she isn't going to find one. I really don't care which genders she likes, as long as she likes *me*.

Finally, she exhales. "I don't know. For a while I thought pansexual was the right label for me, but I just . . . can't seem to get into cis boys. Girls? Very much! Nonbinary people? Definitely! Trans guys? Absolutely. But then a cis guy flirts with me, even a really rare good guy like Austin Barrett, and I am so, so not into it." Her fingers twist around each other like she needs something to do with her hands, and I think about reaching out to take one, but it feels like she needs her space to process. "According to the wisdom of the Internet, 'polysexual' is the best fit, so that's what I'm trying on right now. In my head, anyway."

"And? How's it feel?"

"Like it'd be nice if more people knew what it meant," she says with a twitch of a smile. "But I think I like it. And I'm also good with 'queer.' And really, I just know what I find hot when I see it."

"Meaning . . . me?" I ask with a grin.

A fucking adorable pink flush creeps into her cheeks. "Well . . . yeah."

I laugh and lean over to peck her on the mouth. "You are cute as hell, you know that?"

"Shut up," she says, swatting me away, her skin flaming. "What about you? Gay or bi or . . . what?"

"Oh, I'm super fucking gay." At that, she cracks up, and so do I. "I mean." I gesture down at my flannel shirt and cargo shorts. "I'm definitely not fooling anyone who doesn't wanna be fooled. The only thing that could maybe make me look gayer is an undercut, which I wanna do eventually. A full-on mohawk, maybe. Super short on the sides and soft and spiky on top. I think that'd look cool."

She smiles. "I think so too. So why don't you just do it? Like you said, it's not like you're in the closet."

I tug my upper lip between my teeth. "There's a difference between being visibly but quietly queer and putting it all out there. You'd be amazed by how much people can ignore if they want to. There are literally people who assume I'm in this just to see guys naked in the locker room, because they can't imagine a girl could have zero interest in boys. And while I categorically do not give a shit about them, I don't feel like giving people one more thing about me to tear apart. Besides, I don't need to reinforce anyone's stereotypical bullshit, either.

I'm not good at football because I'm a lesbian; I'm good at football, and I'm a lesbian."

"I hear that," she says on a sigh, fiddling with the ends of her hair. "I don't wanna hear any of that 'But you're a cheerleader!' crap. Like, yeah, I am—what the hell is your point?"

"Oh my God, you're Natasha Lyonne."

"Who?"

I drop into her desk chair. "There's an old movie called *But I'm a Cheerleader* about a cheerleader who gets sent to gay conversion camp. She's played by that actress from *Russian Doll*. We should watch it."

"Like, on a date?" she asks, waggling her eyebrows. "A date of just the two of us?"

"Exactly like that." I roll the chair toward her bed and wrap a pinkie around hers. "Is that cool?"

"Yeah, I guess that'd be all right," she says, and laughs. I love her laugh. I love *making* her laugh.

"Hey, this is me playing hard to get," I say seriously. "Please note my very casual invite."

"You haven't played hard to get for a minute, and neither have I," she points out. "Which is really twisted, because Hard to Get is literally my favorite game, after Seven Minutes in Heaven."

I cup her cheek in my rough, calloused palm, then climb onto the bed with her. "I fucking love that you haven't. Why waste all that time when we could be doing this instead?" Then I kiss her so deeply, the heat liquefies my bones.

We may not know exactly what we are, and we may not be going anywhere, but where we are right at this moment is so. Damn. Good.

- - - - -

Unfortunately, as I wash up the next morning, being careful not to get any toothpaste on the pajamas I slept in and apparently get to wear to school today, I'm still thinking about everything I didn't say the night before. I can't shake the idea of walking into homecoming with her on my arm, of actually *going* to homecoming, looking dashing as fuck in a suit while Amber blows my goddamn mind in something that shows off Those Legs.

I dare *anyone* to give me shit then, especially coming off a win, which we will be.

"Who was that girl who dropped you off last night?"

I'm so used to silence in the morning that the sound of my mom actually speaking to me when I emerge from the bathroom instead of sitting on the couch and staring out the window like she's waiting for her husband to come back from war makes me jump ten feet. But yup, there she is, sitting at the kitchen counter in front of a plate of bacon and eggs, a matching one sitting in front of the empty barstool next to her. Her phone is propped up on a charger—she's FaceTiming with my brothers and dad while they all eat, and they can hear every word.

I should've known there'd be no having privacy in this place, ever.

"Just some girl from school," I mutter as I join them, because that's all I get to say. This is not an opening to introduce my girlfriend to my family.

It could be.

But it isn't.

But it could be.

God damn it.

Why do I want this so badly? Is it about her? Or about me? Because I was perfectly happy keeping things on the DL until we had that fucking date—which was *her* idea, by the way—and now all I can think about is how much fun we could have out in the open.

Who thinks, *Hey, I'd really like to change up this routine I have of sneaking around with my hot girlfriend so we can get pizza or see a movie together?*

"She hot?" Jeremy asks, then cracks up when Jason makes a face.

"No way," Jason declares. "I bet she's butt."

"Bet she's hotter than your last girlfriend," Jeremy shoots back, obviously not realizing he's somehow sort of defending me. "You should ask Jack to introduce you."

"Oh yeah, because that's every high school cheerleader's dream—to hook up with a thirteen-year-old shrimp." They're both being total dicks, but I'm just so happy they're finally talking to me that I let it slide. Of course, that doesn't mean I have to be nice.

"As opposed to a sixteen-year-old lady beast?"

"Oh fu—"

"Hey!" Mama snaps. "All y'all, hush up and eat or tomorrow I'm telling Daddy to give you oatmeal."

That shuts the twins up good, being as they've both compared oatmeal to baby vomit on multiple occasions.

"And Jack?"

"Yeah, Mama?"

"I assume that girl was a study buddy and not a distraction from your schoolwork or football."

Well, I definitely studied something *at her house last night.* "Yep, Mama. She's in my English class. We're reading *The Great Gatsby.*" All that is true, at least. And I even finished the book, thanks to a long bus ride back from last Friday's game during which—as usual—no one said a word to me.

"Good. You know the deal."

"I do." Thank God she doesn't say it out loud yet again. I've heard "If you're not getting an athletic scholarship for this, you'd better be keeping your grades up" more times than I can count. Like I need a reminder that there's probably no future for me in the only thing I love.

It drives me nuts that of all the sports to give myself to, I chose one that barely exists for girls at the collegiate level. And, sure, I could dream of being the next Toni Harris, but even in the impossible version of the universe where I got a scholarship to play football, what are the chances someone's gonna let me on to a college team as a QB?

I do play other sports. In the spring, I'll walk on to the softball team—my true best option for a scholarship—and this past summer, when I wasn't playing football, I was life-guarding and giving swimming lessons. I love basketball, too, especially playing with my brothers in the cul-de-sac near our house.

But there's nothing like football to me. Nothing like the rush of throwing a perfect spiral and watching it land in a pair of capable hands (or semi-capable, in the case of Dan Sanchez), of thundering past a guy who's twice my size, and of that solid, earth-shattering collision when you don't quite make it. Of playing under the lights on a sticky Florida night.

It's worth it. It will always be worth it.

But getting to play *and* openly date a hot cheerleader? I mean, that's the dream.

The very, very, very faraway dream.

And the irony is that all three of us—Amber, Miguel, and I—are out to our families. We're all out to one another. Staying inside the closet for two teams full of assholes feels so fucking pointless.

At least it does to me, but I don't exactly have anything to lose. Clearly, Miguel and Amber feel like they do, so I'll keep respecting the rules of the closet. It's not like going to a high school dance has been a dream of mine for ages; it never even occurred to me to want to until last night.

And I'm sure that want will go away just as quickly.

Any minute now.

Annnnny minute now.

Chapter Nine

-AMBER-

I love Pajama Day. Every girl spends hours picking out the perfect pajamas and neutral makeup to make it look like we just rolled out of bed, and to make all the guys think about rolling *into* bed with us, and meanwhile the guys literally do just show up in whatever they sleep in. (Or whatever they *would* sleep in if they wore clothes to bed—cough, cough, Matt.)

Of course, Jack manages to be an exception to the rule yet again. While the rest of us are in cute and strategically buttoned matching sets from Victoria's Secret, she's wearing a gray ribbed tank top and the same navy drawstring pants she wore to Midnight Breakfast. We've got carefully styled disheveled-looking waves, and she's got that same tight topknot that shows off the world's most lickable jawline.

How does she look so. Much. Sexier. Than everyone else?

"Is she *trying* to look like a boy or what?" Cara asks with a snort, sidling up next to me and catching me staring. "God, it's so sad."

"So sad," I agree, though I'm not talking about Jack when I say it. "I still can't believe your parents let you wear that nightgown to school."

"I mean, I *was* wearing leggings underneath when you picked me up this morning," she reminds me, curtsying. "That helped."

"So sneaky." I tug on one of the thin pink ribbons around the neckline. Cara's parents really do dream of keeping their oldest daughter seven years old forever. But they also have five other kids and a congregation to keep their eyes on, and the more successful her father gets, the more Cara seems to get away with. When I think about how she's managed to get everywhere from Midnight Breakfast to Zach Sawyer's party so far this semester with no problem, it gets easier and easier to picture how she engineered secretly dating Robbie.

"We don't all have moms who literally hand over their own lingerie and tell us to go to town," Cara says with a snort.

"That happened *once*." But it was admittedly hilarious, a desperate move freshman year when I slept in baggy T-shirts every night and all my babysitting money was going into the household gas fund, leaving me nothing for new clothes. My mom managed to dig up some old satin nightie that was wildly inappropriate but sort of passed for acceptable over a T-shirt, and from then on, a pair of cute pajamas became one of my annual Christmas presents so I'd never miss out.

I glance up at Jack again, and this time I catch her eye and she gives me a little smile. It's so hard to keep my face straight (no pun intended), I think I might explode, but Cara's eyes are firmly on me, so I have no choice. At least I know Jack understands, even when she visibly sighs and walks toward her next class.

There's an opening to talk to Jack about coming out now, about coming clean to everyone and just being a couple, the way Crystal and Calvin Jordan got to be, and Taylor and Matt get to be, and Diana . . . well, the way Diana *wants* her and Aidan Manos to be. With the obstacle of Miguel's closet residence out of the way, that just leaves Jack's and mine, and she wouldn't exactly drop any jaws if she announced she wasn't itching to get into the guys' locker room.

Whether she *wants* to be out here is another story, but truthfully, we both know she's got nothing to lose. It may sound cruel, but you don't have to worry about your friends looking or acting differently around you when you don't have any friends. You certainly don't have to worry anyone's gonna think you're checking them out in the locker room when you have the space all to yourself for every single practice and game. As for her position on the team, if this were any threat to her there, she never would've made it this far.

It's tempting, the idea of bringing the date I actually want to homecoming, to get to sit with her at lunch and openly flirt with her in the halls and cheer my little ass off for her on the field and post selfies of us being queer and adorable. But is that really what it would be like? Would I still get to cheer for her if the girls decided they weren't comfortable having me in the locker room or stopped inviting me to victory parties and things like Midnight Breakfast, where she was never truly welcome?

It isn't just the cheering part I'd be giving up if this got me booted off the squad. It's watching Disney movies at Cara's house (and pretending it's a hardship even though I could watch *The Little Mermaid* a million times and never get tired of it) and Squad Saturdays at Diana's pool and blissful summers at cheer camp and stupid games of Truth or Dare and Never Have I Ever on bus rides and that *glow* that comes with having a great pep rally and the possibility of ever getting that C on my sweater, of getting to stand in front of a massive crowd and yell "Ready, steady, go!" and seeing everyone fall in line.

My best chance at being a leader at cheer camp next summer.

Which means my best chance of doing this at the collegiate level.

And most importantly: my best chance at freedom.

Everything I've been dreaming of, just . . . gone.

Stop making issues where there aren't any, I order myself,

freshening up my lip gloss in my locker mirror then handing the tube to Cara so she can do the same. *You're on the
same page. You both want this to stay in the dark. So it will.*

Out of the corner of my eye I see a bunch of the football
guys turning the corner, laughing at one another's pajamas
and playing keep-away with Lamar's ridiculous nightcap. Miguel is right in the middle, wearing a pair of basketball shorts
I know he doesn't sleep in, because his room has lousy air-
conditioning and his nighttime attire is at most a pair of boxers.

In another minute he'll see me, and he'll try to catch my
eye, try to see if I've given any more thought to what he said,
if Jack and I have miraculously changed our minds.

Suddenly, I feel very compelled to be on time to class.

- - - - -

I have no choice but to avoid Miguel for the rest of the
day, which is surprisingly easy since we only have one class
together—physics, in which we're not lab partners, since
they were assigned—and I know where he spends every other
minute of the day. I get my fair share of surprised looks in
the library when I spend lunch there, doing my homework
and sneaking bites of an energy bar I begged off Coach Armstrong, and I head straight home after practice.

But Friday is Books and Balls Day, which also means Game
Day, and it's impossible to avoid the football players when we
spend every free minute with them, posing for yearbook pictures

and selfies and breaking into impromptu cheers in the halls. Books and Balls Day is basically a wild freebie, with everyone dressed up to represent the clubs they're in, from the football team and cheerleading squad to Model UN and the chess club.

"Smile, y'all!" Melanie Stern motions for Miguel and me to squeeze together while she holds up the enormous camera around her neck—I guess she hasn't heard the news you can take pictures on your phone now?—and we dutifully pose with huge smiles and pretend pom-poms in the air. "Beautiful! We definitely need the 'before' pic of our top homecoming king and queen contenders."

On autopilot, I amp up my smile at that, but I hate how hollow it feels. If Miguel and I were both single while doing this fauxmance thing, it'd be hilarious and wildly fun and we'd do ourselves all the way up. Instead, I know we'll both just be thinking about the two people who aren't there but should be.

"And who says they're the top contenders?" I hadn't even seen Diana come over, but suddenly there she is, Aidan in tow. "I think it's time these two got a little competition."

Oh yes, competition. Something I definitely need more of as I watch my grip on the team slip away in favor of those who want to make Jack's life a living hell. God, Diana—can you not just let me have one thing?

"Does this mean y'all are officially a couple?" I ask, maybe a little pointedly, maybe with a little extra eyelash flutter in Aidan's direction to remind him what committing means giving up.

"I don't—" he starts to say, but he's immediately spoken over by Diana.

"Just wait until you see our coordinating outfits for the dance," she says proudly, placing a hand on his chest, meticulous baby-pink nail polish gleaming in the school hallway's fluorescent lights.

It's a total nonanswer, but whatever; I'm not getting into it with her. All I know is that if I don't get to go with my first-choice date, I'm certainly leaving with a tiara. "Good luck with that" is all I offer, and then I drag Melanie's attention back to me by placing a big wet smack on Miguel's cheek that I know he's dying to wipe off.

But all too soon, Melanie's gone, and everyone else falls away and it's only me and my future king: pretenders to the throne. "Have you given it any more thought?" he murmurs.

I could act like I don't know what he's talking about, but it'd just be insulting. "Nothing's changed, Migs."

He sighs. "Yeah, I know. I just thought maybe . . ."

"Maybe what?"

His usually warm brown eyes have a weary look to them I haven't seen in a long time. "Maybe you'd realize you want the same thing I do."

Even though we're keeping our conversation plenty vague, I still feel the need to drag him to a quiet corner. "Look, all else aside, sure, it'd be fun. But there are a lot of things I want and this isn't even close to the biggest one." A little lump forms in my throat as I say it, as if trying to argue with me, and I swallow a few times until it disappears. "And I know you think you want this, but you still have almost your entire senior year left. If this *does* turn into hell, do you really want months and months of that?"

I don't know what response I expect from Miguel, but it isn't a weak little shrug. He really means it when he says he'd throw the team away for Malcolm. He really thinks having a boyfriend would be enough to sustain him here if he no longer had football.

Part of me is jealous. Part of me thinks he's deluded.

And okay, a tiny little part of me wonders if *I'm* the one who's deluded, if I'm gonna keep up this charade for the entire rest of high school while the girl I want to be with is right freaking there, walking the halls friendless, no one knowing how cute she looks in glasses or that she can do the toughest rap in *Hamilton* or that she tells people her favorite movie is *The Boondock Saints* but it's actually *Love, Simon*.

But then I think of my future, of everything I want, and here's the thing: I really like Jack.

But I love me.

-JACK-

This is stupid. This is really, really stupid. I wipe my palms on my sweats and check the time on my phone again. Two minutes. *You have two minutes to come up with an entirely different reason why you asked him to meet you in the middle of nowhere.*

I don't even realize I'm pacing until a particularly large twig snaps beneath my feet. The fact that I'm nervous is a sign I shouldn't be doing this, right? I should not be doing this. I finally have an almost friend on the team and I am going to ruin it, and for what? I don't even know if *she* wants this.

But you can't know if you don't ask for real, and you can't ask for real until you do this.

But you sort of asked. And you sort of know.

I should leave.

But I don't.

When Miguel finally arrives, he's three minutes late, and I have worn every twig in a six-foot radius down to splinters. "You're mixing up your secret rendezvous buddies," he says dryly as he picks his way over to me in the woods of the nature preserve about a mile away from school. I discovered it on a run, and the path around it has become my favorite route ever since, especially when I need to think. I've never even taken Amber here, though I've thought about it. I hate having anyone intrude on it, but I certainly wasn't gonna ask Miguel Santiago to climb through my window. "You want the one with boobs."

And how. "Funny, Santiago. But yes, as you may have guessed, this is about the buddy with the boobs."

"What did Loud do now?"

"She didn't *do* anything." I take a deep breath, hoping this isn't the ask that fucks up a friendship I don't even have yet. "I just—look, I was thinking of asking her to homecoming, but, uh, obviously she already has a date. And I know y'all have your arrangement and you don't wanna be out, but I'd have to kick my own ass if I didn't at least ask if there's something we can do here."

The look on his face is weird and unreadable but doesn't look like anger. "Have you talked to Amber about this?"

"Not really. Sort of. I mentioned something about it, and she shut me down fast because of you. Which is fine!" I add quickly. "I'm not trying to throw you out of the closet. It's just . . . I've changed how I feel about it since I got here. It was that stupid date, making me want stupid things I probably shouldn't want. So I thought I'd check just in case maybe you felt the same way, which, as it comes out of my mouth I realize is even dumber than I thought. I'm new here with no friends and nothing to lose. You're . . . not."

"When?"

Okay, not what I expected him to say. "When what?"

"When did you talk to Amber about this?"

It feels like I'm walking some sort of dangerous line here, and the wrong answer is going to put someone in a world of hurt. The problem is, I don't know what the *right* answer is, or why. "Like I said, I didn't really talk about it with her. It was, like, a two-second throwaway conversation when we were hanging out last night—"

"Last night," he says flatly, and I know I've chosen wrong. *Fuck.*

"Like I said—" I start, but he's already walking away, taking backward steps away from me through the crunching leaves.

"Last night," he cuts in, "she already knew I wanted to come out at homecoming, to bring Malcolm with me. Last night, she could've said yes if she wanted to, and she knows it. And today, when I talked to her about it, she might've mentioned that the only person standing in her way wasn't me or you, but *her. She's* the one who doesn't wanna come out, which would be fucking fine if she hadn't lied to us both."

It feels like I've been sacked by a two-ton linebacker, and I close my eyes against the pain. Of all the shitty ways I imagined this conversation going, this might be the shittiest one I never even saw coming. Not that I don't know that she has her own reasons for wanting to stay in the closet, but to lie about it? To both of us?

I don't know if I get to be mad. I mean, you're never allowed to be mad at someone for not being ready to come out, right? And it's not like we didn't agree to keep this on the DL. So no, I'm not mad.

But I do feel shitty.

Why do I feel so shitty?

Maybe because you want to show her off, Miguel wants to show Malcolm off, and once again, you're the loser no one can be proud of?

Oh yeah, that's probably it.

Miguel, however . . . Miguel is pissed. And if he says a word to Amber about this conversation, she's gonna be even more pissed than he is. For now, I have to focus on talking him down. After that, I'll figure out how I wanna handle this for myself.

But when I open my eyes to pick our conversation back up, he's already gone.

- - - - -

I'm so prepared for the sight of Miguel's bike to beat me to Amber's house that when I jog up her street and don't see it, the only thing I can think is that he's already come and gone. But it's obvious when I ring the bell and get Amber's sunny expression that she hasn't just been face-to-face with her best friend ripping her to shreds.

"Hey!" She sounds a little out of breath, and I look past her and see I caught her mid-workout. Some lady is doing an impossible yoga move on the TV, and my lizard brain can't help derailing for a sec to wonder if Cheer Girl is equally bendy. "What's up?"

I wait for her to step aside to let me in, but she stays blocking the door, and I realize with a flash there's someone inside who is neither Miguel nor her mom. A moment later I get my confirmation when Cara Whelan calls, "Did your mom forget her keys again?"

I know Cara is Amber's best friend on the squad. I know. I know they go back to childhood and I know she lost the guy she was dating and I know she's in pain. I *know*.

But Cara Whelan fucking sucks, and the fact that she's the reason I'm being shoved in the closet sucks even harder.

"I talked to Miguel," I say flatly, because clearly there's no real sit-down conversation in the cards for us right now. "He told me he wanted to take Malcolm to the dance. He told me he told *you* he wants to take Malcolm."

"Keep your voice down," she whispers fiercely, stepping outside in her bare feet and closing the door nearly all the way behind her.

"Why?" I challenge her, even though my instincts betray me and I lower my voice. "To protect you from your 'best friend'?" I use air quotes, because I'm pissed and she deserves me being an asshole. "Because it's clearly not to protect Miguel, like you told me it was, and it's not to protect *me*, like you told *him* it was. So, it looks like the only people you give a shit about are you, bitchy Minnie Mouse in there, and I guess the rest of your homophobic squad."

"So I'm not allowed to have a say in this?" She folds her arms over her chest. "You and Miguel both suddenly decide you wanna come out and I *have* to be on board and out myself, too?"

"No, Amber, you don't," I say on a sigh, and I'm not sure if I'm imagining it, but it looks like she might be flinching when I use her actual name. "You just have to be honest with the people you're *supposed* to care about and not play us against each other because you're too chickenshit to deal with the fact that you're surrounded by assholes."

She sucks in a sharp breath, like nobody's ever talked to her like that before, and maybe they haven't. Maybe she's long overdue for a reality check that she can't play the entire fucking world like puppets on strings. "Anyway," I add before she can get a word in, if she'd even dare to open her mouth again with Cara in a fifty-foot radius, "looks like you got what you wanted after all—nobody left to care about but you."

My parting shot doesn't feel as good as I want it to, because I'm in the same boat. But it's been a while since I've gotten to feel a shred of dignity in this town, and I'll take it.

- - - - -

When my doorbell rings that night, I'm sure it's Cheer Girl, come to apologize or at least talk shit out, but instead I get my second Miguel Santiago interaction of the day. "Something else you forgot to crush me with earlier?" I ask as I let him inside, watching him take in the small living space, the pull-out couch with my stuff piled next to it. Other than Amber, he's the only person who's been to my place in Atherton, and I wish I'd at least cleaned up a little or whatever.

But he doesn't make any jokes about it being smaller than the locker room (which it is) or anything like that. There's no smile on his face at all. Which makes me think he had his own confrontation with Cheer Girl, until he says, "I didn't know about it when we talked earlier. Which is why I'm here now."

My brain is still so squarely in Amberland that I'm caught completely off guard when it turns out she has nothing to do with why he's there. "The guys are gonna throw the game. Word spread around that Terry Lawrence is finally coming to a homecoming game, specifically to see you, and the guys are pissed. I'm sorry. I know this was important to you."

I have to blink about a hundred times while I process what he's saying, and it doesn't help that he won't meet my eyes. Even his hands are jammed in his pockets, like he wants to hide from me as much as possible when he tells me this. "Hold up. You're telling me the team wants to throw the *homecoming* game, of all games, just so they can fuck me over in front of a scout who isn't even really coming to scout me? They wanna look like shit the year they're finally *not* shit just so a girl can't get a chance at a future?"

He closes his eyes for a deep inhale, then slowly sighs it out. "Uh, yeah, that's about the gist of it."

There's no use waiting for an "I tried to talk them out of it," because of course he didn't; what would the fucking point even be? "That's the stupidest fucking thing I've ever heard."

"Yeah, well, Dan Sanchez isn't planning to go to college on an academic scholarship, so."

I might laugh if I weren't so pissed. "It's not like I'm the only one this screws over. If we blow the game, *no one* is getting scouted."

For the first time since he walked in, Miguel looks up at me, his expression managing to juggle looking tired, amused, and irritated. "No one was ever gonna get scouted other than you, Walsh. Everyone knows that. No one would be throwing this if they thought they had a chance in hell at a future in football."

"Maybe they don't have a chance in hell at a future in football because they're too busy being misogynistic pricks to work on their game."

"Maybe!" Miguel throws up his arms in frustration. "Look, I hate this too. I hate that I looked over my shoulder the whole ride here, and I hate that I just sat through that fucking ridiculous team meeting, and I hate that my boyfriend is mad at me and *I'm* mad at Loud and all of us are in a shitshow. All I ever wanted to do was play football and have a few people around to get me through my four years until I could go off to Miami, and now all of that's in the toilet. And yeah," he says, his dark eyes burning into mine, "I really hate the way they treat you and that I'm too chickenshit to stop it. It's not even purely being chickenshit."

"I know."

"If I thought it'd make a difference—"

"I know." And I do. But I don't say that it'd make a difference to *me*. Because everything he's saying, all this drama . . .

214

it's because of me. And I don't have the right to ask for anything else.

Do I?

"No, you know what?" The words are out of my mouth before I can stop them. "That's bullshit. You've never even tried to stand up for me. And maybe that's because you don't actually like me, but you're here right now even though the team would fucking destroy you if they knew, and I don't think that's for Amber. So, what is it, man? Because I gotta tell you, it does not feel great to have you tell me you're brave enough to come out to the team as gay but not as a Jack Walsh supporter. That kinda feels like your own brand of misogynistic bullshit right there."

He opens his mouth and I can see he's got a heated reply planned, but then he closes it. He blinks. "I . . . fuck. I don't know what to say."

"Say 'You're right, Jack.' Maybe even 'I'm sorry, Jack.' I'll definitely take 'I should've stuck up for you sooner, Jack, but I'll start right now, because you've been working your ass off, and having a scout watch you play may be your one shot at having a future in it after high school and becoming a fucking *legend*, and I'll do anything to stop my friends from screwing it up for you.'"

At least he has the decency to look ashamed. But accompanied by his silence, it's not good enough.

"Thanks for the info. You can leave." I don't wait to watch him go, instead heading to the bathroom and turning on the shower high enough to fill the room with steam fast, and to cover the sound of his retreating footsteps and the door shutting behind them.

I had two friends in this entire school—this entire town— and now I'm really and truly alone.

Chapter Ten

-AMBER-

Miguel isn't answering my texts.

This is the first time I can remember him leaving me on read.

Yeah, sometimes he's unreachable when he and Malcolm get a little . . . caught up, and I know never to try him at practice, but otherwise, Miguel is always, always there when I need him.

Except right now.

When he's leaving me on read.

No one fucking leaves me on read.

"You're missing the entire movie," Cara complains, prodding at the goopy pink mask on her face. "If I knew you were gonna text your boyfriend the whole time, I would've at least dragged Kelsey here with me."

"Sorry, sorry," I mutter, turning my phone upside down so that the sparkly pink-and-purple ombre case looks back up at me instead of the glaringly quiet screen. Normally I'd snap at Cara to just *go* to Kelsey's stupid house, then, but she's right— I'm being a shitty host and I *did* tell her we could have a sleepover the night before Books and Balls Day so she could be at her freshest instead of rolling in with the special kind of sleep deprivation that comes from sharing a room with two sisters who both snore. "Do you want more sorbet?"

"I can't eat anything with this stuff on. How long do I have to leave it to give me perfect pores?"

I check the tube. "It says fifteen minutes, but do you want me to point out that you already have perfect pores or nah?"

"Feel free," she says with a smug smile before turning her attention to the TV, where Vanessa Hudgens is twirling around in a tiara.

Five minutes after our masks are washed off and our pores are more perfect than a Hadid sister's, it's Cara's phone that starts beeping like mad. "Is that *your* boyfriend?" I tease before I can think better of it.

If my stupid joke brings Robbie to mind, it doesn't show on her face. "Just some cheer stuff," she says.

"Uh, if it's cheer stuff, why isn't *my* phone lighting up?" I ask, holding it so she can see its dismally dark screen.

The thing about Cara is she's never been a fast enough thinker to be a great liar, but it never stops her from trying. "It's just Kelsey and Claire, uh, talking about how we're all getting to the game."

"It's Kelsey and Claire texting you—you, a person who does not have a car—about how you're all getting to the game. When everyone knows I drive you everywhere."

I know she's going to bite her lip and her cheeks will turn pink before it even happens. It's Cara's standard "Oh darn, I was caught in a lie" move, and she does it all the time because, again, bad but compulsive liar.

For the millionth time, I wonder how she got away with keeping Robbie a secret for so long, but that's a question best left for another day.

"Cara."

She huffs out a breath. "Fine. They're talking about how funny and awkward it's gonna be when we cheer for guys who are throwing the game. Are you happy?"

"What do you mean? Who's throwing what game?" And then it clicks. Jack. The scout. Not even homecoming—alumni swarming the bleachers to watch the game, especially with news of Atherton's first female quarterback—is sacred. "You mean the football team is gonna throw the *homecoming* game? Seriously?"

"See, this is why you're not on the texts," she says, more than a little bitchily. "Between Midnight Breakfast and that whole little cheer at the pep rally, people think you're, like, Team Jack. And as your best friend, I've told them a hundred times that you're not, you're loyal to the team and to us and to Robbie." There's a little flash of pain in her eyes, blink-and-you-miss-it quick but present all the same. "It's not true, though, is it? You're supposed to be our leader next year, but for some reason, you support her. You don't even care who it hurts."

"It shouldn't hurt *anyone*!" It's not the right thing to say to Cara, but it needs to be said. "She stepped in. She lifts up the whole team. They *win* now. And it's our job to cheer them on whether they win or lose, but it *matters* that they're finally winning and that it's a girl helping them do that. We're a fucking cheerleading squad of girls, Cara—how are we not behind the girl we should be cheering on the most?"

"God, you don't get it, do you?" I've never seen the look of disgust on Cara Whelan's face right now, not when Sara's pit bull peed on her tennis shoes or when we got food poisoning the first and only time we tried oysters or when Matt Devlin wore an all-denim suit to the Sophomore Swing dance on a dare. "She's not one of us! She's never gonna be one of us! And you're acting like you have some big gay crush on her and it's pathetic."

The blood goes cold as ice in my veins, and I'm so not used

to this version of Cara that I don't know how to read whether she's trying to insult me or she's genuinely calling me out. Which means there's only one thing I can do, and that's go harder.

"Is it more pathetic than bullying the new girl because you're hanging on to a dead boy?"

Unlike Cara, I don't mask whether I'm calling her out. I see the exact moment she realizes I know, because all the color drains from her face.

"I don't want to talk about him," she tries to bite out, but it emerges in a whisper, as her lies often do. And I realize then that all of this has been her talking about him without actually talking about him, about what he meant to her—what they meant to each other—the only way she can. And even though I'm still angry and sad and frustrated, it takes the fire out of me to see her shoulders fall, her gaze drop, her fingers start twisting around each other like if they break free, they might strangle something or someone.

"I think you do."

Her eyes flash, wet with angry unshed tears. "What do you know about it anyway? You have no idea what I'm going through, with your perfect boyfriend and perfect relationship and perfect mom."

There's so much irony in there, I don't even know where to begin, except that, oh yes, I do. "Oh, so now my mom is perfect? That's interesting, considering how many times you've tried to get me to pray for her because she's queer and unwed."

"At least she would take you to get an abortion."

That stuns me into silence, and it seems to stun Cara, too. I can see how badly she wishes she could shovel the words back into her mouth like a plate of fries from Maggie's, but there's really no going back after someone drops the A-bomb, is there?

"Cara—"

"If you tell anyone, I will kill you. I mean it."

"I really hope you know that I would fucking never." She flinches at the swear, a habit that's harder to break than preaching against premarital sex and reproductive choice, I guess. "I don't even know what happened."

"Oh, you know the story." From tiny, sunny Cara, the weary bitterness dripping from her voice is almost unbearable. "Boy meets girl. Boy secretly dates girl because her family forbids dating. Girl loves boy and gives up the virginity she'd been saving for marriage. Girl gets pregnant, because birth control is a sin. Girl tries to tell her mom and gets an earful of how abortion is the greatest sin. Girl tells boy she's pregnant and is keeping it, and boy gets so drunk in response that he drives into a tree and dies."

Oh.

Shit.

"And the baby?" I ask as delicately as I can.

"Girl goes to cheer camp anyway, because she can't stay

in this town for one more minute, and spends the summer training hard and flying through the air while trying not to think about how she's going to raise a baby who no longer has a father. And then one night, there was nothing to think about anymore."

"The night you skipped Kelsey's birthday party because you had bad cramps—"

"I wasn't lying." A tear drops off her jaw and leaves a dark spot on her lilac shirt. "It just wasn't my period."

I feel sick. I feel . . . I don't even know what I feel. I don't know who this person is standing in front of me, still wearing a tiny swipe of creamy pink mask by her ear. Once upon a time I was the only person she'd have sleepovers with because she wet the bed until she was nine, and now she's opening a whole hallway full of doors I never expected.

Saving herself for marriage has *always* been huge to Cara, and I was sure she was still a virgin and would be until her wedding night. I was equally sure that if she ever *did* break her vow of celibacy, she'd be responsible, and failing that, she'd be really excited to have a kid, especially if it got her out of her cramped house and out from under her parents' thumb. And that wasn't just me guessing—she's said more than once that she thought she'd like to go straight into being a wife and mother, that college wasn't really for her even though she planned to do at least two years at Atherton Community College.

I didn't know anything, it turns out.

But then, Cara thinks she knows me, too. She thinks I have the perfect boyfriend in Miguel because she doesn't know our whole romance is a sham. If she knows *something* is up between me and Jack, she definitely doesn't know that we've been secretly dating for weeks. I'd be a major hypocrite to criticize her for keeping such a huge piece of herself from me, even though we both know I wouldn't have judged her the same way she'd judge me.

"You could've told me. And I'm not mad that you didn't," I clarify. "It's your business. But this must've been completely shitty to go through alone. So . . . why didn't you? You know I would've been okay with all of it."

"Do you seriously not get it?" The sadness in her eyes is quickly replaced by irritation. "It's not about whether *you're* okay with it, Amber. *I'm* not okay with it. My values didn't change just because I strayed from my path for a while. Your validation isn't what I need."

And like that, we're back to Jesus. It always comes back to Jesus. And from what I gather, Cara's version of Jesus doesn't have room for girls who think other girls look impossibly cute in glasses.

"Well, I'm sorry about your fight with our Lord and Savior, but I really don't think He's smiling upon what y'all are planning to do to Jack, either."

"Wow." Cara swipes at her eyes, which suddenly look small and beady to me, and sniffs hard. "So even after all that, you're on her side."

"There are no fucking sides, Cara!" I cannot do this anymore. I can't. It's not worth it. "Jack is not against you! She didn't kill Robbie or—" The rest of the words die on my tongue, but they don't need to be said. "You're the only one thinking that this is somehow penance. You've all convinced yourselves it's a disgrace to Robbie's memory to have a girl absolutely kick his ass at football, and I'm sorry, but that's just fifty shades of deranged girl hate. You're right—I'm not on your side." I stalk over to the front door and swing it open, the only time in my life I have ever kicked Cara Whelan out of my house. It's not lost on me that it might be the last time she's ever *in* my house. "Maybe Jesus can help you."

She sets her jaw but grabs her stuff in a haste and storms to the door, turning to lay one last smackdown. "You're never, ever going to become captain after this. You can forget about that, and if you think I'm rooming with you at ACC, you can forget about that, too."

At that, I can't help but snort. There is no way I'm staying in this town after graduation, surrounded by people who think like this. If that means college isn't in the cards for me, now that I'm throwing captainship away, then whatever. The only thing I want out of life after high school is to live openly, and I *did* want to do it without losing anyone, but turns out that even in the closet, people can prove to you that they're just not worth it.

"Wouldn't dream of it," I say sweetly. "I'm sure you wouldn't want to share your room with a big ol' queer anyway."

Her jaw is still hanging open when I slam the door in her face.

-JACK-

I'm going home. Once the thought hits my brain—for real, and not just an angry aside—it becomes impossible to shake. It's one thing to push back against the hate, to keep playing no matter what. But even when the guys were at their most dickish, they were still my team—they still ran the plays I called and caught the balls I threw and tackled the guys in my way. (As well as they could, anyway; it's not like they turned into superstars overnight.) But if they're not doing that, if we're not a team anymore, then this isn't me quitting; it's me not being able to play in the first place.

I had my shot.

It's over.

The thought keeps me up half the night, and by morning, I know it's the right move. It was barely worth keeping my family broken up before, but it's *definitely* not now. I miss my dad. I miss Jason and Jeremy, even if they're being assholes. I miss Sage and Morgan. I miss the tire hanging in our yard and having my own room and the Megan Rapinoe poster on my wall (for multiple reasons).

But how do I tell them this was all for nothing?

I have a scout coming. A fucking *scout*. How many girls get a *scout* watching them play football, even unofficially? It's the secret dream I never even bothered telling anyone about, the dream I pretended never existed because it was just too ab-fucking-surd to possibly be real. Hell, even with it *being* real, I barely told anyone, because it still felt too good be true.

And it was.

I fucking hate this place.

I flex my fingers, stretching them out like a sunburst and curling them in on my palm over and over again, because if I don't keep my hand busy, I *will* reach out and throw something against a wall. And it wouldn't be enough. Butler was one thing, because it never gave me the promise of anything. But Atherton did. And that makes it so much worse that the past couple of months have turned into an absolute embarrassment. I cannot wait to get out of here, and I'm starting to think that if it doesn't happen right now, I'm going to burn this godforsaken town to the ground.

In a flash, I think about leaving Cheer Girl behind, and just as quickly I remember that's just another thing that's over, another thing I clearly never had the chance to get right.

I won't bail on the game, because unlike these pathetic fuckers, I have an ounce of loyalty and class. Besides, it's not like I can cancel on the scout. The best I can do is show him that *I* can play, even if the team can't, and maybe I'll get considered for a one-time kick or something.

My uniform, which usually fits like a glove, feels too tight in every way today, but I can't stop looking at myself in the mirror, knowing it's probably my last day wearing it. It's not coming back with me as a souvenir; even if Coach let me take it, I couldn't bear to look at it again.

I wonder if the shade of Gator green is something I'll ever be able to wear again without wanting to puke.

My phone lights up with a text, and I hate the little blip of hope in my brain that expects to see Amber's name attached to an apology or even a *Can we talk?* but it's just another text from Sage cheering me on for tonight.

No, not *just*, I remind myself. Sage and Morgan have been as good friends as possible through this entire shitshow; it's not their fault they kept living their lives without me and having fun at the things we were supposed to do together. It's not their fault they've been trying to watch out for me and I've been dismissing all their concerns, or that I gave my fucking heart to a girl who didn't deserve it.

The wave of missing them hits hard in my chest, adding another layer to my determination to make this my last game. I'm tempted to tell them right here and now, but I can't stand the humiliation, or the totally irrational part of my brain that worries if they know how big a loser I am here, they'll decide I'm not worth their time, either.

Tonight, though. Tonight, when it's all over and I am at my fucking lowest and I need my best friends. Tonight I'll tell them.

Home Field Advantage

I keep an eye on my phone while I brush my teeth, watch it with laser-beam eyes while I eat breakfast, willing it to light up with something from Amber or even one of my brothers, but nothing else comes.

I take one last look at myself in the mirror, fully dressed in my Alligators uniform from shoulders to toes, and though all I want is to run in the other direction, I set off for school.

- - - - -

With Amber in my first period, I brace myself for the sight of her, but she never shows. At least wondering where she is makes for a welcome distraction from the classmates throwing balled-up pieces of paper at me when the teacher's turned around with "Catch this!" and "How's my aim?" and "Gonna scout me?" nastily whispered at me. Whether any of them have notes inside, I don't bother looking.

Things don't get better when the bell rings; all the same whispering and pointing is there, even though I'm definitely supposed to be wearing my uniform this time. In fact, the only people being suspiciously nice to me—if you can call flat-out ignoring me "nice"—are the other guys on the team, because they're too stupid to realize that's a way bigger giveaway that they've got shit planned than just being their usual asshole selves.

By fourth period, I've seen every other cheerleader in the junior class, so I know it isn't a squad thing. Not that I care. Not that I'm a little worried. If Amber's proven anything, it's that she's always watching out for herself.

I definitely don't care.

I just need to check the time on my phone.

No unread messages.

Crap.

"Hey." The voice is low in my ear, the sound of someone pretending to be passing by who doesn't want to get caught talking to me. I know it well by now, have heard it from a freshman girl here, a soccer player there—the few people in the school who think what I'm doing is cool, even if they know they're not allowed to voice it. This time, though, it's a voice I'm familiar with. "You seen Loud?"

"Nope."

Miguel swears under his breath, but whatever he's worried about, he doesn't share, and I don't ask. Though I don't need him to tell me that from a "hope to become cheer captain" perspective, this probably isn't a great day to skip.

I want to think she's home soothing a broken heart with a pint of ice cream or whatever, but I know better. She's probably just getting Gator green stripes in her hair.

The telltale rush of air that would accompany Miguel moving on with his day doesn't come, and even though I wanna take the opportunity to leave him in the dust, my feet won't make the movements my brain wants them to. It's like part of me still thinks there must be a decent guy in there, and I don't know why. Queer solidarity? Some sort of invisible rainbow-striped bond?

"Listen, I wanna help."

Oh, maybe that's why.

Still, if there's one thing I've learned in Atherton, it's never to get your hopes up, even around the people you think could be your friends. "Hell of a way of showing it, by whispering to me in the corner like I'm some kind of criminal creep."

"It wouldn't exactly work if people knew we were talking," he points out, and as if he'd just summoned them, Matt Devlin and Lamar Burke round the corner and start heading in our direction. "Meet me in the art room at lunch."

Well, he certainly found the place most likely to contain zero people who care about football.

Still, the thought of getting my hopes up again exhausts me. There's nothing one guy on the team can do at this point. The others have given up their pride in the game—there's nothing left for them to lose. But every day I'm here I risk tearing my family further apart, losing my best friends, losing my *mind*.

It feels good to be in control for once, even if just to tap the final nail in my coffin. "Thanks, but I'll pass." And for the first time since I got to Atherton, I'm the one to walk away.

Chapter Eleven

-AMBER-

"Pick up, pick up, pick up," I chant at my phone, but like the last six times, it isn't working. Whatever, it doesn't matter—I've reached those I most need to reach, and hopefully, they'll take it from there.

I switch over to my texts, which have been flooded by Miguel all morning. It's a relief to see he isn't too mad at me to yell, but I'm not sure how much longer that'll last if I keep ignoring him. However, I've already missed half the day for my mission, so I don't have time to get into it with him now. I type out a quick *Coming now, explain later,* do a brief check of my hair, makeup, and uniform, and bounce out the door.

It's a little overly hopeful, still showing up in my uniform. If I get caught skipping the entire morning, they'll keep me from cheering tonight. But it's worth it, I think. I hope.

It feels right, anyway.

I'm just walking into school when the message I've been waiting for comes in—a simple *They're in* followed by a thumbs-up emoji.

I exhale the breath I've been holding for the last twelve hours.

The second I get inside I'm accosted by Diana and Zoe, as if they've had radar on the front door this whole time. "Where have you been?" Zoe practically hisses, dragging me toward the caf. "I covered for you in physics and Spanish, and I heard Austin did in English, but you are this close to being tossed out of the game tonight. Please tell me you came with a doctor's note." She glances behind me and the look on her face gets even angrier. "Where the hell is Cara?"

The part of me that had been wondering if Cara ran straight to the team with the news that one of their bases flies a rainbow flag relaxes. It's clear that Diana and Zoe don't know a thing, and though that won't stay true for long, it's helpful for today. At least I wasn't *completely* delusional all those years of being friends with Cara.

"Haven't seen her today," I say truthfully, thoughts cycling through my mind.

Cara *never* skips school, because she knows all it'll take is one or two absences until her parents use it against her. They're dying to switch her to homeschooling, which really just means keeping her around to help take care of the littlest littles. So why is she skipping today?

I thought Cara was not so subtly throwing her hat in the ring for captain by leading the charge for the anti-Jack rebellion, but if she skips out on homecoming, there's no coming back from that. Was I wrong the whole time? Or did she only just decide to pivot away?

And of course, if it's not gonna be me (and it's certainly not), and if it's not gonna be her (and it's certainly not), then . . . who's it gonna be?

Somewhere along the way, that became the least important question.

Because the most important one doesn't have a thing to do with Cara.

I haven't tried getting in touch with Jack, and I'm not going to. She's right to be pissed, and nothing I can say is gonna fix it. But tonight we'll see if anything I can *do* will fix it, and that's what has me bouncing in my tennis shoes.

Or it's what *had* me bouncing in my tennis shoes. An "I mean business" glare from Diana dries that right up. None of this will work if I don't get out on the field tonight, even if it means pretending I'm all in for plan Fuck Up Jack's Life.

"What, are you two in your first fight ever?" Diana snaps. "Great day you chose for it."

"We're fine," I lie, because if they smell blood in the water, they'll never drop it. "Guess we both had shit to do today, and I'm here, so I bet she will be soon too. Maybe she's having trouble getting a ride."

"Whatever," Zoe says with a roll of her eyes. "Just get to the gym. Crystal and Nia are waiting."

My stomach grumbles at the mention of skipping lunch for a squad meeting, and I wish it hadn't been too filled with butterflies all morning for me to eat in between detective work, plotting, sending awkward messages, and making even more awkward phone calls. I'm gonna have to beg another one of those nasty energy bars off Coach.

While Zoe and Diana hunt the halls to see if Cara's shown up, I make my way to the gym. There, I get another minute of "Ohmygodwherewereyou thankgodyoureherenow" from Crystal and Nia, and then I join Kelsey, Sara, Ella, Claire, and Virany in their stretching corner while we wait for Zoe, Diana, Taylor, and, of course, Cara.

"I was wondering when you were gonna show," Kelsey says immediately, because of course she does. I don't know when she and Cara became besties, but I'm guessing if anyone knows where C is right now, it's her.

"So nice to know you were worried about me, Kels!" I say sweetly. "Everything is fine. Just wanted to make sure my hair looked extra shiny." *And good luck calling me out on that.*

As expected, that shuts her up, and Virany picks that perfect moment to beckon me over so we can pair up for partner stretches.

When Diana and Zoe arrive two minutes later, joined by Taylor, it's clear they've had no luck tracking down Cara, either in person or by phone. Which sends them straight back to me. "Are you sure you don't know where she is?" Zoe's voice drips with disbelief.

"I really don't," I say, keeping my focus on the various muscle groups of my arms and legs. "Maybe Kelsey does."

Everyone's heads swivel to look at Kelsey, who narrows her eyes at me. "Of course I don't know where she is. I would've told you already. Besides, *I* was here this morning."

"Well, she's not answering texts *or* calls," says Diana, her face grave.

Crystal mutters a swear under her breath. "Okay. We'll have no choice but to change it up. Ella, you're flying in Cara's place tonight, and we'll bring up Mandy from JV to cover you, though that isn't gonna work for the Gator Grind. . . ." She pulls out her choreo notebook and does some quick scribbling, continuing to murmur her thoughts while the rest of us watch her work—Crystal's process is not exactly collaborative. Even Nia keeps quiet, silently flexing in anticipation of a more leg-heavy routine.

"Should some of us go out looking?" Ella asks, ever the sweetheart. The girl doesn't have a cutthroat bone in her body.

If *I* were getting my first shot ever at lead flyer, I sure as hell wouldn't be looking to change that up. "I'm getting a little nervous. It was one thing when we assumed they were together," she says, gesturing toward me, "but if they're not—"

"She's been gone all of five minutes longer than Ammo was," Kelsey cuts in. "I'm sure she's fine."

I'm sure she is too, but it does bug me not to know where she is, even if our friendship *is* over.

And then, with a flash, I realize that I do.

Because if there's one place Cara Whelan would go after telling me about her gravest sins, one place where she'd ignore a barrage of frantic calls and texts, it's the home of Confession itself.

"You think it's *fine* that two members of the squad have missed half a day when the homecoming game is in a few hours?" Crystal demands.

Sara and Kelsey exchange a smirk, and I realize that either Crystal's a *very* good actress, or she has no idea that the team is planning to throw the game tonight. But Sara and Kelsey do, and judging by the way Virany's biting her lip, she does too. And now I wonder if I'm giving Cara too much credit by thinking her absence has more to do with Jesus than Jack.

I scrutinize the rest of the team, trying to figure out who's in on it and who isn't. Either Kelsey was lying and knows exactly where Cara is and what she's up to, or she wasn't, but she *thinks* she knows. Kelsey doesn't want anyone looking for her, and Ella does. And I know Kelsey's in on it, which means Ella isn't.

Nia is too dedicated to Crystal to be part of any plot that doesn't include her. The same is probably true for the rest of the seniors. But other than Ella—sweet, unassuming Ella— everyone else seems seriously suspect.

Which means about half the squad has been plotting and consciously leaving me out of it.

But it also means half the squad hasn't. And maybe there's something I can do with that.

"Kelsey, you're a member of Cara's church, right?"

"Yeah, why?"

I turn to Crystal. "I bet that's where Cara is. Praying on the game. You know how spiritual she is, and how much pride she has in the team. I'm sure she just lost track of time asking God to watch out for the Gators and deliver us a win in front of the alumni. Maybe Kelsey could go check there, since she's familiar with the building and everything."

I have no doubt Kelsey's scowling at the back of my head; I'm pretty sure I can feel my hair singeing. But I keep a sweet smile on my face when I turn around. "You wouldn't mind, would you? Cara obviously wouldn't want to miss tonight's game, and I'm sure everyone would feel better knowing where she is for sure." She opens her mouth, and I cut off what she's going to say before she can even try it. "I'd go myself, but I wouldn't want anyone to have to cover for me for any more of the day, seeing as I already missed the morning. Which I am so, so sorry about," I add to Crystal, plus Nia, Diana, and Zoe for good measure. "Maybe Sara can go with you, since she doesn't have to practice with a new flyer." That still leaves Virany, Claire, and Ella here, but I can deal with that.

"Okay, fine," Crystal says with a wave of her hand, too involved in her own plotting process.

Now, to press my luck. "Virany, maybe you can go to the office to have them page Mandy here?"

When no one steps in to stop her, she shrugs and goes. Of all the cheerleaders on the squad, she's dead last in actually giving a shit about it, and even if she's in on the plot against Jack, I would guess her commitment level is squarely at "Sure, until something more interesting comes along." You can always count on her being willing to do something as long as it's not what she's already doing.

And now it's down to Claire, who I know full well is crackable. So here we go.

"As long as we're doing some reworking for tonight, this morning I had a sudden realization for how to update our 'All Our Gators' cheer—part of why I was late was because I was writing it down and making copies for everyone." Of course, by "sudden realization" I mean I pored over it for an hour, but they don't need to know that. "I know we've had some trouble with, um, some names rotating in and out of the QB spot, but I finally figured out how to make Jack's name fit." I hold up the stack I spent way too much time on and start handing it out before anyone can object. "It's really a tiny nothing change—just switching Matt and Lamar, and changing 'Excellent' to 'Preeminent,' and then it totally fits!"

The enthusiasm in my voice is matched by exactly zero expressions, but at least Crystal's eyes are scanning it, her mouth sounding out the beats. Taking their cues from her, Nia, Diana, and Ella start doing the same. They may not have wanted to take a minute to do this themselves, but there's no honorable justification for refusing it when someone else has done the work.

"I don't think we should be making any changes without everyone here," says Claire, an edge of desperation in her voice. "This is just begging for us to make a major screwup on the field tonight."

"You really don't think Cara, Sara, Kelsey, and Ella can handle this?" I ask, letting my voice fill with the subtext of "Wow, you must think they're total idiots."

"That's not what I mean," Claire says hotly. "God, this is why—" She cuts herself off and looks around the room, but the only person there who knows how she was going to finish her sentence is me.

This is why we left you out of our plan.

But I'm not the only one they left out, and they're not finding anything but confusion and a hint of anger among the seniors.

"This is why what, Claire?"

Butter would not melt in my fucking mouth.

You'd have no idea from the way she's looking at me that Claire and I have known each other for years, been good enough friends to ride bikes together down the path behind her house in the springtime as kids and go shopping for the best Cheer Camp Casual that Thrifty Nick's had to offer just this past summer. It's scary to think how much has changed so quickly, and scarier still to know this is only the tip of the iceberg, assuming Cara hasn't outed me yet.

But if captainship is gone, and my sort-of girlfriend is gone, and my best friends are gone . . . what else really matters at this point?

Claire doesn't answer me. Instead, she whirls around to face everyone else, hands balled into fists. "No one was happy when Jack came here and joined the team. Not one of you. So why are we pretending she belongs? If you write her into that cheer, you're saying she has a place on our team."

"And if we don't, we look to every single person in the stands like we don't really support the Gators," I shoot back. "Is that who you wanna be? We're cheerleaders. This is our *job*."

"Welcoming some lesbo with open arms is *not* my job."

Both the sentiment and the word hit harder than I expected, and standing tall physically hurts when all I want to do is curl up into a ball. But this is it—this is when I see how the other girls view me, even if they don't know it.

The room is silent, charged, the air feeling like a weighted blanket on my fiery skin.

And then, into the quiet, a voice I absolutely do not expect speaks up. "So let me get something clear," says Nia, her voice as soft as always. "Wanting Jack gone—was that ever really about Robbie for you and the others? Or was it always because you're a raging homophobe?"

Nia. Of all the girls on the team to stand up, it's the one I've least bothered to get to know. The one who had nothing to offer me to get ahead, because she always just felt like another limb of Crystal's. I know this is Claire's moment of shame, but right now, it's seeping into me, too, just a little bit.

Claire opens her mouth, and shuts it. None of us have ever been confronted by Nia, and I wouldn't know how to answer her any more than Claire does. Piss her off, and you're pissing off the captain. And Claire seems well past having pissed her off right now.

"Ella, maybe you can join Virany in the office and have them page Dayna to join us too, since Claire won't be cheering tonight," Crystal says, and we turn and look at Claire, who's never once been benched. She's on the verge of tears, and I *almost* feel bad for her, until my brain replays the way she spat the word *lesbo* a solid fifty times in a row.

No, the only person I feel guilty about—the only person I care to make things up to right now—is Jack, and as Crystal turns to the rest of us and says, "Okay, let's give this a shot— we'll work on the moves later" while holding up the paper I copied at the Copy Shop two towns over this morning, I

pray this will go at least the tiniest way toward helping me
do that.

-JACK-

At some point, Amber showed up to school—I spot her in the
hallway for a split second before last period—but if she sees
me, she doesn't acknowledge it. Which is fine. She's this close
to becoming a distant memory, even if she doesn't know it yet.

I leave my phone in my locker all morning, full of untyped
texts to Sage and Morgan letting them know I'm coming
home, photographs unsent of me in my uniform with my
middle finger extended toward the mirror that lines the door
of the coat closet that's doubled as my storage space. There is
way too much shit living in my brain rent free, and tonight,
as soon as the buzzer ends the game, I know I'm going to
explode with it. But right now, the combination of fury and
relief pent up in my brain flows through my veins like the
sharpest adrenaline, and despite everything—*everything*—the
only thing my body wants to do is channel it into football.

It's how I'm built. They can't screw that out of me.

Books and Balls Day has everyone wearing their passions
on their sleeves. The chess team members are easily picked

out by their all-black or all-white attire, capped off with horse heads, cone-shaped hats, or crowns. The Model UN kids have their flag tees, and in some cases even hair spray-dyed to match. The debate team literally had shirts made for this, all of which say "Go Ahead: Judge Me" in block letters. And of course, everyone with uniforms, from the band geeks to the tennis team to the cheer squad, is sporting them.

If I had a friend to ask, I'd pose the obvious question about what the kids do who aren't in any clubs or on any teams, but I don't. There are a few kids who don't look like they're showing off any particular attire, but once I see a bunch together, I realize they're the skaters, and they're just dressed the same way they always are, wallet chains and all.

I get it, how so much of who we are is shaped by what we spend our time doing—me and football, Sage and baking, Morgan and cosplay, Amber and cheerleading—but what happens when you don't spend your time that way anymore? I'm not gonna stop being a person just because I stop doing the thing I love most in the world.

I'm pretty sure.

I'd kill for a weight-lifting period right now, something I'll keep doing even after I'm gone from this team, from this sport, but there's no lifting on game day, and I'm not about to break those rules. I'm going out on my own terms, which means resisting the urge to skip American history and sneak out to the weight room.

Instead, I sit through class, thinking, as usual, of how much of our collective history is bullshit, which in turn makes me antsy to go to college so I can get the education I've been missing out on, which of course brings me back to sports and the way I was planning to *afford* college. . . .

Not that a football scholarship was ever a real question. I'm not stupid enough to think a scout happening to be there was gonna suddenly change that. (I might be stupid enough to dream about it, but I'm not stupid enough not to know it's nothing more than a dream.) But I need to be able to walk on to *some* school's softball team in the spring, or I can kiss that dream goodbye. Coach Sundstrom guaranteed I'd be able to do that in Atherton, but Coach Witherspoon at Butler is the vindictive type, and even though she's technically never had to go a season without me (and still wouldn't if I make it back this month), she might just be pissed enough at me for bailing to refuse to give my spot back.

Why is it that no matter how I look at this, no matter what I do, I'm well and truly fucked?

History blends into calculus and it doesn't help that absolutely no one is listening to a damn thing a single teacher has to say today. Even the teachers clearly don't wanna be doing this. Mr. Koenig literally points to equations on the board with a foam finger.

I wonder if they'd be so excited for tonight—if people would be chanting the cheers under their breath without even realizing it, if they'd be pouring chocolate milk out in the cafeteria for Robbie, if they'd be yelling "Go Gators!" at every football player they pass in the hallway (even me, occasionally, if the person didn't know better or get a good glimpse at the uniform)—if they knew their pathetic heroes were planning to throw the game to spite a girl.

God, I want to show them all so badly.

Another thing I really wanna do? Skip this farce of a pep rally, where I'll not only undoubtedly be ignored again but forced to watch the girl I like be one of the people doing the ignoring. But I don't wanna give anyone the satisfaction, so when the bell rings and the announcement ushers us toward the gym, I square my shoulders, push past everyone who'd rather pretend I didn't exist, and go take my spot at the back of the line.

I expect the guys to avoid eye contact entirely, so I'm not prepared when they're suddenly all smiles, holding up their hands for high fives and saying shit like "Heard Terry Lawrence is gonna be at the game—that's awesome." They're nothing but snake-oil grins and obvious fronts, and you can tell which of them think they're charming enough to pull it off.

Imagine Dan Sanchez thinking I believe there's any friendliness behind that fist bump. Im-fucking-*agine*.

And still, I return it, because instinct. Because they'll make it worse for me if I don't, and yes, there is a "worse" in there somewhere. Because even if they're built to give up, I'm not.

One by one, the players get called into the gym, names echoing in the air like they're meant to be remembered, even if they won't do anything to earn it. I wish my name could get buried in the middle, sandwiched between the applause of Matt Devlin and Lamar Burke, but the QB goes last, because in any other world, the QB is the star, the one you clap for the loudest.

I take a deep breath and let my mind float to the things that bring me peace. Lifting in my grungy little gym at home with the quiet buzz of grunting and clanking iron. Sage's lemon meringue pie. Marathoning ESPN Classic when I'm sick. Looking up at the stars while listening to Hayley Kiyoko. Every single suit worn by Cate Blanchett in *Ocean's 8*. Playing ball with Jeremy and Justin in the cul-de-sac.

The last one stings, but not as badly as it used to. They'll have to forgive me when I return home and bring Mom with me. They're my brothers. They have to.

Turns out, that tiny ribbon of fear snaking through my ribs that worries they won't is the perfect distraction. Before I know it, "And finally, your quarterback, Jaclyn Walsh!" rings out loud enough to shake the walls.

I try not to wince at my full name—the one I've asked every single person in this school to stop using, to no avail—and jog into the gym. The cheering is considerably quieter, the crowd less animated, but none of it matters, because there is a single flash of lightning drawing absolutely everyone in the room's attention.

Amber McCloud is doing a solo tumbling run. It's fucking incredible, watching her defy gravity, her legs slicing through the air like a single tanned blade. And when she's done, she barely takes a breath before snatching up the megaphone and shouting "Give me a *J*!"

The crowd, too stunned to do anything other than respond on autopilot, goes ahead and gives her that *J*.

And an *A*.

And a *C*.

And a *K*.

And then she's off again, cartwheeling and flipping like her life depends on it, bringing the entire room to its feet.

I know that if I look at the rest of the squad, I'll see a group of girls that absolutely wants to strangle her with their pompoms. And if I look at the team, I'll see something similar.

But I can't look anywhere except at Amber, her chest heaving with exertion, her face flushed and glistening with sweat, and her eyes—her eyes looking right back at me, soft and sorry and hopeful and just inches above where her teeth worry the lower lip of her nervous pink mouth.

As apologies go, it's not a bad one.

But it doesn't change anything, literally or figuratively. I look away, get in line, and wait for this to end so I can focus on absolutely nothing but the feeling of the Gator grass beneath my feet one last time.

Chapter Twelve

-AMBER-

Okay, so, it wasn't all fixed with Grand Gesture #1. That's okay.
Even though the rest of the squad looks like they want to pour
fire ants down my spankies, and Jack is determined to freeze
me out with enough ice power to rival the North Pole, I feel
good. Like I did the right thing. Like I showed what's important to me. Like I stood behind the squad (who they should be,
at least), the team (who they should be, at least), *and* my girl
(who I'd like to be, at least).

At least I know my mom would be proud.

And it helps me breathe a little easier to see that Miguel

looks like he might be too, if the fact that he sneaks me a tiny smile is any indication. I don't think I can go through with the rest of this if I don't have him in my corner.

For the rest of the pep rally, I fall perfectly in line, ignoring the glares from the contingent of girls determined to embarrass Jack at every corner. Of course, Crystal and the rest of the seniors don't look too thrilled with me either—that wasn't exactly a sanctioned move—but I hope they at least get why I did it.

And if they don't, they will soon.

Still, when the marching band is done with their performance, Dan Sanchez and Matt Devlin have made their nauseating speeches about how they're going to crush Kennedy High (oh, are you, now?), the step team's brought everyone back to their feet, and we've done our final routine, Crystal yanks me by the arm and pulls me over to the side. "Ammo. What the hell?"

Out of the corner of my eye, I see the football players file out, and once more I quickly catch Jack's eye before she leaves. "Is that not what we rehearsed?" I ask innocently, turning back to Crystal.

"Amber."

I exhale sharply and meet her warm, dark eyes. "You heard Claire. You know this isn't about honoring Robbie."

"Just because it isn't for her doesn't mean it isn't for other people."

"And how is this honoring him, Crys? Is the position

just supposed to shut down? No one gave Tim shit when he stepped in, and he sucks."

"Tim was the team's QB3. This was the slot he was set to inherit when Drew up and left."

"Well, he did, and he failed, and they had to get someone new, and Jack is the someone new, and she's *really* good. And we're punishing her for it because . . . what? Because she's a girl who dared to prove you don't have to be male to kick ass at football? Because she hasn't been an Atherton Alligator for life? Literally none of that is her fault, and frankly I think the fact that she's a girl is pretty badass."

"Yeah, I see that," Crystal says, arms crossing her chest. "Are you really gonna tell me that this is all about school spirit for you?"

I square my shoulders. "If you want to ask me something, ask it."

"Fine. I think you like her. I think you liked Veronica, too. And I don't know what that means about you and Miguel, but I do think you're thinking with your . . ." And there she falters, because for all that Crystal can whip us in line and run a tight ship of girls in tiny skirts, she's never vulgar about it.

And then, because I'm done denying it, because I came here to do something and I'm going to see it through, I say, "I do. And I also care about this squad and this team and this school. The same as I'm sure it would've been for you if Calvin had been on the team."

I watch her try to compute the idea of me and Jack being

just like her and Calvin, a wholesome all-American duo that likes sports and movies and going out to eat and whatever. Honestly, it's hard for *me* to compute, after all the stupid hiding we've been doing. But the thought of getting to date like normal people, of getting to have nights like we did at Gutter Kittens but at Maggie's, movie theaters, or the beach . . . Hell, even the thought of getting to wear her letterman's jacket in public sends a little shiver over my skin. My whole time at Atherton, there's never been an openly queer couple outside of the theater kids, and being the first isn't exactly my dream.

But being with Jack is.

"I guess that answers why you were so adamant about fixing that cheer for tonight," she says, and I'm so relieved that the first words out of her mouth aren't anything hateful, even though I've never heard Crystal be hateful in her entire life. "And I'm guessing that isn't all you have planned."

"Still a joint effort with school spirit," I assure her, "but yes. I'm sorry for going rogue. But I'm proud of her. And I'm excited for her, about the scout. And I want this night to be magical for her, as it should be. And I think everyone should want that, but they don't, and they don't want a captain who does. So, okay, that *C* isn't in my future," I say, gesturing toward the letter stitched onto her uniform. "I can handle that. Probably."

"I know you've been working hard for it," she says sympathetically. "Everyone does. But—"

"I know."

"And no matter your motivation, these aren't exactly team player actions."

"I know."

"Coach gave me a serious earful and—"

"I know." I offer her whatever fraction of a smile I can muster. "Trust me, I know. I just wanna cheer her on tonight, and then I'll fall in line or ride the bench or turn in my pompoms—whatever Coach decides, okay?"

She gives me a quick nod, and my heart squeezes at the realization she may not fight for me. There isn't much she can do when Coach gets it into her head that someone needs to be disciplined, but it'd be nice to feel like *someone's* on my side after all the friends I just shed.

Please let this be worth it, is all I can think as I trudge along after Crystal. *Please, please, please let her forgive me.*

-JACK-

Okay, so I feel the tiniest bit guilty about Amber getting reamed for cheering for me. It would've been cool as hell if I could've gone right up to her afterward and given her a huge, obnoxious kiss like I'm sure countless quarterback/cheerleader pairings have done in the past. But we are so fucking far from that scenario, it's not even funny, and I'm done trying to be with someone who has no interest in changing that. For all I know, and certainly for all everyone else knows, those flips were every bit as much about showing off her skills in her campaign for captain as for cheering me on, if not more so.

Who the fuck knows if it was about me at all, at this point?

Still doesn't stop the guys from making their shitty jokes about it as we chow down before the game. "Careful, Santiago," Sanchez says to Miguel, gnawing the last scraps of barbecue chicken off the bone. "You see that cheer your girl had for Walsh? I thought she only cheered like that for you. Something we should know?"

I suck in a breath, but Miguel barely even blinks. He's no stranger to this shit. "If you think that was something, you should see how we both cheer for your mom, Sanchez. You'd lose your fucking mind."

The rest of the guys crack up and talk shit, their mouths full of the chicken, rice, green beans, and corn bread cooked by the Student Athlete Moms Association. Objectively, the food is at least as good as anything my mom cooks, but it may as well be dirt for all I can enjoy it.

What would it feel like to say, "Yeah, fuckers, there *is* something you should know—she tastes like peach lip gloss, has the softest skin I've ever felt in my entire life, and can bend in ways you can't even imagine"? What would it feel like to admit that I can't stop turning that cheer over and over in my head, letting myself feel like it was at least a little bit about me, and that it feels surreal to have someone that talented in my corner?

What would it feel like to just . . . tell the truth? To *live* the truth?

Guess I'll never know.

I do know what it feels like to stab the shit out of a pile of green beans, but it's not as satisfying as you might think.

I'm finishing my food in silence when I feel a kick in my foot, too pointed not to be intentional. I look up, ready to glare daggers at the offender, only to see Miguel trying to catch my eye. He gives the slightest shift of his chin downward, and I realize he's trying to tell me to pull my phone out of my bag—a strictly verboten move, but one I can probably get away with since Coach is flirting with Devlin's mom.

I slip my phone out as quickly and quietly as I can and check my texts. There're just two words: *Open Sesame.*

The words tug at a memory from my days of studying the playbook this past summer like it held all the answers for the ACTs. I was obsessed, committing every single word of it to memory, even the plays that came with notations that they were almost never used.

Plays like Open Sesame, which is basically just a rushing touchdown, but hasn't been part of Atherton's playbook in forever; they haven't had a QB who was a solid runner in the last decade, and they haven't exactly been scrambling to change it up for the one they've got now. I *could* pull it off, but it means having a receiver to work with, and I guess this is Miguel offering himself up.

Can I trust him? Or is this just more fuckery?

I think back to that night at Gutter Kittens, to our conversation in the nature preserve, to Miguel telling me this morning that he wants to help, and I decide trusting him is the best chance I've got. I give him a quick nod, then slip my phone back into my bag before we can get caught. It's just one idea, one play, but God, it would feel good to be able to show off what I can do to the scout, just once.

And yeah, okay, it'll feel good to stick it to everyone else, just once.

When I turn back to my food, it's nice to find that for the first time all day, I have an appetite.

— — — — —

I've been so distracted by everything that it isn't until I'm alone in the locker room, tightening up my bun, that I realize I haven't heard from Sage and Morgan since early this morning. Most game days they send me a selfie of the two of them with "Go Jack!" dancing somewhere on the screen in flashing or vibrating letters. The first time, they even sent a picture of cupcakes with Gator-green icing Sage had made and piped *J*s and footballs onto. (They also sent videos of our friends eating them and sticking out green tongues, along with *Sorry—*

cupcakes stay inside city limits, because they suck, but even that made me laugh.)

Today . . . nothing.

The elastic around my hair makes a satisfying sound as it snaps, and then, as if thinking about them conjured it up, there's a text from Morgan: *Good luck tonight!!*

A few seconds later, Sage adds, *Oh yeah! Good luck!*

Okay, not loving being an afterthought, and a text is pretty weak for them, especially since they know it's my biggest game so far, but it's something. They haven't forgotten about me. They're still going to welcome me home with open arms.

I exhale deeply.

So many things to stress about. So many questions. So many people caught up in this mess.

At least I know not to bother looking for texts from my brothers.

I look into the mirror and slap my cheek so hard, it immediately flushes. "Stop being so fucking emo, Walsh," I order myself, because there's no tough-talking coach around me to do it. The pep talks happen in the guys' locker room, and shockingly, I've not been invited. Of course, they pretend the weak-ass minute on the field is the real deal, but I know where the actual coaching is happening.

I slap my other cheek, hard, and put on my helmet, just in time to hear us being announced onto the field.

Naturally, they wouldn't bother waiting until I was ready. I rush to catch up with the flood of bulky yellow shoulders and bright green numbers, just barely emerging at the tail end of them.

And then. A rush of volume.

Applause. Whistling. Screaming. The homecoming crowd is officially in town.

Except.

"Jack! Jack! Jack! Jack!"

The fuck?

I peel off my helmet and look up into the stands, immediately regretting removing my protective headgear when I feel an unfamiliar prickle at my eyes.

They're here. Sage and Morgan, and what looks like an entire bus full of old friends I've barely kept in touch with. My parents and brothers. Cousins. *Grandparents.*

Holy shit. I have a fucking *cheering section.*

I have never, ever had a cheering section. And with so many people in the stands who don't know the politics of treating me like a human person at this school, their cheering is infectious. Contagious. Strangers who haven't been here in months or years are picking up the chant of my name and all I can think is *Please listen to this, Terry Lawrence. Please, when you see my entire team throw me under the bus, remember this moment that proved that out there in the world are people who want me to succeed.*

And because I am a stupid fool with a stupid heart, I hazard a quick look at Amber, who doesn't seem surprised at any of this. Who looks thrilled and . . . accomplished.

And it clicks that she had something to do with this. I don't know what. I don't know how. But I know with every cell of the blood pumping through my veins that the girl who pulverized my heart is doing everything in her power to put it back together.

I glance at the team, and they look *pissed* . . . except for Santiago, who absolutely cannot keep the goofy smile off his face when he catches my eye. He finally wipes it clean when Sanchez spies it and glares at him, but he winks one last time, and I wink back.

Maybe we can't win, but we can sure make the people who are here for us proud.

And that is what I'm gonna fucking do.

We huddle up and Coach gives us the usual—fight hard, do your best, make Atherton proud. Miguel and I exchange another glance, just to confirm we're going ahead with our plans, and we break. But before we can get into formation, while the cheerleaders are still riling up the crowd, Coach says, "Walsh, c'mere a minute."

My heart freezes up and I worry he caught that one glance, that somehow he knows everything about what we have planned. But all he says is, "Big game for you tonight."

"Yes, Coach."

"You feeling ready?"

Am I feeling ready? I would be, if it were a normal game. If all I had to do was play and let my hands do the work. But that's not what I'm up against tonight.

Does he know that?

"I'm feeling really grateful for the opportunity," is what I say. "And that so many friends and family showed up." Fuck it. "I've really been missing that support."

He nods gruffly. "You're a good player, Walsh. You are."

"With all due respect, sir," I bite out, "I know that. And I know this was my one shot to play and I'm grateful for it. But this isn't what it should be. And I don't know"—I cut myself off before I can say "what you expected out of bringing me here," because that skirts way too close to talk of illegal recruitment—"what I expected when I came here," I say instead, "but this hasn't been what I signed on for." Deep breath. "And I don't know if I want to keep doing it."

He gives me a jerky nod, like he's been expecting this since that first and last two-a-day when everyone treated me like a joke. And that only makes me angrier. Because he's seen it this whole time, and it's been his job to fix. But he's cared more about making a crowd of whiny babies happy so he can keep his cushy job coaching losers to failure because everyone's given up on winning for so long, they don't even know what to do with it when it lands in their palms after a perfect spiral.

I open my mouth to say more, to tell him that I'm going to run this game my way, but then the ref calls out, "The coin

toss will take place on the center of the field!" and I let myself
melt back onto our bench, kicking up a little extra dirt in my
cleats as I leave him behind me.

Because he can't even get a coin toss right, Devlin calls
"Tails," and of course we lose. Kennedy's captain looks directly
at me and says, right into the mic, "We'll kick. I wanna see what
their girl can do."

Devlin smirks, and as I feel the frisson of glee on both sides
at the expectation I'm gonna fall on my ass—literally or meta-
phorically, I guess—I open my mouth to snap about how I'm
not "their girl," only to have someone else's voice cut me off.

"Yo, she can do *anything* your bitch ass can do with her
eyes closed, punk."

Miguel. Dear God. As the ref turns to control my foul-
mouthed teammate while the rest of the guys jeer, the urge to
kick so much ass that he'll never have to eat those words pumps
fast and furious through my blood.

And with that in mind, defense lines up.

For this, at least, the team actually tries, as anxious as everyone else is to put me on display. Dan makes the catch and
runs it up to the forty-yard line, so at least we're in good field
position.

He has no idea how much he's about to regret that.

I exchange a glance with Miguel before sizing up the defense. This could go one of two ways. Either Kennedy's going
to try to intimidate me because they think I'm a wee little girl
who'll go absolutely numb at the sight of five or six big strong

boys clambering in my direction, or they'll go weak on me and focus their defense on the guys who actually frighten them.

Let's find out.

I line up under Zach Sawyer, praying he has enough self-respect not to fuck up the snap, and call "Hike!" Thankfully, he doesn't let himself look like a complete douchebag by messing it up, and as soon as the ball hits my hands, I drop back and see Kennedy's chosen Option B, sending a pathetic three-man rush after me.

I roll out of the pocket and pretend for half a second like I'm searching for an open receiver, just enough to make Coach think this really was a spontaneous call, and then I tuck it under my arm and run downfield like the fucking wind, keeping the sideline in my sights for when I inevitably get plowed. By the time I take a hit to the side that knocks me out of bounds, I *know* I've gotten a first down, and the roar of the crowd only confirms it for me.

The team, unsurprisingly, is not as thrilled. "What the fuck, Walsh?" Dan demands, coming up to crowd me. "That's not the play!"

"Oh crap, sorry about that. Guess your girl fucked up." Can they see my shit-eating grin behind my mouthguard? I hope they can see my shit-eating grin behind my mouthguard. "Let's try that again. I'll get it right this time."

"You better," Devlin says menacingly, and the other guys murmur their agreement, except for Santiago and, I can't help but notice, Burke.

Is he just being quiet, or is it possible he's not as convinced as the other guys to throw this one? He's never treated me quite as horribly as they have, always choosing to ice me out rather than actively be an asshole. Having one more guy on our side would definitely help.

Do I wanna chance it?

I decide to keep it in my back pocket in case I get desperate, but for now, I'm sticking with Santiago. We line up again, and there's not even a pretense at being happy we got a first down, but that's fine; I'm feeling cocky as shit now and I know—I *know*—this is gonna work. I exchange a glance with him, just brief enough to confirm we're going ahead with the plan, and then we line back up while everyone around me mutters into the wind. I bought us all the yardage I could, but I'm not gonna get away with it twice, so I hope he's ready to run like hell.

They add one more guy on me, which leaves Santiago practically open. I only gain a few yards this time, but it's enough to get off a lateral pass and then watch him take off, down, down, over . . . Holy shit. I keep waiting for the sound of bodies colliding and hitting dirt that never comes, and it isn't until I hear the crowd going absolutely insane that I realize I'm actually seeing what I thought I saw.

"Touchdown: Gators! Number seventeen, Miguel Santiago, just took it seventy yards into the end zone! Unbelievable!"

Unbelievable isn't even the word for it. Hot damn. I'm running after him before I even know what I'm doing and we chest-bump right there on the field, everyone getting an eye-ful of the fact that we're clearly on a team here. I'm sure there are a million questions why, but I'm not answering to *anyone* right now.

Of course, Seth Mathison flubs the extra point, but it's tough to say whether that's intentional or he just sucks that hard. Even when he gives Sanchez an exaggerated wink, I'm still pretty sure it's a cover.

To the surprise of no one, our defense gets utterly trounced, and by the time I get the ball back, we're down 7–6. I'm mostly relieved this isn't gonna be a shutout, but still manage to get another first down by throwing a bullet straight to Santiago. He's tackled immediately—guess they're catching on to the fact that practically speaking, I only have one real receiver on this team—but at least we gain some yardage.

Santiago stays on the ground a minute longer than he should, and I know it's time to give him a break, even if it means burning any shot at another first down. This time, I do follow the playbook, and send a twenty-yard pass down to Sanchez, knowing there's no chance in hell he'll catch it and the best I can hope for is that it won't be intercepted.

It isn't, but he doesn't catch it, either, making a big deal of motioning that I threw it out of his reach, even though my seven-year-old cousin sitting in the stands could've jumped high enough to grab it.

The crowd groans, and I almost wish I could see Dan's expression behind his helmet. I guess he's used to hearing disappointed fans, so maybe this is a nice bit of nostalgia for him.

On the sidelines, the cheerleaders are doing their best to keep the crowd pumped, and I weigh my options. I could run again, but it's too early in the game to risk a second hit. Returning to Santiago would probably catch them off guard at this point, but I don't want to risk him getting injured either.

"Walsh, where's your head at?" Coach snaps me back to attention in the huddle, and whew, he is definitely pissed at me, but really, what's the point of this? He can tell me to pass to Sawyer or Sanchez or Devlin, but we all know what the result's gonna be. Or maybe everyone knows but him. Either way, it's a waste, which means it's either me or Santiago risking our limbs again. Or maybe we won't even get that far, if they're pissed enough to let the rush through to bury my ass in the dirt.

And then, a voice in my ear. "Statue of Liberty. I can do it. I'll get us to the forty at least."

It's Burke. I seek out his dark brown eyes beneath his helmet, and he looks sincere, but maybe he's just a better actor than the rest of them. "I won't screw you," he adds. "I know the guys are . . . whatever, but my brother's up there. My mom and pops are up there. I can't promise you Mathison will make the kick, but I can get us closer to the end zone."

It's a ridiculous choice of play at this point in the game, but surprises can only help me, especially if it means getting someone else on my side. "Yeah, all right. Get Coach on board. I don't think he's gonna listen to me right now."

I watch from a few feet away while Burke makes his case to Coach, and it's clear Sundstrom's not buying it. So we run yet another play that gives Sanchez a chance to show off how much he sucks before Coach mercifully gives our plan a shot and calls Statue of Liberty. There's a flicker of irritation in his eyes when they land on me while he makes the call. I'm in for some shit later. But for now, I close my eyes and pray I can trust Burke as much as I hope I can. I drop back, fake to Santiago—he's just the most believable target, for anyone who's been paying attention—and hand it off. True to Burke's word, he gets the nine yards we need to go for a field goal, and I let out the breath I've been holding since the tail end of my last "Please don't fuck me over."

Now it's up to Mathison, which blows. But whether or not he takes us up to 9–7, everyone, including Terry Lawrence, can see who's been putting in the work here. My running, throwing, and strategy have all been on display tonight, and while my leadership abilities could probably use some work, I've done the best I can. I don't know how much is left in me, or in Santiago—not without the rest of our team. But I'm going to keep giving it everything I have.

Doesn't hurt that it brings me a lot of joy to see Amber breaking into a new gleeful cheer and knowing I'm part of why.

I'm grateful my helmet hides that I can't take my eyes off her when I'm not playing. On a squad full of hot, peppy girls, she got the nicknames Ammo and Loud for a reason. The only thing more powerful than her killer legs is her voice, and every time it cheers my name I want to melt into the grass.

I swig my water as Mathison takes his place on the field, and turn away just before he kicks. I can't watch him miss again, and my gut says he's going to. Crowd reaction tells me I'm right, and the scoreboard staying at 7–6 confirms it. God, that kid sucks.

Defense replaces us on the field and I chug my water and let myself watch the cheerleaders launch into a new routine. Amber is flawless, as usual, and when she does a cartwheel without even using her arms, it makes me want to fight every single person who's ever made her feel like she's just a short skirt. No chance in hell I could do that shit.

"Walsh!" Coach barks, and I tear my eyes off the squad. "Over here."

I jog over obediently, knowing I'm about to be ripped a new one. "Hey, Coach."

"Walsh."

I tear my helmet off and swipe at my sweaty forehead. "You know they're throwing this game, right?"

"What are you talking about, Walsh?" We both look at the field, where Zack Sawyer takes a shoulder to the gut and falls on his ass. "That was—that's not throwing the game." *They're just bad* goes unsaid.

"Not defense," I clarify, even though I have no idea. "You

really think Sanchez missed that throw by accident? Did that look out of his range to you?"

"You're reading into things, Walsh," says Sundstrom. "And you can't just pull plays out of your ass to make yourself look good for a scout."

"Do I *really* have to prove to you that I'm here for the team, Coach? I've done everything you've asked. *Everything.* I've learned every play, including, yeah, Open Sesame. I know every single player on this team's strengths and weaknesses, every blind spot. You *just* asked me how I was feeling about tonight and here's my answer: I feel good about it with people I can trust. And I think we can win it with people I trust. So, if you trust *me*, you'll let me win this for us."

"That's not how this works. Let me talk to the team—"

"With all due respect, sir, we both know how this really works. There's only one real question here, and it's how badly you care about winning tonight."

We stand in a fiery face-off until the inevitable happens: Kennedy scores, and whether that's because our team is intentionally blowing it or they just suck is irrelevant. We're losing, and if I'm right, we're not getting back up.

"What's your plan?" he finally grunts.

I lay it out, my brain calculating and recalculating with each move how to make this work if Burke, Santiago, and I run every play that matters. To his credit, Coach listens, but he cuts me off when I say we can get away with Open Sesame one more time.

"It won't work twice," he says bluntly. "Not just because the other team won't fall for it again, but because you and Santiago will run yourselves out. Use Barnes."

"Barnes? Barnes has been riding the bench the entire season. You're gonna put him in?"

"Your turn to trust me," Coach says.

So I do.

By the end of the first quarter, we're down 14–6, but there's nothing I can do to control the defense. What's more important is that Coach was right about Barnes, and I saw exactly why—he's the most passable of the second-string, but he never gets a shot because our fearless captain rarely sits. Tonight, though, it was easy to bench Devlin when he intentionally flubbed a catch and handed Kennedy an interception, and there's no way in hell Sam Barnes was missing his chance to finally show what he can do.

At the half, though, Santiago, Burke, and Barnes are bruised and exhausted, and I know we've probably hit the end of the line. I expect us to take a massive beating in the third quarter while they rest up and get refreshed, but Kennedy's QB1 rolls his ankle, and our second string takes a cue from Barnes and uses a rare opportunity to show off. Not that they can score for shit, but defense *does* manage to keep the Cougars to a single field goal. By the time we line up for the last quarter, 24–12 on the board, I know the odds of us winning are in the toilet, but they haven't been completely flushed.

Then again, I'm not sure it matters. Either way, I've looked fucking awesome, and there's no way this crowd, including Terry Lawrence, is missing it.

No way my family's missing it.

No way Amber's missing it.

If one thing's clear, it's that I'm the star of this team, and everyone else throwing the game just makes them look like they can't touch me—which they can't. But obviously it's triggered something, because when I call the play for the Downtown Dance, Matt snaps. "Fuck that," he declares, back on the field now that Sam needs a break. "Gator Grab. Let's go."

"You're not Coach. Coach makes the calls."

"And I'm the captain. Don't you fucking forget that, you little bitch," he mutters, his voice so low, Coach can't hear it from where he stands. But that doesn't stop the rest of the team from picking it up and snickering, declaring "Gator Grab" to each other in stage whispers.

It's the stupidest of all possible power moves, again requiring a split-second decision. If I let him have his call, will they actually play it through and get a first down? Because defense has been riding our asses all game and Downtown Dance was getting us, like, three yards at best. But if they fuck it up, I've let him take control for nothing.

Whatever—let him whip his dick out and wave it in the wind.

"Green, forty-two! Green, forty-two! Hike!" Devlin can't catch for shit tonight, but he's way too proud of his running to fuck that up. While I run back and let the ball fly in the most perfect spiral I've thrown all night, he manages to get halfway down the field, where defense has left a hole. His hands would have to go numb to miss this catch, but he's so stunned I actually followed his move that he almost drops it anyway, rolling out of bounds the instant it's in his mitts.

First down. Okay. Let's go.

- - - - -

Either Devlin knows making me look bad is now a lost cause or he's just feeling the high of doing something right for once, but there's no bullshit on the next play—just another solid pass that gains us six yards, and then it's back to the Walsh-and-Santiago show for another first down.

The crowd is *roaring* now, and you can actually feel the mood on the field change, feel who was going reluctantly along with the shitty plan but doesn't want to go back to losing. Even Devlin is clearly getting desperate to look good, or at least he knows Coach will bench him if he fucks up one more time. Finally, *finally*, we start playing like an actual team, and when we finish the play with a touchdown, even Mathison is feeling the spirit enough to score the extra point. (Just barely, but who's measuring?)

Blessedly, defense stays on a streak of not sucking, and we hold Kennedy to twenty-four. However many eyes there are in the bleachers, it feels like a thousand times that number are lasering holes into my uniform. The pressure is daunting, no question, but it's also . . . kind of awesome? That it's even a question we could turn this around, that all these Atherton people believe *I* could turn this around. . . . I mean. It's *very* fucking awesome.

Deep breath. Line up. Behind me, I swear I see Devlin make the sign of the cross, and I'm surprised it doesn't send him bursting into flames. Then I block everything out of my brain and focus on nothing but Sawyer's hands, the ball hitting my gloves, the fake to Burke followed by the real thing to Sanchez. He's sacked so hard and fast the ball flies off his fingertips, but honestly, it's almost worth it just to watch him get knocked on his ass.

Second down, we run a play that has me passing to Santiago, and I really hope Malcolm is in the stands somewhere watching his boyfriend have the game of his life, because he's truly crushing it. It isn't a first down, but it's close enough that on the next play, I run us there.

We're still down by five, which means nothing but a touchdown is gonna do it. Burke gives me a nod, and I return it, grateful that even with Sanchez continuing to be useless and Devlin suspect at best, the win remains possible. We line up again, and at the snap Burke takes off like a shot, hands at the ready, and I let the ball soar. He nabs it from the air and cradles it to his body like he's protecting a baby from an explosion, which isn't all that far off given the hit he takes. But it's a first down, again, and suddenly, I know beyond a shadow of a doubt that we are going to win this game.

And after another completion—reluctant credit to Devlin for that one—and another play that brings us so close, I can practically lick the end zone, I run it in.

And we win.

We win this impossible fucking game and I can finally breathe.

Holy shit.

A body slams into me and my first thought is that Sanchez and Devlin are about to kick my ass in front of everybody, but it's Santiago, and then it's Burke, and then Barnes, and oh God this is what it feels like to be on a team.

Shit, I might be crying.

The crowd is going absolutely bananas, and I pick out my family and friends and find they're all on their feet, even Jeremy and Jason, and it feels like everything is forgiven right now even if it won't be tomorrow. And it feels so good, I don't want anything in my life to be broken anymore. I want to talk to Amber. I want to work shit out even if it means two more years of hiding in her room and dates nowhere but at Gutter Kittens.

I turn to catch her eye, to smile, to try to mouth a request to talk later, but all I get in response is a smirk. And then she and a couple of the other cheerleaders break away from the squad and come to stand about six feet away from the bench.

"Ready, steady, go!" she yells, and all eyes turn to her, including the majority of the squad left behind, who clearly have no idea what's going on. The three of them—Amber, Crystal, and Nia, I see now—do a bunch of funky dance moves while the crowd cheers, and it ends with them lifting her up, a tiny pyramid of three with Ella Chow backspotting. (Insert a self-pat on the back for teaching myself a little about cheerleading.) Even without a megaphone, we can clearly hear her yell "Home-C-O-M-I-N-G!"

"Home-C-O-M-I-N-G!" Crystal, Nia, and Ella echo back.

"Home-C-O-M-I-N-G!" Amber repeats, pom-poms waving in the air. "Home-C-O-M-I-N-G! Jack Walsh, will you go with me?"

Silence.

Just . . . complete and total silence. Every guy on the team turns to gawk, even—especially—Miguel. Every cheerleader, too. Even I have no idea what to say.

Well, actually, I do. "Hell yeah, I will."

And then there's cheering again. And whistling and catcalling and I know it isn't all friendly, and I know the team is whispering and snickering and *none* of that is friendly. But I don't give a shit. Because she's hopping down from the pyramid. Because she's running over here. Because my brain is working on autopilot, picking her up and swinging her around and kissing her in front of the entire. Fucking. School.

Somewhere in the back of my brain it occurs to me that maybe I'm not thrilled at a scout seeing *this*, but I'm done being anyone other than who I am. If anyone watching can't handle me having a girlfriend, they can't handle *me*.

Still, no one needs to see two people of any gender making

out for too long, so we force ourselves apart, grinning like idi-ots. "I'm forgiven?" she whispers.

"Not even close," I whisper back. "Now I have to spend tomorrow looking for a suit."

She laughs and squeezes my hand. "Sage and Morgan said they'd be very happy to help with that. And maybe tomorrow you can get your hair cut, too. If you want to."

My heart swells a little bit at the suggestion. I know what she's saying, and she's right; the cat's out of the bag. It's time to look like me too. "Yeah?"

"Yeah. But for now . . ." She yanks the elastic out of my messy hair and pulls it up into a neater, photo-ready knot, and there's something about how she isn't bothered by any of the sweat or grime or how rank I must smell that sends the butter-flies fluttering even harder. "Much better."

"I'm suitable to be a cheerleader's girlfriend now?"

She winks. "Well, you *are* the quarterback."

Chapter Thirteen

-AMBER-

"Will you stop fidgeting? You're going to make me smudge it."

I sit obediently, admiring my newly polished fingernails while my mom finishes winging my eyeliner. Ordinarily, I'd be getting ready with a few other girls on the squad, but, well, nothing about taking my football player girlfriend to homecoming on a day's notice is ordinary.

If we were doing this normally, I'd be picking up Miguel and maybe a couple of friends who need rides. Instead, I dug hard into my savings and took out a loan from my mom to make this night as special as possible to make it up to my two favorite people.

Of course, that left nothing for a mani-pedi, but thankfully, my mom is as talented with a nail polish brush as she is with an eyeliner brush. And a bronzer brush. And a contour brush. For someone who rarely wears makeup, she is pretty damn skilled with it. When she finally lets me take a look in the mirror, my immediate reaction is to catcall myself. If only I knew how to whistle.

"You look gorgeous, sweetheart." She kisses the top of my head, taking care to avoid the curls I've painstakingly ironed into my hair. My cheeks shimmer with highlighter, my eyes look otherworldly aqua, and even I want to kiss my lips, which are the perfect bubble-gum pink to match my lace halter dress. "I hope tonight is wonderful for you. I know you've worked really hard at it."

To hear that, most people would think I had something to do with planning the dance, which I didn't. But my mom knows I spent hours getting in touch with Jack's family and friends to beg them to make the drive to Atherton for the game. She knows I stayed up half the night writing and rewriting cheers and routines to make Jack look as beloved as possible and prove she has leadership skills.

She knows it meant that I threw away getting captain, that I might have thrown away being on the squad entirely, and she supported it anyway.

"Mom, I—" My attempt at a mushy sentiment is immediately cut off by the sound of a doorbell ringing, and I freeze in my seat.

She's here.

My first ever queer date—well, first ever queer date who's actually into *me*—is here.

And I'm going to the dance on her arm. In front of everyone.

Holy crap.

"Would you like me to get that?" Mom asks, clearly holding back laughter as she takes in my panicked expression.

I shake my head, but it still takes me a few seconds to actually slip out of the chair. I slide on my silver heels and check myself in the mirror one last time, making sure Jack will get the full effect of my sexy but delicate look, and then I open the door.

And promptly slip on my own drool.

Okay, not literally, but it does feel like a serious danger when I see Jack in all her hot glory. If my mom weren't here, I definitely could not be held responsible for my actions.

The hair that was always knotted away as an afterthought is now front and center as a platinum mohawk. The sides look so smooth and soft, my fingers instantly itch to brush over them, and the rest is artfully tousled in that sexy just-got-out-of-bed way. I'd think she *had* just gotten out of bed if not for the rest of her looking immaculate.

The suit is . . . good God. It's deep green velvet with

cropped pants rolled at the cuffs and a pristine white dress shirt buttoned all the way up. In truest Jack fashion, she's foregone heels to pair it with immaculate white tennis shoes, and a watch with a thick brown leather band and a face the size of a saucer glints from her wrist.

Dapper is the word that comes to mind.

Well, it's the clean word, anyway.

"Hi," I somehow manage despite my mouth going completely dry.

"Uh, hi." She scratches behind her ear as her eyes travel up and down my dress and back again. "You look, uh." Her eyes dart to my mom, standing a few feet behind me. "Hi."

"Hi, Jack." If my mom's trying to keep the laughter out of her voice, she is desperately failing. "Nice to see you again. Take good care of my daughter tonight."

"Yes, ma'am."

"I trust there'll be no—"

"Oh my God, Mom, stop. No one believes you're a master enforcer and you know we'll probably both drink a tiny bit and neither of us is driving and obviously neither of us will be doing drugs. Can we go now?"

"Hug and kiss, first."

I let out a big huffy sigh, but when it comes time to wrap my arms around her, I squeeze a little tighter and longer than usual. I know how lucky I am to have a mom who supports me in everything I do, who doesn't blink at the fact that a girl in a suit is taking me to homecoming. I give her an air-kiss so as not to smudge my lip gloss and then grab Jack by the arm and yank her out the door before she can even finish calling out "Bye, Ms. McCloud!" like the suck-up she is.

The door's barely closed behind us before I find myself up against the wall of our building, Jack's mouth hot on mine. I let myself melt into it immediately, one hand stroking the soft velvet of her jacket while the other brushes her newly shorn hair. It takes until we're both just about out of oxygen before she finally pulls back, rests her forehead against mine, and says, "Sorry. I just. You look." She laughs breathlessly, the scent of minty mouthwash ghosting over my lips. "So fucking good."

"Trust me, I get it," I say, coasting my hand over the tips of her mohawk, careful not to disturb it. "Oh, I get it."

"You like it?" she asks.

"Uhhh, yeah, I like it." I tilt my head up to kiss her again. Even with me wearing heels, she's still a couple of inches taller than me. "Was I not clear?"

"I may have been a little nervous about it," she confesses. "Kind of a big change. But now that I'm all out, I felt like I should actually look like *me*."

"Agreed," I say, twining my fingers with hers. "And it does look like you, which is part of why I love it."

"What's the other part?"

"Umm, the 'you look really fucking hot' part. Again, was I not clear?"

She squeezes my hand. "Nah, I just like hearing you say

it." She nips at my lower lip. "Are you absolutely sure you want to go to this dance thing? Because that looks like a pretty big limo and I'm gonna guess there's a divider in there."

"That is . . . extremely tempting," I admit, gently tugging her toward the stairs down to said limo, "but unfortunately, there are a couple of stops to make on the Amber McCloud apology tour, so that may have to wait."

"Ahh." We get to the limo, where the driver—Stefan—is standing and holding the door open for us. We thank him and slide in, our hands never moving from their clasped position. "So this is another double date."

I exhale deeply. "Here's hoping."

– – – – –

It takes all my best pleading to get Miguel dressed and in the car, complete with repeating "I got a freaking *limo!*" about a thousand times, but by the time we round the corner to Malcolm's house, he's bouncing with even more excitement than we are. Miguel had texted him to get ready in his school dance best, and Mal delivered, emerging in a pair of perfectly fitted jeans and a tailored blazer. Together, we share a bottle of sparkling cider—the only thing my mom would allow—and take turns being complete tools and sticking our heads out the window.

"All hail the rainbow brigade!" Malcolm yells, and the rest of us laugh and yank him back down. With Jack and I having very publicly come out last night, we know the focus tonight is going to be mostly on Miguel, and we want to make sure he has as good a time as possible. Even if that means letting him have control of the music.

It's way too short a drive to school, despite having Stefan take the longest way possible, and by the time we arrive, everyone is staring: people might get limos for prom, but no one gets them for homecoming.

Then again, we're not just anybody.

"Nice ride!" someone calls out, and I blow a kiss out the sunroof, giving no fucks as to whether it was sarcastic or not. Jack exits first, and I scramble out to take her arm and wait for the guys. For all the fun we had on the way here, this is a massive and terrifying moment for Miguel, and I wish I could reach into the limo and take his hand, but I'm not the person he needs holding him steady right now.

Miguel and Malcolm emerge together, and if possible, it seems like the crowd has grown outside. But when they take each other's hands and the gawking and whispers really start, we all about-face and march straight into the school, focusing on nobody but each other, on nothing but celebrating ourselves with terrible music and even worse punch.

-JACK-

I've always hated being talked about, but tonight it's proving particularly hard to get to me.

It might be that it's really tough to distract from the ridiculously hot girl on my arm and the scent of sweet floral shampoo wafting off her big glossy curls.

It might be that I finally feel like I look like myself.

It might be that if I proved anything this weekend, it's that I can take on anyone in this room.

It might be how Miguel, for all his obvious nerves, is fucking glowing in Malcolm's presence.

It might be any of those things.

But of course, we make it about five feet into the gym before we bump up against Sanchez and Devlin, and being talked *about* fades into the woodwork, because they are definitely talking *to* us.

"Y'all know this is a school dance, not a fucking Pride parade," Sanchez spits, his stink eye practically rolling in its socket as he struggles to figure out which of his teammates is more deserving of it.

"Don't worry, Sanchez," Santiago says, puffing out his chest. "No one's confused into thinking y'all have anything to be proud of. Everyone saw the game last night."

"Burn!" someone says cheerfully from the crowd of bystanders.

"Shut the fuck up, Barrett," Devlin snaps.

But Barrett won't shut up, and I realize it's Austin from my English class—the guy who's always blatantly staring at Amber's legs. I knew he had good taste. "He's right, though. Neither of y'all could catch for shit last night. If anyone deserves to be here—with whomever the fuck they want—it's these two." He gestures at me and Miguel.

"Hear, hear!" someone else calls, and a whole bunch of voices echo.

"So this is how it's gonna be?" Devlin snarls. "No one gives a shit who we have to share our locker room with anymore? No one gives a shit that Robbie's gone?"

"You don't have to be an asshole to prove you give a shit that Robbie's gone."

The voice is quiet, but it's so unexpected that it renders everyone else silent. I don't know where Cara Whelan's been hiding—especially *this* Cara Whelan—but she's back, and she has clearly got something to say.

Taking advantage of the silence, she turns to Amber, whose nails are digging into my arm so deeply, I can feel them through my suit jacket. "I owe you an apology. I didn't know what to do with my grief and I took it out on you." She glances at me. "Both of you." And then, she turns to Miguel. "And you. I knew what he was doing to you."

Miguel looks like he wants to spit fire in response, and I don't blame him. "You ever think of stopping him, maybe?" he snaps, and Malcolm reaches for his hand and squeezes it.

"You know what hell it is, being on a team with someone who's blackmailing you? Having to work with someone who wants to ruin your life?"

Whispers spring up like brushfires, and all I can think is *I do*. No wonder Miguel was willing to piss off everyone else to come to my side.

"I can't imagine," she says, her eyes on the floor. The way her jaw is working at the words, it's like she's prying everything out with a crowbar. And maybe that's what it feels like, because if there's one thing I've learned about Atherton, it's that people don't take kindly to dragging Robbie Oakes through the mud. "I should've stopped him. And I should've told you I knew the truth about y'all," she adds to Amber. "I was in love with him and it all sounded right, but you *are* the one person who's always been there for me. And I don't wanna hurt you for anybody. Even if I don't . . . understand everything about you."

Well, I could've done without that last part, and judging by the tic in Miguel's jaw, he could've done without any of it. It seems to be enough for Amber, though, or maybe she just needs some little sense of closure. For the first time that night, she lets go of my arm, going to hug Cara. I feel strangely cold without her body heat. But a moment later she's back, and all feels right with the world, especially when Cara declares she just wanted to say that and now she's going home.

With so much to process, everyone's forgotten about the four of us for a minute, and we quickly escape to the drinks

table. "So what happened with the infamous Terry Lawrence?" Santiago asks. "Did you get to talk to him?"

It's still hard to believe this part is real, especially since the
only people I've talked to since the game are Amber and my
family. "I did."

"And?"

"And he said he'll be back next year to check me out for
real for UWF, and we'll stay in touch, but it's looking good."

"Holy shit!" Miguel engulfs me in a huge hug, and Malcolm and Amber join in, and soon we're laughing and dancing and truthfully if Sanchez and Devlin are even still in the
room, I have no idea.

This *is* a goddamn Pride parade, and I am proud as hell to
be here.

- - - - -

People who've never spoken a word to me before come up all
night to congratulate me on the game, to compliment my hair
or my suit, and to tell Amber and me that we make a cute couple. It's all a little surreal from a school that's hated on me so
hard, but if this is my chance at a fresh start, I'm gonna take it.

My phone beeps with a text, and I pull it out to see a message from my mom with a picture of my family—my whole
family, minus me—blowing kisses, our white clapboard
house in the background. We had a long family night after
the game, all of us squeezing in at the breakfast bar in the

apartment and pounding on-the-house takeout from Maggie's while we talked about where we're gonna go from here. We agreed to try having my mom spend a few days there and Dad and the twins spend a weekend here every month, and tonight marks my first night on my own.

Well, I don't really plan on spending it on my own, but.

Sage and Morgan are still on the road; they texted from a rest stop halfway home, begging for pictures, mostly so Morgan could brag endlessly about their impeccable eye. It was awesome to get to spend the day with them, and not just because they took me shopping and convinced me to buy this suit. I still can't believe Amber reached out to everyone to get them over here, but the truth is, I should've done it myself. Sage and Morgan would have dropped everything if they'd known I needed them, which is part of why I refused to tell them. Needless to say, they were not thrilled about that.

There's been a lot of pride swallowing this weekend, that's for damn sure.

"Can I have everyone's attention?" Principal Seacord is tapping on the mic, and oh *God*, I forgot about this stupid king and queen shit. Judging by Amber's quiet groan in my ear and Miguel's not so quiet "kill me," they weren't thinking about it either. Which is slightly more problematic for them, seeing as they're nominated. "It's time to name your homecoming king and queen. But first, let's get the whole court up here."

"Yes, let's!" I say sunnily to Amber and Miguel, both of whom shoot me death stares.

"If you step more than a foot away from me while he's up there, I'll end you," Malcolm warns me.

"Sweet deal."

The potential kings go up first, and Miguel gives Malcolm's hand a quick squeeze before taking his place with Matt Devlin—who steps aside like Miguel's very presence might turn him gay—Austin Barrett, Aidan Manos, and Mason Blackfoot. Then it's my turn to lose Amber to the stage, and Malcolm and I immediately reach for each other as we watch her go up.

For those who somehow haven't caught on to the recoupling, there aren't any questions raised by Amber and Miguel moving to the ends of their lines so they're standing as close to each other as possible. But it's clear Seacord knows what's up, because when he announces, "Your homecoming king is . . . Miguel Santiago!" it's immediately followed by a muttered "Oh boy" he definitely did not mean for the mic to pick up.

"Congrats," I murmur to Malcolm. "Your boyfriend is homecoming king. Not many people can say that."

"Just me and your girlfriend," he shoots back, and we both snicker while we wait for the announcement of queen.

"And your queen is . . ."

"You just announced the queen!" a voice yells out that almost definitely belongs to Dan Sanchez.

Miguel grabs the mic from Seacord and yells back, "Yeah, and my first royal order is to shove my foot up your—"

Seacord grabs it back and helplessly declares "Amber

McCloud!" which gets an enormous holler from me and Malcolm, but we're not alone. It's not the *whole* squad that's lining up and cheering, but it's Crystal and Nia and Ella and Virany and it's enough. Everyone spreads out to give Amber and Miguel room for their spotlight dance, and somewhere in the distance I imagine Seacord has run off to his office for a drink.

Malcolm and I go ahead and dance next to them, and when the song is over, we take our partners back. "So," I say to Amber, playfully adjusting the shiny tiara on her head. "Homecoming queen. That feels like potential future captain material."

"Pretty sure the captain dream is fairly dead," she says, winding her arms around my neck. "But that's okay. The odds of winning a scholarship are, like, one in a bajillion anyway. I think I just wanted . . . *something*, you know? Something of my own. Something that maybe certain family members couldn't ignore."

"And you're over that now?"

"I am. Turns out, there are people who actually like me just as I am and don't require I win any special prizes for their affection."

"Like who? I'm only in this for the crown, baby."

She smirks. "You were that confident I'd win, huh?"

"I voted for you at least twice."

"I really hope you play football more honestly than you vote for homecoming queen."

I shrug. "Eh. If Tom Brady doesn't, I don't see why I should have to."

"Touché." She pulls me down for a kiss, and if I hadn't known by this point that this was all worth it, I sure as hell do now. "So, am I remembering correctly that you have your entire apartment to yourself tonight?"

God, I love the way this girl thinks. "You are."

"Good, good. The Rainbow Brigade is gonna need a bigger meeting space. I don't think Drip is gonna cut it anymore."

"Amber."

She flutters her eyelashes innocently. "Did you not want to continue this double date all night?"

"I'm going home." I turn to leave, and let Amber immediately pull me back.

"You can't go yet," she says in a teasing voice. "I still have the limo for another hour."

"Just sitting there empty?" I raise an eyebrow.

"Just sitting there empty," she confirms.

We hold a shared gaze for a few seconds that feel like an hour, and then we're out of there, Amber holding on to her crown for dear life as we tumble into the parking lot and I give Stefan an extra twenty to take a hike somewhere.

"This is a little cliché, don't you think?" Amber says as she drops her heels on the floor of the car and helps me out of my jacket. "Quarterback and cheerleader doing it in a limo at a school dance?"

"They really do call you Loud McCloud for a reason, don't they."

She gives me an impish smile, sly and innocent all at the same time. "Why don't you find out?"

I unbuckle my mammoth watch, leave it on top of the jacket, and turn around to see Amber's already shed her dress. I am going to die. "What does a girl have to do to get a personal cheer?" I ask, my voice gone embarrassingly raspy.

"You seem pretty good with your playbook," she says, pulling me down on top of her and pressing her mouth to mine. "Let's see if you've got one more win in you."

-The End-

waves pom-poms

Acknowledgments

I can acknowledge (no pun intended) that it's a little weird to have a dream imprint, but Wednesday has been mine since its inception, and I'm so grateful to have now published two books with an incredibly amazing team there. Thank you, always, to my delightful editor, Vicki Lame; her lovely assistant, Vanessa Aguirre; my fabulous publicist, Meghan Harrington; marketing extraordinaires Alexis Neuville and Brant Janeway; the whole excellent team of production editor Carla Benton, production manager Jeremy Haiting, and copy editor Kaitlin Severini; the managing editorial team

Acknowledgments

of Eric Meyer and Elizabeth Catalano, and, of course, those responsible for making this book look so gorgeous I can only hope my words live up: text designer Devan Norman, cover artist Alex Cabal, and legendary cover designer Kerri Resnick. Many thanks, too, to Bethany Strout and the entire team at OrangeSky Audio, and to Natalie Naudus and Lori Prince for breathing the most beautiful life into Amber and Jack.

To my wonderful agent, Patricia Nelson—thank you for constant support, quick email responses, as-needed phone calls, and general wonderfulness. I am so grateful for all the pieces you've picked up and everything you've put back together, and I can't wait to see what else lies ahead with you.

A tremendous debt of gratitude to everyone who lent their expertise to various areas of this book. The brilliant Sarah Henning and Maggie Hall went way above and beyond, and *Home Field Advantage* is so much better for their tremendous help and that of Lauren Gibaldi, Lindsay Myers-Humlie, Kelly Head, David Nino, and Mark Oshiro. Any remaining errors are mine, except for Amber's distaste for Mountain Dew, which is, frankly, her problem.

I'm also hugely grateful to A-M McLemore, who pushed me through to the end of writing this book with one insightful phone call; Marieke Nijkamp, who is forever one of my first readers and greatest cheerleaders; Katherine Locke, recipient of a truly embarrassing amount of my angst, but who's always there for the joy in equal amounts; Jenny Bent, who gave this book its title during a generous phone call years ago; 'Nathan

Burgoine, who helped change the course of this book with a single Twitter thread; and DongWon Song, who first made Wednesday my home.

Given all the circumstances of when this book was written, edited, and published, there's no way I would've gotten through it without having so many incredible and admirable fellow author-parents for empathy, venting, support, and encouragement. I feel so lucky for the lifeline of these group chats. And to all the authors whose texts and DMs help make this industry feel smaller in the best way, including but definitely not limited to Jenn Dugan, Lev Rosen, Cam Montgomery, Jennifer Iacopelli, Sona Charaipotra, Tess Sharpe, Jess Capelle, Sharon Morse, Becca Podos, Becky Albertalli, Swapna Krishna, Emily Henry, Phil Stamper, Meryl Wilsner, and, of course, Maggie—thank you. Publishing during a pandemic sucks, but you all make it suck a little less.

I'm so thankful to the authors I admire so deeply who lent their kind words to this book—Lev, JRo, Kelly, Rachael, Meryl, and Chelsea, you are all quite literally awesome and I appreciate your support (and your own work!) so much. And, of course, huge thanks to the bloggers, Bookstagrammers, booksellers, librarians, educators, and BookTokers who've shared my work with readers, especially Rachel Strolle, Farrah Penn, Laynie Rose, and Danika Ellis.

To whatever family and friends actually still read my books, thank you and I love you. To my family and friends who will never see this line, that's okay—I love you, too. To

Acknowledgments

Yoni, my parents, my in-laws, and my siblings who have done their best to give me the time and space needed to do this thing I love, I am forever appreciative and so incredibly lucky to have you.

But the biggest thank-you of all goes to my children: you may have done your best to stop me from working as often as possible, but you gave me the maternity leaves that allowed for this book to get written, so let's call it even.